Lead Me to the Slaughter

Graham Ison

© Graham Ison 1990

Graham Ison has asserted his rights under the Copyright, Design and Patents Act, 1968, to be identified as the author of this work.

First published in 1990 by Macmillan London Limited.

This edition published in 2017 by Endeavour Press Ltd.

Table of Contents

Chapter One	5
Chapter Two	16
Chapter Three	26
Chapter Four	36
Chapter Five	47
Chapter Six	56
Chapter Seven	65
Chapter Eight	75
Chapter Nine	84
Chapter Ten	93
Chapter Eleven	102
Chapter Twelve	112
Chapter Thirteen	125
Chapter Fourteen	133
Chapter Fifteen	142
Chapter Sixteen	155
Chapter Seventeen	166
Chapter Eighteen	177

Chapter One

There was a patch of blood on the road. It was quite a large patch and had seeped into the pleasant pink-coloured surface. Someone had chalked a circle round it.

'What's that?'

'Blood, sir.'

'I can see it's blood, Jack. Whose blood?' Tommy Fox studied it as he walked carefully round the perimeter of the chalk circle. He always walked carefully. Fox was a man who set great store by his appearance and his rivals suggested that such care was to preserve his expensive shoes and his immaculate suiting. Those who did not know him were inclined to describe him as a dandy... which was a mistake. Despite his cockney raffishness, Fox was a thorough man. It was one of the factors that had been considered when he had been elevated to the rank of Detective Chief Superintendent and, later, given operational command of the Flying Squad. The other factor was that he held the Queen's Gallantry Medal for disarming a violent criminal.

'One of the security guards, sir.'

'What happened to him?'

'Decided to be a hero. Got two cartridges in the legs. Reckon they'll have to amputate one of them.'

Fox shook his head. 'They will do with these things,' he said. 'I thought you'd got all this buttoned up, Jack. Sounds to me as though your snout needs a good smacking.'

Gilroy shook his head. 'Got the job right, sir. Got the place wrong. He reckoned they were going to blag them at the bank, not on the hoof.'

'Hope you didn't pay him, this reliable snout of yours.'

Gilroy grinned. 'That'll be the day,' he said.

'Anyway, what's the score?' Fox looked around, at the security van, a gaping hole cut in its side, then at the abandoned chain-saw that had done the cutting, and at the two cars, one in front of the armoured van, the other behind.

'Brought it to a stop here, guv'nor.' Gilroy waved a hand broadly across the whole scene.

'I'd more or less worked that out for myself,' said Fox.

'Sawn-off shotguns, chain-saw — '

'How many in this little team, Jack?' Fox interrupted again.

'Four, apparently. Plus the wheelman in the getaway car. Well, van actually.'

'Van?' Fox raised an eyebrow.

'Yeah, a transit.'

'Any details?'

Gilroy hesitated. 'There's a witness, sir. P'raps you'd like to talk to him.'

'Where is he?'

'That's him, over there.' Gilroy pointed to a man walking back and forth in the ditch.

'What the hell's he doing, Jack?'

'Looking for his car keys. He pulled up behind this lot when they were at it. One of them shoved a shooter up his nose, took his car keys and slung'em in the ditch.'

'Fetch him over.' Fox turned to a uniformed PC leaning against a police area car. 'Here,' he said, 'go and find that gentleman's car keys. He's assisting the police with their enquiries... which is more than you're bloody doing.'

The PC didn't know Tommy Fox but recognised authority when he saw it and promptly took off.

'This is Mr Deacon, sir.'

Fox shook hands. Deacon was about sixty, with wispy grey hair and a worried expression on his face that looked as though it lived there.

'My inspector tells me you saw this robbery, Mr Deacon.'

'Yes, that's right. I came from down there.' Deacon pointed. 'As a matter of fact I was just popping down to the village to get some tobacco. I didn't realise I'd run out until I went to — '

'Just the details, Mr Deacon, please,' said Fox patiently.

'Yes, well as I say, I came round the bend in the road and there was this van, where it is now. There were some men pulling boxes out through the hole and loading them into their van. Two of the security men were lying face down over there with their hands on their heads.

The other poor fellow was there...' Deacon pointed to the drying patch of blood now being photographed by one of the team from the Yard's SO3 Branch. 'I wanted to help him, but one of the men ran over to me and put this gun against my head. I didn't even get a chance to get out of the car.'

'What was he like, this man?'

'A big chap, wearing a balaclava. You know, like you see the IRA wearing on the telly.'

'Did he say anything?'

'Yes, he said something like, "If you know what's good for you, grandad, you'll have seen nothing." Then he took my keys out of the ignition and threw them in the ditch.'

'What sort of accent did he have?'

Deacon gave that some thought. 'None really, not that you'd notice.'

Fox nodded. That usually meant that they'd got London accents. 'How many of them were there, altogether?'

'Four, I think, all wearing balaclavas. Oh, and one in the van, the getaway van. He was just sitting there with the engine running.'

'This van,' said Fox. 'Did you get the number?'

'Oh yes.' Deacon looked pleased with himself. 'I wrote it down and gave it to this gentleman.' He indicated DI Gilroy.

'False plates, guv'nor,' said Gilroy. 'We've checked. And those two are nicked.' He pointed at the abandoned cars that the robbers had used to stop the security van.

'Anything else about the van?'

Deacon shook his head. 'Nothing that I can remember, no.'

Fox turned to Gilroy. 'We'll have this little team, Jack. I want everyone on this. D'you hear? Everyone!'

'Right, guv'nor.' Gilroy turned away, unhappy. It was unfortunate that Fox had been out and about in his car when the call came through and had been close enough to reach the scene and interfere. Gilroy, as a competent DI, was quite capable of doing what was necessary, and didn't need his detective chief superintendent breathing down his neck. But Fox loved mixing it, as he called it, and refused to stay at his desk. Most detective chief superintendents found that the paperwork attached to their job tended to keep them away from the cut-and-thrust of crime. Fox would have none of it, and frequently upset his commander by overlooking the administrative demands of his post.

Tommy Fox appeared in the doorway of the Flying Squad office at New Scotland Yard and scowled. 'Where's Mr Gilroy?'

'Out, guv,' somebody said.

'Out where?'

A detective stood up. 'I'll have a look in the Duty Book, sir.' He walked across the office to the A3-sized binder that was kept permanently open on a central table and ran his finger up the page. 'Meeting informant in the Walworth Road, guv... on Carter Street's ground.'

'I know where the Walworth Road is,' growled Fox. 'What time's he supposed to be coming back?'

' "Back conc" , it says here, sir.' The detective looked up and grinned. It was the recognised and invariably used abbreviation for 'back at conclusion'.

'Doesn't it always,' said Fox irritably, and made his way down the corridor to his office.

Twenty-four hours had elapsed since the raid on the security van at Cobham, just two hundred yards inside the Metropolitan Police boundary. But that was not all. Exactly an hour later, fifteen miles away — and again just inside the boundary — another cash-in-transit van belonging to the same security company had been attacked. But on the second occasion there had been no independent witnesses, and both guards had denied seeing a transit van similar to the one used in the raid at Cobham. Tommy Fox had to admit that for the team to have used the same van a second time would have been chancing their arm just a little too far, but apart from that the MO was identical. The only conclusion that Fox drew was that the team must have an inexhaustible supply of chain-saws.

The robbers in the second heist, the guards had said, had fled in a Ford Granada which the police had later found abandoned in a lay-by near Heathrow Airport. Altogether the thieves had netted over three hundred thousand pounds in the two raids.

'These cash-in-transit people are getting a bit slovenly,' said Fox when Gilroy eventually returned from his sortie into south London. Gilroy had a coterie of informants, most of whom could usually be found in the pubs in or around the Elephant and Castle. 'What's the word, Jack?'

'Not a dicky-bird, guv'nor. Nobody's saying anything.'

Fox moved his hand slowly across the top of his desk and flicked a fly into eternity. 'They've had three hundred grand off, Jack. The bastards have got to have put it somewhere. There's no way they're going to be able to launder that lot in a hurry.'

Gilroy nodded. 'From where they did the hit, there's a thousand places they could have picked for a slaughter.'

'Yeah, but I'm not going looking for it, Jack.' Fox stood up and walked across to a framed map of the Metropolitan Police District on his wall. It was one of the few old ones still remaining and showed all the divisional letters of the force as it had been for nearly a century before a new commissioner had decided to mess it all up and impose eight administrations where previously there had been only one. 'They've certainly got plenty of scope. Lots of nice country there for a slaughter.' It was one of the perversities of criminal slang that a slaughter was a place where stolen goods were secreted; a slaughter had nothing to do with killing. 'I think we'll have to set a trap.' Fox carefully lifted the collar of his jacket and then smoothed it back into place. 'But first we'll have to find one member of this team. That's down to you, Jack.'

Detective Inspector Jack Gilroy was as unlike a Flying Squad officer as it was possible to imagine. Just touching six feet tall, he was a youthful-looking man who wore rimless spectacles and for most of the year affected a waistcoat. What made him valuable to Tommy Fox was that for the last three years he had been a member of the Yard's Criminal Intelligence Branch and had only recently been transferred — following lengthy negotiations between Fox and Murdo McGregor, Gilroy's previous commander — to SO8, as the Flying Squad was officially styled.

'This team, Jack,' said Fox, 'that's had these two tickles on this so-called security firm...' He blew gently between clenched teeth, an eloquent criticism of a company that seemed to have failed in its primary duty. 'Should be done under the Trades Description Act. Bloody cowboys, they are.'

'Yes, sir.'

'I want these villains, Jack.'

Gilroy took off his spectacles and carefully wiped them. 'Are you sure it was the same team, sir?'

'Got to be, hasn't it?'

Gilroy shook his head. 'I'm not so sure.'

Fox looked surprised. 'Come on, Jack. Look at the facts. Same company owned both vehicles. Same MO. And both just inside the MPD. Probably an inside job.'

Gilroy knew the signs: Fox was thrashing about. 'But the van, sir...'

Fox frowned. 'What about the van?' he growled.

'Wasn't used in both jobs, sir.'

'Would you have used it in both? The moment they'd pulled the first one, they'd have known that every copper in London would be looking for it. Well,' he added reflectively, 'every copper in London had better be looking for it. No, mister, that bloody van's not come to light in twenty-four hours. It's got to be holed up in a slaughter somewhere. And I want it... and the little firm that goes with it. Get among them, Jack.'

'Getting among them' had a rather different meaning for Gilroy than Fox visualised. Tommy Fox was one of the old school of detectives who firmly believed in making frequent visits to the pubs, clubs and racecourses he knew to be haunts of the wicked. And it worked. The sight of the operational head of the Flying Squad in some low boozer south of the Thames would cause a severe outbreak of astonishing introspection and an uncharacteristic interest, by the patrons, in the inside of their glass of beer. A similar visitation to, say, Kempton, Sandown, Epsom, or, worse, Wimbledon, Haringey or White City would create a paroxysm of activity among the less honourable tic-tac men.

Gilroy was unimpressed by this. Apart from anything else, he had been trained as a criminal intelligence officer and was a committed computer man. It usually meant that when he and the team of detectives he led eventually paid a visit, someone was going to get nicked... for something that would stick. But just because he often worked with a computer didn't make him a soft touch. He was a hard man, and could play villains at their own game. He simply liked to be certain of his facts first, rather than play a hunch. Fox would never admit it, but it was more effective than his method.

Sometimes, of course, events called for a combination of both methods. And this seemed such an occasion.

Gilroy started work. The record of every criminal who had ever been involved in a payroll heist was brought up on the computer screen and examined. Those who were in prison were eliminated, as were others known to be in exotic places for health reasons. One or two others were ruled out too, like those who operated only outside the Greater London area. Finally, Gilroy was able to present Fox with a list that contained a mere nine names.

'We'll play this low-key, Jack,' said Fox. 'Get the hounds out. Find out where they are and what they've been up to. Nothing direct until we're certain we've got one of them. And then...' He smoothed Gilroy's list with his hand and smiled, serenely.

Needless to say, Fox had a plan and he had explained it carefully to the Flying Squad in a short briefing. Fox trusted his men and credited them with still possessing the intelligence and unscrupulous cunning for which they had been selected in the first place.

There is an element of live and let live in the unceasing war which is waged between the police and the forces of evil, but this undefined discretion is, from time to time, suspended. And Fox had just suspended it. From now until the security van robbers were apprehended nothing and no one would move. Search warrants would rain like confetti and be executed relentlessly until the occupants of the Flying Squad's targets were dizzy. In short, London's villains were in for a hard time... harder than usual. And they would be squeezed until someone squeaked.

It is in the nature of things that this uncomfortable atmosphere — like a hot and humid summer's day — will make tempers short, and the sort of hooligans whose profession is to relieve others of their property and wealth will eventually become so frustrated that word will go out to give the Old Bill whatever it is that they want so that relations can be restored to some semblance of normality.

The upshot of this carefully conceived and executed stratagem was the arrival of Detective Inspector Jack Gilroy in a public house in the Rotherhithe area of London — a public house much frequented by persons known to the police. Gilroy was alone. The sort of business he had in mind to transact was such that he preferred to do so in the absence of witnesses.

The pub was gloomy. The woodwork — which was a dominant feature — was blackened with the grime of years, and the ceiling, once white, was brown with several generations of exhaled cigarette smoke.

'Hallo, Dancer.' Gilroy perched himself on the leather-topped stool next to a foxy-faced little man with shifty eyes.

'Dancer' Williams shot a nervous sideways glance at the policeman. 'Mr Gilroy! What you doing in here?'

'Same as you were doing at Epsom last week,' said Gilroy. 'I'm on business.'

'I never went nowhere near Epsom last week, Mr Gilroy, so help me.'

Gilroy grinned at Williams' reflection through the tarnished mirror at the back of the bar. 'Saw you there myself,' he said. 'Had your hands in more pockets than the Chancellor of the Exchequer.'

'Play it straight, Mr Gilroy. You know I wasn't nowhere near there.'

Gilroy took a packet of cigarettes from his jacket, lit one, and dropped another on the bar in front of the anguished Williams. 'And who d'you think the magistrate's going to believe, Dancer? You or me?'

'You're after something, Mr Gilroy...'

'Now you're getting a bit shrewd. Yeah, sure I'm after something. The little firm that did two security vans the day before yesterday and — '

'Christ, Mr Gilroy, don't ask me that — '

'Don't interrupt, Dancer, it's rude,' said Gilroy. 'As I was saying, the firm that did two security vans and had it away with about three hundred grand.'

'I don't know nothing about it, Mr Gilroy, so help me, I don't.' Williams looked depressed and studied his beer with a consuming intensity.

'Well then, Dancer, p'raps you'd better start listening around. Really listening, I mean.'

Gilroy slid off the bar stool and grinned at Williams' reflection. 'Be lucky,' he said.

The phone call, when it reached Gilroy anonymously from Dancer Williams, gave him a name. To no one's surprise, it was a name that featured on Gilroy's list.

'There you are, Jack,' said Fox. 'Whittled down from nine to one in one foul swoop.'

'Fell swoop,' murmured Gilroy.

Fox grinned. 'I know what I mean, Jack,' he said.

The name was Perkins. Harry Perkins. And Harry Perkins was a brilliant snooker player. If Perkins' devotion to the game had not been interrupted at regular intervals for the purpose of spending a period in one of Her Majesty's Prisons, he could have been a world-class professional. As it was, Perkins was to be found most days of the week at a billiard hall in Stockwell. He was rarely short of a partner for a frame or two, but none of them would take him on for money.

Jack Gilroy sauntered into the billiard hall and looked around. The clientele, for the most part, did not know who he was... but they knew what he was. Gilroy did not know Perkins either, not by sight that is.

'Harry Perkins about?' he asked of a pimply-faced youth who had just missed a sitting red.

The youth nodded briefly towards the next table where a tall, skinny individual was pocketing red balls with relentless dedication. For once he had no partner.

'Harry Perkins?'

'Who wants to know?'

'Detective Inspector Gilroy, Flying Squad.'

'Oh yeah!' Perkins' cue ball kissed the pink and disappeared into a far pocket. 'Sod it,' he added.

'Oh, bad luck,' said Gilroy. 'I want to talk to you.'

'Oh yeah? What about?' Perkins recovered the white ball and steered it back behind the balk-line with the side of his cue.

'A certain little heist two or three days ago. In fact, two heists two or three days ago.'

'Dunno what you're on about.'

'I'm on about three hundred K,' said Gilroy. 'And I'm here to talk business.'

'What sort of business?' Perkins looked along his cue, but glanced up at the detective briefly.

'Not here,' said Gilroy. 'Across the road in the boozer.' He walked out.

Perkins leaned on the bar and gazed reflectively at the pint of bitter Gilroy had bought for him before his arrival. 'I drink Scotch,' he said.

'Take it or leave it,' said Gilroy.

Perkins took a sip of the warm beer. 'What business?'

'I've been talking to faces.'

'Oh yeah.'

'And one of them tells me that you're involved in these two little jobs, Harry. Don't mind if I call you Harry, do you?'

Perkins shrugged and shot a sideways glance at Gilroy. 'So?'

'No one else knows,' said Gilroy.

'What's that supposed to mean?'

'My guv'nor knows where the slaughter is. Where you've got it stashed.'

'You don't expect me to believe that, do you?' Perkins grinned. 'Why would you come down here to tell me that?'

'Between you and me, he's going to repossess it,' said Gilroy. 'That'll be half the battle.'

'And the other half?'

'The names. Nobody's got any names. Except me. And I've got yours.'

'What are we talking here, Mr Gilroy?' Perkins suddenly realised that this conversation was not taking the customary course. In his experience, the filth didn't invite you to have a drink and then nick you.

'We're talking a little percentage to stay shtum.'

Perkins nodded slowly and then took another sip of beer. He wiped his mouth with the back of his hand. 'And if I don't play?'

'Very silly, that'd be.'

'Supposing I go down the Yard and tell 'em what you just said?'

'How much form you got, Harry?' Gilroy knew the answer to that.

'A bit.'

'That's right. Are they going to take your word against mine? Or are you wired up?' Gilroy ran his hand quickly down Perkins' shirt front. It was half a joke. Gilroy knew that villains of Perkins' calibre didn't go around perpetually carrying recording equipment on the off chance of the Old Bill soliciting bribes.

Perkins turned to face Gilroy for the first time since he had entered the pub. It was a sign of the increasing confidence that comes from the comparative security of dealing with a bent copper. 'We only had the one off,' he said. The thought that Gilroy might be wired up had obviously not entered his head.

'Pull the other one,' said Gilroy. 'It's got bells on it.'

'Straight, Mr Gilroy. Just the one.'

'OK, but if you're trying to have me over...' He left the threat hanging in the air. 'How much?'

'Hundred grand, give or take.'

'Let's settle for a premium of ten K, then.'

Perkins looked shocked. 'That's a bit steep,' he said. 'It'll have to come out of my cut.'

'That's your problem. I reckon you scored about twenty grand each. Talk to your friends. See if you can defray the overheads. Look at it this way: it's five per cent less than VAT.'

'You've got no evidence,' said Perkins.

'How d'you know?'

'Because if you had, you wouldn't be here negotiating now.'

'But you've just told me...'

Perkins grinned. 'That's the sort of verbal you might have got away with a few years ago,' he said truculently, 'but not any more.'

It was bravado. He knew that this Flying Squad detective could stitch him up a treat, and with his form he'd go down like a ton of bricks. 'All right,' he said. 'I'll meet you back here tomorrow, same time.'

Gilroy laughed cynically. 'Don't be funny, Harry,' he said. 'I'm not falling for that. You and half the Complaints Investigation Bureau, I suppose.'

Perkins looked hurt. 'Would I do a thing like that, Mr Gilroy?'

'Yes,' said Gilroy. 'I'll find you. Be lucky.' He slapped Perkins on the back and then ostentatiously wiped his hand on his trousers.

Perkins left it for a quarter of an hour and then walked casually down the road and made a phone call.

Chapter Two

Tommy Fox knew with the instinct of twenty years' experience of pursuing the unrighteous that Harry Perkins would make for the nearest telephone box. Not that Perkins would have done so had he known that Gilroy had in his possession Fox's signed authority to play the part of a copper on the make. Gilroy had insisted on having it in writing. He knew that things of this sort could go terribly wrong and that if he was suddenly confronted by a couple of heavies from the Yard's Complaints Branch, it might happen that people forgot all about the set-up in which he had been involved. Not that Tommy Fox was like that, but it paid to be cautious. Gilroy hadn't liked the idea, but Fox had convinced him. 'Not in the dream factory now, Jack,' he had said. 'This is the real world of cops and robbers.'

Fox had had a bit of trouble getting a Home Office warrant to put an intercept on the phone box that Perkins had made for, and the one at the snooker club. The snooker club wasn't so bad, but some toffee-nosed bastard at Queen Anne's Gate had said that the Home Secretary was not at all keen on tapping public call boxes. It abrogated people's civil rights, he had said. Fox was unimpressed and had drily observed that 'nicking three hundred K off 'em' didn't do a lot for their civil rights either.

The call that Perkins had made went out to Alfred Barnes, a villain known as 'Silver' because of his white hair. Mr Barnes had an office in Clapham from where he conducted various dubious business transactions under the all-embracing heading of general dealer. When he received Harry Perkins' call, Mr Barnes became very agitated and swore at Perkins for talking to the police at all, let alone the Heavy Mob, as the Flying Squad was unaffectionately known to the criminal fraternity of which Silver Barnes was a member.

Silver Barnes was not greatly taken with the idea of parting with ten thousand pounds just to sweeten a detective whose informant had put the finger on one of his business associates... and, by implication, on Barnes himself.

The loot would have to be moved, pronto, and before Perkins' next meet with DI Gilroy. Barnes didn't believe that Tommy Fox knew where the slaughter was, any more than Perkins believed it. It was obviously part of Gilroy's ploy of unsettlement to make Barnes and his team feel more vulnerable than usual, but Barnes was not prepared to chance it.

Barnes decided that he would leave the other three members of his team in comfortable ignorance for the time being. To remove the proceeds of the robbery to another place that they didn't know about would undoubtedly make them more willing to part with a percentage of their share to buy off Gilroy. It was a dangerous business, but it was a chance that Barnes had to take. The van would have to be got rid of too.

Some time previously, Barnes had bought in one of British Telecom's cast-offs and had spent some time restoring its original yellow livery so that it could pass for the real thing. It was this van that he intended to use to transport the cash. And he intended that he and Perkins should be booked up. It didn't pay to take risks and there were too many dishonest people about, just waiting to get their hands on a substantial sum of money.

*

Commander Murdo McGregor, head of the Yard's Criminal Intelligence Branch, was justly proud of his surveillance team which until recently had been led by DI Jack Gilroy. He still regretted the moment of weakness when he had sanctioned Gilroy's transfer to the Flying Squad but was fair-minded enough to acknowledge that it would give the inspector wider experience and a consequently better chance of promotion.

The static observation which had been set up in Stockwell just before Gilroy's meeting with Harry Perkins was a routine operation similar to hundreds of such jobs that had been undertaken by SO11 Branch in the past. So was the observation at Clapham which had been put on immediately, the intercept on Perkins' call to Silver Barnes had told them where to mount it.

It was the next part that was going to be the real test. Mobile surveillance was never easy. London's traffic saw to that.

Nothing happened until nine o'clock that night, by which time the surveillance teams had been in place for nearly eight hours. Not that any but the most acutely observant would have noticed. The nondescript vans and cars, and even the motor-cyclists, merged into the south London milieu as perfectly as a chameleon took advantage of its temporary habitat. But it was gruelling and there was always a danger of being compromised, particularly at this time of the year when the schools were on holiday and the streets of Stockwell and Clapham were filled with apprentice criminals looking for something to do... or something to nick.

One of the vans, a beaten-up and filthy Ford Transit — but with a superb engine — was crewed by Detective Sergeant Jefferies and Detective Constable Trinder. At about four in the afternoon, Trinder had become aware that a group of youngsters had gathered on the pavement.

''Ere,' said one loudly. 'There's a bloke in that van. You can see the slits.'

'What are we going to do, skip?' asked Trinder. 'If we don't get rid of them, we'll show out.'

'Nothing to it, lad,' said Jefferies. He stood up and opened the rear door of the observation van. Sternly he surveyed his young audience. They, in turn, stared stoically back.

'Told yer,' said the spokesman.

'Your dads all got television licences, have they?' asked Jefferies loudly.

There was a stunned silence and then suddenly the group broke up, running in all directions.

But the surveillance went well. Completely oblivious of his followers, Harry Perkins drove to Clapham and made his way to a lock-up in one of the back doubles near Venn Street. It was not an arrangement which had been made in Perkins' telephone call to Barnes that morning, and the watchers could only presume that there had been another conversation between them from a phone other than the two monitored by the police. Ideally, Fox would have arranged for an intercept to be put on Barnes' phone within minutes of Perkins' telephone call that morning, but he knew that the Home Office would never move that fast to issue a warrant.

The door of the lock-up was opened from the inside to admit Perkins and was quickly closed again. The surveillance team had held back so as not to arouse suspicion and consequently were unable to see who was already inside.

Patiently, the police waited another twenty minutes before the doors of the lock-up were opened again and a yellow Austin Maestro emerged. It paused briefly while Perkins shut the garage doors, locked them and climbed in beside Silver Barnes. Both men were attired in overalls that would enable them to pass as Telecom engineers.

All this information was passed by radio to Tommy Fox whose powerful Ford Granada was parked on Clapham Common. It was unusual for the Flying Squad chief to take a personal hand in an operation of this sort, but as the thieves had thumbed their noses at him by doing two robberies only an hour apart, he felt they were entitled to some specialist treatment.

'Right,' said Fox to his driver. 'Let's go.'

'Right, guv.' The driver started the engine and then looked sideways at Fox. 'Where to, guv?' he asked.

'I don't know,' said Fox. 'Listen to the radio. You're the driver.' He eased his seat back a few notches and stretched his legs as the car moved off.

The surveillance team's running commentary was precise, and the Flying Squad, who were not involved in that part of the operation, were able to follow the same route without difficulty.

Not once did the bogus Telecom van exceed the speed limit. On occasions like this, Silver Barnes and other villains going similarly about their nefarious business, were faced with a problem. Keeping to the speed limit was often, in itself, regarded with suspicion by patrolling police cars, but if they exceeded it, they were almost certain to be stopped and asked some very awkward questions. On this occasion, Fox was hoping as fervently as the villains were, that that would not happen.

It was a tiresome business. Out through Merton. Then Wimbledon. And on to the A3. The in-town following was not too difficult: there was plenty of traffic about. But when Barnes and Perkins reached Esher and turned into Copsem Lane, it became a task for a solo motor-cyclist.

At last the message that Fox had been waiting for came through. The van had taken a turning off Copsem Lane, driven for half a mile and into the grounds of a house that couldn't be seen from the road.

'Got 'em,' said Fox, and removing the radio handset from its place in the glove compartment he gave instructions to the Flying Squad team.

Fox's car drove slowly through the gateway, the headlamps fixing Barnes and Perkins in the act of returning to the van, each of them carrying two nylon holdalls. For a moment the two robbers remained motionless, then they dropped the holdalls and turned and ran towards the back of the house. Fox remained in the car and smiled. A few minutes later the two reappeared, handcuffed, accompanied by a number of Flying Squad officers, the little procession shepherded by Detective Inspector Jack Gilroy.

Fox got out of his car and, pausing only to fasten the centre button on the jacket of his immaculately tailored suit, strolled across.

'Both tooled up, guv'nor,' said Gilroy, displaying two pistols.

'Well, well,' Fox said and tinned to examine the two prisoners. 'Mr Barnes and Mr Perkins, I presume?' The two robbers scowled but remained silent. 'Thomas Fox... of the Flying Squad,' he said with a smile. 'And in case you were under any illusions, gents, you're nicked.' Fox tinned to DI Gilroy. 'What's in the bags, Jack?' he asked.

'Money, guv'nor,' said Gilroy. 'Lots of money.'

'Oh dear, how unfortunate.' Fox took a step closer to Barnes. 'What I want from you is an explanation. Like where you got this money from...' He kicked lightly at one of the bags. 'And who helped you to acquire it.'

'Aren't you supposed to caution me?' asked Barnes sarcastically.

'Don't be ridiculous,' said Fox. 'You know the rules. Now don't tell me you're not going to co-operate.'

'I've got nothing to say,' said Barnes with a sneer.

'Oh dear!' Fox turned to Gilroy. 'Have you hit him yet, Jack?'

Gilroy moved closer. 'Not yet, sir.'

Fox looked pensive. 'P'raps you'd better give it some consideration.'

'Now hold on!' A look of sudden fear appeared on Barnes' face. He had fallen foul of the Flying Squad before. They were nasty bastards and they didn't always play by the rules.

'I thought we'd wait until we got to the nick, guv'nor.' Gilroy played along, but he had never struck a prisoner in his life.

'Which is the local nick?'

'Cobham, sir.'

'Oh yes, of course. Very nice little nick is that. Isolated. You can't be overheard.'

'Unfortunately,' continued Gilroy, 'it's closed at nights. We'll have to go to Esher.'

'What a shame,' said Fox. 'We'll just have to try not to disturb anyone.'

The night-duty custody sergeant at Esher police station was a bit put out. Usually the most that he had to deal with was a drunken driver who had zoomed through the division in his BMW on his way to the stockbroker belt, and had been caught by traffic officers — the Black Rats — waiting in cover on the A3. On those occasions, the custody sergeant was in command. But now he was confronted by a detective chief superintendent and at least two DIs, apart from a handful of detective sergeants all of whom, the custody sergeant was convinced, had a scathing contempt for the Uniform Branch.

'Where's the canteen, squire?' asked DS Percy Fletcher.

'We don't have one. Just a meal room,' said the custody sergeant. 'There is a kettle,' he added helpfully. The Flying Squad officer's suit made him feel inferior.

DS Fletcher stared at him for some seconds. 'Bloody hell!' he said.

Tommy Fox settled himself in the DI's office and picked up the phone. 'Get me the Press Bureau at Scotland Yard, my dear, would you please?' he said to the middle-aged lady on the switchboard, who, unbeknown to him, had tutted at having to put down her knitting.

'This is Thomas Fox... of the Flying Squad,' he said when eventually he was connected.

'Evening, Mr Fox,' said the Information Officer.

'I should like it to be widely known,' said Fox, studying the revealing portrait of a young lady on the absent DI's calendar, 'that the Flying Squad has just arrested two suspects called Barnes and Perkins in connection with the recent security van robberies — Cobham and Heathrow — and that same are at this moment assisting the police with their enquiries.'

'Right, Mr Fox. Where are they being held?'

Fox paused only briefly. 'Bow Street,' he said and put the phone down.

He strolled down the stairs, through the charge room and into the interview room. 'Is he talking to you yet, Jack?' he asked as though Silver Barnes wasn't there.

'Not a dicky-bird, guv,' said DI Gilroy, 'but Perkins wants a private word.' He grinned.

Fox opened the door to the front office. 'Let me talk to Perkins, skip, will you?'

'Yes, sir. D'you want him brought up?' The custody sergeant hurried through with the cell keys.

'No thanks. I'll make it a house call.' Fox walked through into the cell passage and waited while the sergeant opened the wicket and inspected the occupant of Cell Three prior to unlocking the door. Perkins was lounging on the bed and made no move as Fox came through the door. 'You got something to say to me, Harry?'

'You bet I have.' Perkins' attitude was surly. 'That copper out there... Gilroy — '

'Mr Gilroy? What about him?'

'He's bent.'

'Good gracious! What on earth makes you think that?' Fox smiled. Those who knew him better than Perkins did would have interpreted it as a dangerous smile.

'He tried to blag me for ten grand.'

Fox nodded sympathetically. 'In the boozer opposite the billiard hall in Stockwell, you mean?'

Perkins sat up sharply, propping himself on one elbow. 'How d'you know that?'

'I sent him,' said Fox mildly. 'Seemed to be the easiest way to get you to talk to your mate Barnes. He's going to be well pleased when he finds out.' Fox turned in the doorway. 'You ought to be more careful, putting stories about like that, you know, Harry. Mr Gilroy can get very nasty when the mood takes him.' He paused. 'He might even sue you for slander.' Fox slammed the cell door with a resounding bang and walked back into the interview room. 'Jack.' He signalled to Gilroy to follow him. 'What I want you to do,' he said, once they were out of Barnes' hearing, 'is to get your team back to the slaughter and wait.'

'What for?'

'The rest of them,' said Fox. He smiled an evil smile.

'What makes you think — ?'

'Very simple,' said Fox. 'I have just released the news to the Press Bureau that these two have been nicked... just in case some big-mouth here hasn't done it for me already.' He swept a hand round the charge-room as if to indicate the entire staff of the station. 'But I have said nothing about finding the proceeds of the robbery. Ergo, Jack, the remainder of the firm, who you can bet your boots weren't told what Barnes and Perkins were up to this evening, will hear the sad news and immediately rush down here like the Seventh Cavalry to liberate the loot... I hope.'

Jack Gilroy nodded slowly. 'I like that, guv'nor. I like that very much... or I will if it works.'

*

It did. Having been briefed by the Press Bureau, radio and television stations and the morning newspapers informed the nation that, following raids in various parts of the capital, two men had been detained. At least two members of the great listening public were very interested in this snippet... passionately interested, in fact. Namely a Mr Lambie and a Mr Grover, who drove hell-for-leather to Cobham.

Once there, they made straight for the changing room alongside the swimming pool very close to where Perkins and Barnes had been arrested less than twelve hours previously. They opened the door to find themselves peering at the wrong end of a Smith and Wesson which gently wavered from Lambie's navel to Grover's navel and back again.

'Good morning, gents,' said Gilroy.

They turned. Rapidly. Only to find their escape blocked by another armed officer.

'The guv'nor said "Good morning".' DS Percy Fletcher's revolver lazily indicated that they should put their hands up.

'What's bloody good about it?' asked Lambie.

'Well,' said Fox, resting his feet on the small table in his office and accepting a cup of coffee from DC Swann. 'What do we know so far, Jack?'

'Apart from the four in custody and seventy grand from the first job, nothing, sir. We're still short of the wheelman, thirty K from Cobham and the take from the job at Heathrow. The van they used at Cobham was in the lock-up at Clapham.'

Fox shook his head slowly. 'Two choices, Jack. It's either at Cobham, or it's somewhere else.'

The disparity in rank between Gilroy and Fox prevented the DI from pointing out that that was bloody obvious.

'And,' said Fox, walking across to his wall map, 'given that the slaughter where we nicked them is mid-way between the venues of the two jobs, my money is on it being there somewhere.' He jabbed a forefinger at Cobham before turning to face Gilroy. 'So find it, Jack.'

'Find it?'

Fox nodded. 'Yeah!' He sat down again propping his feet on the occasional table once more, and finished his cup of coffee. 'How big's that drum, Jack?'

Gilroy shrugged. 'An acre, maybe less... three quarters.'

'Rooms? How many rooms?'

'Three reception rooms, six bedrooms, two bathrooms... one en suite —'

'All right, all right. You're not a bloody estate agent.'

'It's a big house, guv. Swimming pool and changing rooms, three-car garage ... '

'Right. I want it searched. That money's got to be there somewhere.'

They wrecked it. Floorboards came up, mattresses were slit open, chimneys were swept. Nothing!

'Right,' said Fox. 'Dig!'

'Dig, sir?' Gilroy looked horrified.

Fox nodded. 'Got to be there somewhere, Jack.'

'We could get a helicopter, sir.'

Fox looked at his DI, searching for a tell-tale smirk. 'What would you do with a helicopter?'

'The lab boys have got one of those machines — infra-red or ultra-violet, or some damn thing — that tells you if the earth's been disturbed.'

'See through trees, does it?' asked Fox acidly. He was suspicious of many modern aids to crime detection.

Gilroy shrugged. 'I don't know, sir.'

Fox put his hands behind his head and yawned. 'Well, Jack, I don't care how you do it, but do it. And...' Gilroy paused at the door. 'Do let me know if the earth moves for you, Jack.'

*

It took a week.

'Well?' asked Fox.

'No money,' said Gilroy. He was speaking on the telephone from the Cobham house. 'But we've just found a body.'

'Oh!' said Fox. 'Whose is it?'

'Dunno, sir. Female anon.'

Fox put down the receiver. 'Sod it,' he said and then shouted through the open door of his office. 'Swann!'

'Sir?'

'Get my car up.'

Chapter Three

The Flying Squad do not like murders. It is not that they have any moral objections, or fastidiousness, or even scruples about the taking of human life. In fact, they accept that it is part of the murky world in which they live and operate: a sort of profit and loss account of criminality. It is simply that they do not specialise in the investigation of murder.

The news that DI Jack Gilroy and his team had found a body did not therefore fill Tommy Fox with unrestrained joy, especially as it had been his own idea to dig up the garden.

'Well?' Fox stood at the back of the house and gazed at the canvas screen that had been erected around the grave, and at the cluster of support staff: photographers and 'sockoes', as scene-of-crime officers were known, and at the mountain of equipment which had been unloaded from their fleet of white vans now cluttering up the drive of the house.

The pathologist, Pamela Hatcher, walked towards Fox, pulling off her rubber gloves. 'Hallo, Tommy,' she said. 'Don't tell me that the Sweeney have caught a murder.' She was nearing fifty years of age, slender, and wore her long greying hair in a single pigtail... at least, when she was working.

'Bloody well looks like it,' said Fox gloomily. 'If you're certain it's a murder.' His devious mind was working out ways in which he might be able to lumber this unwelcome enquiry on to someone else. But he knew from previous experience that the chances of doing so were remote.

Pamela Hatcher grinned. 'I should think so. I know the cost of funerals is high, but she's buried in her day clothes in a shallow grave.'

Fox grimaced. 'How long's she been there?'

'Not long.'

'Is that the best you can do?'

'Give me a chance, Tommy. I'll tell you when I've done the post-mortem ... perhaps.'

'Cause of death?'

'Ditto,' said the pathologist.

'Thanks.' Fox walked across to the screens and stepped inside, trying to avoid getting mud on the tooled leather of his elegant McAfee shoes. On a board beside the hole lay the putrefying body of a woman. A little of her brown hair remained, but it was really the earth-stained red dress that gave an initial indication of her sex.

'Can't see any obvious signs of injury.' Pamela Hatcher was standing behind Fox as he surveyed this latest piece of human detritus to come to the notice of the police. 'But then I wouldn't expect to, not with the body in that state. No doubt the PM will tell a different story.'

'Like natural causes?' asked Fox hopefully.

Pamela Hatcher laughed. 'Like hell,' she said.

*

'D'you remember the murder of a soldier called Reg Watters, at Duisburg in Germany?' asked Pamela Hatcher.

'No. Should I?'

'Not from your own experience, I didn't mean. It was in the 1950s. He was killed by his wife's lover. Chap called Emmett-Dunne.'

'I was at school then,' said Fox.

'So was I, but he was killed by a karate-type blow across the throat. It was thought to be suicide at first — '

'You mean people actually commit suicide by hitting themselves across the throat?' asked Fox, but he was smiling. He did actually remember some of the vague details of the case.

'No,' said Pamela Hatcher, sitting down and pulling off her rubber boots. She thrust her feet into a pair of shoes and stood up again. 'The murderer simulated a hanging. But the PM, when they eventually got around to it, showed that the horn of the voice box had been fractured. Not something you could achieve with a hanging.'

'Very good,' said Fox, glancing at his watch. 'Is this all leading somewhere?'

'That's what you've got in there,' said Pamela Hatcher, jerking her thumb in the direction of the theatre where the mortuary technicians were roughly reassembling the body of the woman that Jack Gilroy and his men had found. 'I don't mean a rigged suicide. I mean a fractured horn on the voice-box.'

'And?'

'She was almost certainly killed by a blow to the front of the throat, probably with the edge of a hand. Whose hand is your problem, Tommy.' Pamela Hatcher smiled. 'Oh, and by the way, she was three months' pregnant.'

*

Fox laid the pathologist's report on his desk. 'Pamela Hatcher reckons that she had been dead about two weeks or so,' he said. DI Gilroy nodded. 'Apparently there's something in the soil around there that preserves dead bodies. Useful to know, that,' he added.

'It didn't look very preserved to me, sir,' said Gilroy.

Fox shook his head slowly. 'A comparative term, Jack, a comparative term. If it hadn't been for the soil in that particular place, the body would have been in an even worse state.'

'Oh!' said Gilroy and paused. 'And the cause of death?'

'As previously stated,' said Fox. 'A chop across the throat.'

The whole thing was unsatisfactory. Due to the limitations of the Police and Criminal Evidence Act, a millstone which Her Majesty's Government had hawked around as a piece of legislation designed to assist the police, Messrs Perkins, Barnes, Lambie and Grover had appeared before a Bow Street stipendiary magistrate and been remanded to Brixton Prison. They had appeared at Bow Street despite having been arrested in Cobham because Tommy Fox didn't hold with what he called local arrangements... and that included benches of lay justices. He had, therefore, had his prisoners transported to London and charged at Bow Street Police Station, but a short walk across the station yard to the court.

All this had happened because the police had insufficient grounds for extending the period of the quartet's detention prior to their being charged, or for seeking a remand into police custody after they had been charged. As the villains' solicitor had pointed out to the magistrate in the most unctuous of tones, the police had recovered the money and they had four men in custody. What else did they want?

The only highlight in the morning's proceedings had been a short exchange between the said solicitor and the beak. Right in the middle of the solicitor's impassioned plea for bail, the magistrate had interrupted. 'There will be no bail in this case,' he had said mildly.

The solicitor shuddered to a stop in mid-flow. 'You make it very difficult for me to continue, sir,' he had said.

'That was my object.' The magistrate had smiled and written 'RIC' in the large book in front of him.

None the less, Fox had got the distinct impression that the court was doing him a favour in remanding his four prisoners in custody rather than releasing them on bail.

That, however, was history. On the day that Gilroy and his team had found the woman's body at the slaughter in Cobham, Barnes and Co. had appeared at Bow Street for their first remand hearing. Fortunately they had been put down again, but that created problems. Every time that Fox and his officers wanted to talk to the robbers — there was no doubt in Fox's mind that they were guilty — they had to journey to Brixton to do it. And the sterile surroundings of one of Her Majesty's Prisons was not exactly conducive to a little homely chat about the inmates' futures.

Nevertheless, the four were each interviewed independently but refused absolutely to discuss the Cobham job in the absence of their solicitor. They further denied any involvement in the Heathrow job and when the question of the woman's body was raised, they as good as dismissed it as a Flying Squad stitch-up.

'We've tried ID-ing her on fingerprints, sir.' Gilroy appeared in the doorway of Fox's office.

Fox looked up from the Court and Social page of *The Times*. 'Yeah?'

'Nothing, sir. She's not on record,' said Gilroy.

'Find her dentist, Jack,' said Fox. 'See if he can identify her from his records.'

It wasn't that easy, and Gilroy knew it. He arranged for a dental surgeon to examine the teeth in the nameless body, but it was no help.

'As far as I can tell, Mr Gilroy,' said the dentist, 'this woman had perfect teeth. I can't see any trace of her having received dental treatment in her life.'

'You mean that I'm unlikely to find a dentist who'd treated her?' The dental surgeon shrugged. 'She may have had a regular scale and polish. Some people do, others don't bother. I can make you up a chart of what we've got here, and I can wish you the best of luck. But that's all I can do.' He peeled off his rubber gloves and washed his hands. 'She is British, I suppose?'

Gilroy looked puzzled. 'Does that make a difference, then?'

The dentist grinned. 'Does really, doesn't it? It's no good asking around the dentists in Britain, if she just happened to be here on holiday from, say, America... or France.'

'Thanks a lot,' said Gilroy. 'Can't you tell?'

'I've just said that she's received no dental treatment,' said the dentist. 'If you mean are foreigners' mouths different, the answer generally is no... if they're of Caucasian stock.'

'It wasn't that,' said Gilroy, smiling. 'I just thought I could smell a whiff of garlic.' None the less, he sent out copies of the chart made by the dentist. He got no replies. Not because the dental profession is ill-disposed to co-operate with the police, but simply because on this occasion it had nothing to tell him. It left him wondering if there was something in what the dentist had said about the corpse being foreign.

*

'Terrific.' Fox folded his newspaper untidily and dropped it in the waste-paper basket. In his view it was very unreasonable of unknown victims of violent crime not to have previous convictions and thus enable the police to identify them without too much trouble. 'Missing persons?' He was not hopeful of identifying the woman that way either, but it had to be done. He knew that on the one occasion that the police didn't bother, the answer would be there. Fox sighed. But the enquiry couldn't really start until they knew who the mysterious woman was. Murder enquiries often started with the victim's friends and acquaintances and then worked outwards. Until that was done there was no one to talk to. 'Pictures, then, Jack.'

'No go, sir.' Gilroy knew the routine as well as his detective chief superintendent, and had already had photographers of the Yard's SO3 Branch assess the dead woman's face. But there was no way that they could make it look alive enough to prepare portraits of the victim for publication in *Police Gazette* and in *Confidential Informations* in the hope that one of the publications' readers — all of whom were policemen — would be able to put a name to her. It had been a vain hope. Even with all their skill, the photographers had to confess that they were unable to do much with a face that had been interred for some time and that any photograph they took of her would bear no resemblance to the woman when she had been alive.

Tommy Fox fired his next directive. 'Find the previous occupant of that house, Jack.'

'Yes, sir,' said Gilroy with a sigh.

*

'Good morning, madam.' DS Percy Fletcher was impeccably polite when the mood took him... like now. In the days when the wearing of hats was *de rigueur* for CID officers, Percy Fletcher was the sort of officer who would have raised his hat as a preamble to arresting a female suspect. 'I'm a police officer, madam.' And in response to the woman's look of scepticism, produced his warrant card. 'We are making some enquiries to try and trace the whereabouts of your next-door neighbour.' He smiled. 'Well, that is to say, your nearest neighbour.' It was a flattering acknowledgement that the woman lived in a very large house and that none of her neighbours could exactly be described as 'next door'.

The woman opened the door a little wider. 'You don't mean the Reverend, surely?' she asked.

'Pardon?'

The woman moved out on to the doorstep. 'You are talking about that house there, aren't you?' She pointed.

'That's right, madam.'

'Yes,' she said, retreating once more. 'That was a Reverend gentleman.'

'Well I'm blessed,' said Fletcher. 'Do you happen to know his name, by any chance?'

The woman smiled serenely. 'I'm afraid not, officer,' she said. 'We tend to keep ourselves very much to ourselves round here, you know.'

'How do you know that he was a Reverend gentleman, then?' asked Fletcher, frowning.

'He used to wear a clerical collar.' She lifted one eyebrow in a sarcastic and crushing assessment of Fletcher's intelligence and detective ability.

Three other neighbours living nearby confirmed that the previous occupant of the house had been a clergyman. They rarely saw him, had never seen any family, and presumed that he lived alone. And the last time that anyone had seen him had been some three or four weeks previously.

*

DS Fletcher kept at it.

The clerk in the Community Charge office at the local council carefully wrote down the address and went away to a back room. When he returned, he was carrying a computer printout. 'Yes,' he said. Fletcher noted that he had adenoid trouble. 'The charge-payer in question...' He coughed affectedly and glanced up. 'Is the Reverend John Calvin.'

Fletcher flicked open his pocket book. 'Would you spell that?'

The clerk did so. 'He pays his charge regularly, and in full. The next payment is not due until next April.'

'Thank you,' said Fletcher, and went upstairs to the electoral registration department. The list of voters showed that the sole voter on the records was the same John Calvin.

But Fletcher's visit to the local public library was less successful. The Reverend John Calvin was not listed in *Crockford's Clerical Directory*.

'Well now, there's a thing,' said Fox.

*

The initial search of the house had been conducted in an effort to find the proceeds of the Heathrow robbery, which Fox was still convinced was down to Barnes and Co., but had only turned up the body of a woman. It had failed to provide any clue to the disappearing clergyman. That in itself was suspicious. A deserted house normally has some clue to the identity of the last tenant, particularly when, as in this case, he seemed to have disappeared leaving all his belongings behind. There was a razor in the bathroom, a dressing-gown behind the bedroom door, and dirty linen in a clothes basket on the landing. But nowhere could the police find photographs or personal documents that would indicate the present whereabouts of the Reverend John Calvin.

'You're an educated sort of bloke, Jack,' said Fox. 'This Reverend Calvin...'

'Yes, sir?'

'Got to have a guv'nor, hasn't he?'

'A guv'nor, sir?'

'Of course, Jack. In this world, everyone's got a guv'nor of some sort.'

'Well, I suppose he'd be a bishop, sir.'

'Yes,' said Fox thoughtfully, 'I suppose he would. Find him. Ask a few questions, eh?'

'Yes, sir.'

*

Jack Gilroy was not over familiar with the line-management chart of the Church of England, and in any case there was nothing to indicate that the Reverend John Calvin had been a member of that particular church, as opposed, for example, to being a Roman Catholic, a Methodist or even an American television pastor. But Church House seemed a good place to start. Fox described it as their Force Headquarters.

Gilroy walked across Victoria Street from Scotland Yard and through Broad Sanctuary to Dean's Yard. After one or two false starts, he was shown into a tiny office where a rather austere and elderly grey-haired lady politely enquired what she could do to help.

Gilroy outlined his problem.

'A murder, you say?' She raised an eyebrow and smiled. 'Don't get many of those.' She shook her head. 'Go on at this rate and we'll soon have to have a crime correspondent for the *Church Times*.'

Particularly around Wimbledon fortnight when some of the clergy in England seemed to spend their time bustle-punching young ladies who have come to watch the tennis, thought Gilroy. But he decided that it would not be helpful to his enquiry to give voice to that sort of observation. 'I must emphasise that there is nothing to connect Mr Calvin with this particular matter,' said Gilroy, 'other than that the body was found in the grounds of his house. It may have been put there since his departure.' He didn't believe it, but he didn't want anyone getting to Calvin before the police. It was a forlorn hope, but he had to try.

The woman opened several drawers in a card index system and looked through a number of files in a large cabinet, but found no reference to Calvin. Gilroy assumed that she was demonstrating the extent to which the establishment of the Church was willing to assist the police. But at the end of it all she was only able to tell him the name and address of the bishop to whom Calvin might have been answerable if his parish was near where he lived. But there was nothing in the records to indicate that John Calvin existed, much less that he was the beneficiary of a living anywhere.

'Of course,' said the woman, 'he may have been an overseas clergyman who had come home to retire. How old was he?'

'I have no idea, I'm afraid,' said Gilroy. 'The people we have spoken to suggested that he might have been anything between thirty and sixty.'

'There you are, then,' said the woman with a smile.

'As you say,' said Gilroy thoughtfully. 'Here I am.'

*

It was about six o'clock that evening before the Bishop was able to see Gilroy.

'My dear Inspector, my apologies for keeping you hanging about. Come in, come in. Have a seat.' The Bishop rose majestically from his desk and walked across to a cocktail cabinet. 'I'm sure that you'll take a glass of whisky.' He smiled beatifically.

'Thank you.'

'Now what can I do to assist?' The Bishop sat down opposite Gilroy, in a leather armchair beside the empty fireplace of his study.

'The Reverend John Calvin,' said Gilroy. 'Do you know of him?'

The Bishop looked thoughtful. 'No...' he said. 'Name doesn't mean anything. You've tried *Crockford's*, I suppose?'

'Yes. He's not there. I've tried Church House, too. The lady there suggested that he might have retired from abroad, or something similar.'

The Bishop stared into his whisky as if seeking the answer there. 'Mmm! Possible, but generally speaking we know about chaps like that. Keep an eye on them, as you might say. Just in case they need anything. Can't say I've ever heard of him, though. What was the address again?' Gilroy repeated it. 'Could try the vicar. Chap called Smith.' The Bishop smiled. 'Here,' he said, rising from his chair, 'I'll jot the address down for you.' He paused. 'More whisky?'

*

The Reverend Smith was no help either. He had never heard of John Calvin, and was quite convinced that any clergymen in the area — retired or otherwise — would be known to him.

Gilroy tried Archbishop's House in Ambrosden Avenue where the Roman Catholics kept their records, and the administrative offices in Matthew Parker Street where the Methodists kept theirs, both fortunately within walking distance of New Scotland Yard, just in case they had heard of the missing clergyman. But even Gilroy had to admit that Calvin was an unlikely name for either a Roman Catholic or a Methodist.

*

'It looks very much as though the Reverend John Calvin is not a clergyman at all, sir,' said Gilroy.

'Bad luck,' said Fox. 'That just makes your job a bit harder, doesn't it?' He smiled. 'Another thing, Jack.'

'Yes, sir?'

'We still haven't found the wheelman.'

'No, sir.'

'Find the wheelman, Jack.'

'Yes, sir.'

Jack Gilroy was not at all happy with the idea of traipsing around the streets looking for something which could be discovered with much less effort. He too visited the Community Charge department of the local authority.

'You told my sergeant that the Reverend John Calvin always paid his poll tax on time.'

'That is so,' said the adenoidal clerk.

'Good,' said Gilroy. 'Perhaps you would tell me how he paid.'

'One moment.' The clerk went to a filing cabinet. 'By cheque,' he said. 'For the full amount. Of course, it is possible to pay by ten equal instalments, with a bank standing order, but Mr Calvin always —'

Gilroy held up his hand. 'Yes, I know,' he said. 'All I want is the name of his bank.'

Chapter Four

There is a provision contained in Section Nine of Part Two of the Police and Criminal Evidence Act 1984 which allows an inspector of police to apply to a circuit judge for a warrant to inspect the bank account of any person suspected of having committed a crime. Gilroy swore an information that the dead body of a woman had been found in suspicious circumstances in the house of a person who had now apparently fled, that the police wished to interview him and that enquiries by other means had failed to find him. The judge agreed that a warrant should be granted as that seemed to be the only way of tracing the aforesaid person. Even though Calvin was ostensibly a clergyman, it was not unknown in the annals of crime for a Clerk in Holy Orders to commit a serious offence.

The bank manager to whom the warrant was addressed was unhappy about revealing any information concerning his clients... ever, but was phlegmatic enough to know when he was beaten. But he looked marginally brighter when he returned to his office with a manilla folder in his hand. 'I'm afraid the account has been closed,' he said.

'How? Did he withdraw all the funds?'

'No. They were transferred to another bank.'

'Which bank?'

'Webster's and Hyde's.'

'Never heard of it,' said Gilroy. 'Where is it?'

'Twentyman Street, Toronto,' said the manager. 'That's in Canada,' he added with a smile.

*

Inspector Colin Fitzgibbon was an officer of the Royal Canadian Mounted Police. For the last three years he had been at the Canadian High Commission in London as the Legal Attache, a name conjured up to avoid the criticism of the civil liberties bower-boys who might take grave exception to the presence of a foreign policeman in their midst.

'Well, Jack, we'll do what we can. I'll be in touch.'

A week later, Fitzgibbon was in touch.

'Your guy's gone, Jack... if he was ever there.' The Canadian handed a report across the desk. 'Funds transferred to Australia... Melbourne. Our guys checked the address that was given. It didn't exist.' He shrugged. 'The address of the Melbourne bank's on there. Hope it turns up more than the Canadian one did. Sorry!'

'So am I,' said Gilroy.

*

There wasn't a policeman at Australia House. The Legal Attaché there really was a lawyer, and much as he would have liked to help, there were proper channels. The proper channels were the International Criminal Police Organisation: ICPO to the police; Interpol to the popular press. The telegram was sent from the National Central Bureau at Scotland Yard to the ICPO Headquarters at St Cloud on the outskirts of Paris, who sent it to the Australian National Central Bureau in Canberra. They acknowledged it and advised that the matter would be referred to the State of Victoria Police.

The enquiry eventually landed on the desk of Senior Constable Crosby of the Melbourne Criminal Investigation Branch, a member of the Fraud Department. It wasn't that the police in Melbourne had been led to believe that the Reverend John Calvin was involved in fraud. It was just that Fraud Department officers were more conversant with banks and knew ways of getting the information that they required by the quickest possible route. But Australia is no different to most other places when it comes to bank accounts, and Senior Constable Crosby — like Detective Inspector Gilroy in England — had to get a warrant.

'Account's closed,' said the bank manager, walking back into his office with a file and kicking shut the door with his foot. 'Drew all the cash out and shot through by the looks of it. What's it about anyway?'

Crosby shrugged. 'Search me,' he said. 'Some enquiry from the pommy police. Seems they found a body in his back garden.'

'Oh, right,' said the manager. 'I've got an address for him. Any help?'

'Yeah, could be.'

*

It was raining as Crosby drove out of the city along Spencer Street. It was cold too — the middle sixties Fahrenheit — but this was autumn. The address he had been given was a well-kept bungalow in one of the less attractive suburbs to the west of Melbourne, and Crosby hunched his shoulders against the rain as he ran up the path. The woman who answered the door was sun-tanned, of medium height and had dark hair. She had a bare midriff, wore white jeans and was smoking a cigarette. She held a picture magazine against her chest.

'G'day. I'm from the police, here in Melbourne,' said Crosby.

'G'day.' The woman held the door firmly ajar. 'Can I see your credentials?' She smiled and subjected the well set-up and beefy detective who stood on her doorstep to a lingering appraisal.

Crosby produced his warrant card. 'There y'go,' he said. 'Senior Constable Crosby.'

The woman glanced briefly at the document and opened the door wide. 'Cold, isn't it? Why don't you come in?' She led the way into the living room and turned off the television. 'D'you want a beer?'

'No, thanks.' Crosby took out his pocket book. 'Would you be Mrs Calvin, by any chance?' he asked.

The woman shook her head. 'No way,' she said. 'I'm Mrs Howard.' She shot the detective a sideways glance. 'Roberta Howard,' she added. 'Bobbie to m'friends. You sure about that beer, constable?'

'Yeah, quite sure. D'you know anyone called John Calvin, then? Reverend Calvin he is.'

'Reverend?' Mrs Howard giggled. 'Only ever seen a Reverend once,' she said. 'That was the day I got married. What a mistake that turned out to be.'

'How long have you lived here, then, Mrs Howard?' Crosby emphasised the Mrs.

'About three weeks. I'm only renting.'

'You and your husband?'

She shook her head. 'Just me,' she said. 'I'm here all by myself. M'bloody husband's still across in Adelaide, and as far as I'm concerned be can stay there.' She pulled on the knot of her shirt, stretching it tight over her breasts.

'Never heard of anyone called Calvin, then? He was s'posed to have lived here.'

'No.' She shook her head.

Crosby shrugged. 'Oh well,' he said, 'that's the way it goes. Can I change my mind about that beer?'

'Sure.' Bobbie Howard walked through to the kitchen. 'I suppose your job's a lot like this?' she shouted.

Crosby had stood up and was wandering around the room. 'How d'you mean?' He heard her open the fridge.

'Routine stuff... and getting nowhere.'

'Yeah!' he said. 'Happens all the time.'

Bobbie walked back into the room. 'Mind a tinny?' She handed him a can of beer.

'Nah!' said the policeman. 'Never drink it any other way.'

'What made you think you'd find this bloke here?'

'What, Calvin? The pommies think he's here some place. I reckon it's a bum steer, but we have to follow it up. I shall just write it off.' Crosby grinned at her and drank his beer down at a gulp. 'Thanks a lot, Mrs Howard. You've been very helpful,' he added, standing the empty tin on the coffee table.

'That's all right, constable,' she said, and ran her tongue round her lips. 'Always willing to oblige the police.'

*

'There's a message here from the Melbourne police, Jack.' Fox waved the telegram as Gilroy entered the office. 'About your man Calvin...' Gilroy noted the careful way in which Fox was slowly shifting the weight of the investigation on to him. 'He's disappeared.' Fox looked searchingly at his DI as though it was his fault that Calvin had avoided the clutches of the State of Victoria Police.

'What do they have to say?' asked Gilroy.

'Could be hopeful,' said Fox. 'The local Old Bill went to an address in Melbourne that they got from Calvin's bank — the bank account's closed incidentally — but there was no trace of him. There's a Mrs Howard living at the address now and she'd never heard of him. So the Melbourne boys ran a check with the estate agent. They'd never heard of Calvin either, but they told the police that the address had been rented by some bloke called Donald Close before Mrs Howard moved in.'

'So far he's been to Canada and Australia,' said Gilroy. 'Perhaps he's gone to the States now... or even India.'

'That'd certainly be a problem for you,' said Fox, and Gilroy got the distinct impression that his detective chief superintendent had washed his hands completely of the murder that had got in the way of a decent blagging.

'Was there anything else, sir?'

Fox studied the telegram. 'Yes,' he said. 'Melbourne did some checking with the Australian immigration people. They've turned up a date of birth for Calvin... for what it's worth. But what makes it interesting is that he arrived in Australia with a bird called Ivy Close.' Fox sniffed. 'Sounds like the name of a road,' he added.

'Ah,' said Gilroy. 'Donald Close and Ivy Close. Looks as though it's starting to come together.'

Fox looked up, a broad grin on his face. 'Yes,' he said, 'particularly when they obligingly tell us that, according to her passport, Ivy Close's maiden name was Barnes.'

*

Jack Gilroy had got fed up with doing all the leg work himself. One did not claw one's way to the dizzy heights of detective inspector in the Flying Squad just to do the leg work. He sent a team of detective constables to St Catherine's House to search for a birth certificate for John Calvin. They were able to make short work of it, having been provided with a date of birth by the Australians. And because Gilroy had told his men to look for it, they found Calvin's death certificate as well. He had died, aged four and a half, following a road accident in Reading. Then they searched for a Donald Close... but they didn't find him. At least not a Donald Close with the same date of birth. There were quite a few other Donald Closes and they selected the three who had been born within a year of John Calvin. Gilroy received the information with a sigh. It was the old ploy.

'How's it going, Jack?' Fox caught Gilroy in the corridor.

'Haven't finished yet, sir. We did a passport search on John Calvin, though.'

'And?'

'This is him.' Gilroy juggled with the file he was carrying and handed Fox a form with a photograph attached to it.

'So?'

'I had DS Fletcher take it round to the neighbours — Calvin's neighbours, that is — and they think it might be him.'

'Only think?'

'Yes, sir.' Gilroy looked apologetic on behalf of Calvin's neighbours. 'But there is one interesting point. You remember that I went to see the local vicar ... chap called Smith?' Fox nodded. 'Well according to that' — he pointed at the form in Fox's hand — 'Smith is shown on there as having countersigned the form and the back of the photograph, certifying that it's a good likeness.'

'And he didn't, I suppose.'

'Exactly, sir. I sent Fletcher to see Smith. He denies ever having seen Calvin and certainly didn't sign any forms.'

'Another Smith, then? It's a common name.'

Gilroy shook his head. 'No, sir. It's Smith's address. Calvin could have got it out of *Crockford's*. Come to that, he could have got it out of the phone book. Anyway, Fletcher showed Smith the signature, and he just laughed. Said it was nothing like his, and showed him what his own looked like. Anyway, Calvin's dead. The real Calvin, I mean.'

'Anything else?'

'Yes, sir,' said Gilroy. 'Smith said he was glad it wasn't a clergyman after all.'

'He's got more confidence than I have,' growled Fox. 'I blame Frederick Forsyth and John Stonehouse for this, you know,' he continued. 'If Frederick Forsyth hadn't explained it in *The Day of the Jackal*, and if prosecuting counsel hadn't explained in open court what Stonehouse had done, no one would ever have worked it out. Well, Jack, what now?'

'I'm about to let my fingers do the walking, sir,' said Gilroy enigmatically.

*

Jack Gilroy seated himself at a VDU of the PNC, which is what policemen call a visual display unit connected to the Police National Computer. Of John Calvin there was no trace. But that was to be expected. A child who had died at four and a half years of age could hardly have acquired a criminal record, and if the bogus John Calvin had inadvertently acquired one, he would promptly have disposed of that identity and assumed another.

Donald Close was a better bet however. He had a criminal record. The photograph on the file which Gilroy obtained from the National Identification Bureau showed him to be the same man as the John Calvin on the passport. Aged thirty-five, he had come to the notice of the police on several previous occasions. But he was a late starter. And he had been a clergyman. Aged twenty-seven before he first appeared in court, Close had been arraigned for attempting to relieve one of his parishioners — the chairman of a large company — of a substantial sum of money by means of a blatant blackmail.

'It seems,' said Gilroy, accepting Fox's invitation to sit down and spreading the papers on his knees, 'that Close had learned that the chairman of this company was having an affair with a very attractive and much younger woman. Instead of giving counsel and advice according to his Christian principles and beliefs' — Gilroy looked up and grinned — 'Close suggested to the chairman that Mrs Chairman might be distressed to learn of the matter. He further suggested that the payment of a sum of money into Close's bank account might resolve the problem to their mutual satisfaction. It wasn't put quite as obviously as that, of course.'

'Of course,' murmured Fox.

'There was some fanny about a new roof for the church, except that the church had had a new roof only the previous year. But unfortunately for the Reverend Donald Close, the chairman's wife not only knew of her husband's affair, but was having one of her own.'

'Oh dear,' said Fox mildly. 'So what happened?'

'Reading between the lines,' said Gilroy, 'it looks as though they were both over the side, by mutual agreement.' He laughed. Policemen were always amused by things like that. 'Probably something to do with the income tax laws,' he added.

'So what did he go down for?' Fox was getting a little impatient.

'He was remanded for nuts and guts.' It was policemen's jargon for mental and medical reports. 'And the inevitable social report.'

'Don't tell me. Such a good boy at home. Can't understand this one-off aberration, et cetera...'

'Nearly.' Gilroy smiled. 'Seems he'd had the best of everything. Good school and on to Oxford. Got a rowing blue there, and a degree in theology. He told the probation officer who interviewed him that he'd taken theology because it was easy... and so was the job you could get with it when you came down. But he wasn't really cut out for the Church. Seems it didn't pay enough. Particularly once he was married. A bit flighty by all accounts, his wife, and very expensive. At least, that was his story. Mind you, sir, according to this, he liked a bit of rich living himself and he got into debt. The blackmail was seen by him as an easy way to settle with his creditors. Apparently the Learned Recorder was not too impressed by Close's last visit to Henley Regatta. Turned up in a hired Rolls-Royce, complete with chauffeur, a large hamper from a well-known firm of West End provision merchants, and several cases of the finest champagne.'

'Can't really criticise the fellow for having good taste,' said Fox without the trace of a smile. 'What did he get?'

'Four years, sir.' Gilroy grinned. 'And he was unfrocked. Which is why he doesn't appear in *Crockford's*.'

'Sounds about right.' Fox leaned back in his chair. 'And what about this Barnes woman?'

'Haven't got anywhere with that so far, sir.' Gilroy tapped the file. 'According to the "antecedents" on here, Close's wife's maiden name was Yates.'

'Well now, isn't that interesting?' said Fox, suddenly leaning forward. 'What's this Barnes woman's name again?'

'Close, sir,' said Gilroy.

'Yes, I know that.' Fox looked sharply at his DI. 'Her first name, I mean.'

'Ivy, sir. Ivy Close.'

'Oh yes, of course. What age did the Aussies say she was?' Gilroy glanced down at the file. 'Thirty-one, sir.'

'Mmm,' said Fox. 'Could be her.'

'Who could, sir?'

'The unidentified body.'

'There's something else, sir,' said Gilroy.

'Yes?'

'This man Close. I said he'd got a rowing blue at Oxford. Well he's still very keen on rowing. Never been known to miss Henley Regatta.'

'Really? When's that held?'

'Beginning of July usually, sir.'

Fox glanced at the calendar. 'That's about three weeks away.' He pondered the likelihood of a man travelling from Australia — if he was still there — just to attend a bit of a boat race. 'I don't suppose there's a photograph of this Ivy Close on there?' asked Fox, pointing at the CRO file that rested on Gilroy's knees.

'No, sir.'

'Pity. What about the house? Any photographs there?'

'No, sir. Nothing.'

'Right.' Fox stood up. 'Get up to Fingerprint Branch, and get them to go through every one of the unidentified prints that we've got from this job so far. See what that turns up.'

*

The only prints that turned up belonged to members of the Flying Squad, and that made Tommy Fox very suspicious indeed. Not that he suspected his own officers: policemen had to open and shut doors, and it was no good using a handkerchief like they do on television. The Flying Squad's fingerprints were where they should have been: on edges and sides, where it was unlikely that there would have been any others. But the fact that the house had been cleaned of all other prints indicated that they were dealing with a team of professionals.

Not that Fox had much doubt about that. 'There's a link here, Jack,' he said.

'Yes, sir,' said Gilroy. He had come to that conclusion some time ago, as soon as he had discovered that Donald Close had arrived in Australia with a woman whose maiden name was Barnes.

'It wouldn't surprise me to find that the Reverend Donald Close was the missing wheelman, Jack.'

'Doesn't sound his style, guv'nor. I mean, it's not as if the getaway vehicle was a hearse, is it?'

Fox glowered at Gilroy. 'That, Jack,' he said, 'is not funny.'

*

Barnes, Perkins, Grover and Lambie were all in custody, remanded to stand trial at the Central Criminal Court, and the money from the robbery at Cobham was in police possession. Unfortunately the same could not be said of the missing wheelman or the ex-Reverend Donald Close.

In common with most senior officers, Tommy Fox believed himself to be more competent than his men in all matters, so he decided to interfere. Furthermore, he was a believer in combining business with pleasure and spent a day at the races. It was some time since he had visited Sandown

Park, but its close proximity to Cobham added some attraction on this occasion... being but a few miles from the scene of the heist.

'Well, Mr Fox, fancy seeing you.' As if by magic, the barman produced a large Scotch and placed it in front of the Detective Chief Superintendent.

Fox nodded his thanks and added water from the jug on the bar. 'Heard anything?' Carefully, he unbuttoned the jacket of his elegant suit. Today he was wearing a well-cut Prince of Wales check, ideally suited for mingling with the racing fraternity.

'A snippet,' said the barman, hardly moving his lips. 'Wait till the first race is off, Mr Fox. It thins out in here then.' He grinned and wiped the bar with a damp cloth.

Some ten minutes later, the pre-race rush having subsided, the barman put another Scotch on the bar in front of Fox. 'There's a little tickle coming off, Mr Fox, so I've heard. Payroll job in Richmond.'

'Interesting.'

'Word is that it's the same team that done the Heathrow snatch ... the one that happened the same day as that one just down the road from here.'

Fox didn't believe that. He was still convinced that the four men he had in custody were responsible for both blaggings. But Tommy Fox was a man who kept his counsel. 'Go on, then.'

The barman leaned closer. 'I heard it on the vine, Mr Fox. Payroll job at a building company. Quite a few grand's worth by all accounts. Ain't heard nothing on dates yet, but you can put your pension on it being a Thursday. That's the day they deliver.' He placed Fox's glass under the optic once more, and left it there for a seemingly interminable time. Then he put it on the bar in front of Fox. 'If it comes off, Mr Fox...'

'Don't worry,' said Fox. 'I'll see that a grateful security company knows how to show its appreciation.' He swallowed the Scotch and walked out on to the terrace. By the end of the day he had won eighty-five pounds. Things, he thought, were starting to get lucky.

*

'The van, guv'nor,' said Gilroy, 'The one that was used in the Cobham job.'

'What about it?' asked Fox.

'They've come up with an ident on one of the prints... apart from the four we've got in, I mean.'

The van had been unearthed in the lock-up at Clapham shortly after the arrest of Perkins and Barnes, and thoroughly examined for fingerprints. As was to be expected, Perkins' and Barnes' prints were in it, as were those of Grover and Lambie. There had been, however, a fifth set, a set which Fox had idly thought might belong to Donald Close. But they didn't match. Which was no more than Gilroy had expected. As he had said, a blagging — even as wheelman — wasn't the unfrocked clergyman's style. Consequently the Fingerprint Branch had set out to discover the identity of the missing fifth man.

'Who is it, then?'

'Charlie Boakes, guv.'

'And who the hell's Charlie Boakes, poor sod? With a name like that, he's got to be a villain, hasn't he?'

'Got two previous, sir. Both armed robbery. Got probation the first time — '

'Probation?' Fox sounded scandalised.

Gilroy grinned. 'He was only eighteen.'

'And the second one?'

'He was twenty-three then. Got a five-year stretch.'

That's better,' said Fox. 'Anything on your clever intelligence files that says he usually runs with Barnes and his lot?'

'No. I think he's a journeyman wheel artist. Works for the best payer.'

Fox nodded. 'Find him, Jack.' He stood up, stretched and yawned. 'Now then. Richmond.'

'What about Richmond, sir?' Gilroy looked puzzled.

'There's a job coming up there,' said Fox mysteriously, 'and it's yours.'

Chapter Five

Gilroy sat in his car. Waiting. The building company's offices were several streets away from where he was parked, but an observation post in a room over a chemist's shop opposite the target kept him informed of every movement. Gilroy's team had become very familiar with the street's features, and its routine. Far too familiar, in fact. They had been staking out the offices for nine days now, and this was the second Thursday, the day of the week when the money was delivered.

Fox had become more impatient on each successive day that Gilroy had reported to him. He knew that there were to be four or five robbers taking part in the raid — even knew the names of two of them — but had now reached the stage when he was beginning to doubt his informant. 'We'll give it another few days, Jack,' he had said, 'and then I'm going down to Sandown to take a certain snout apart.'

And then it happened. On the very next Thursday after Fox's declared intention of sorting out his informant.

'It's on, guv.' The flat unemotional tones of the officer who was keeping observation galvanised the police into action.

It happened like lightning.

As the security van pulled up in front of the building company's offices, a Vauxhall Carlton closed with it from one end, and a BMW from the other. But just as quickly, the four Flying Squad cars that were lying in wait, out of sight in side-turnings, accelerated into the street. DS Fletcher's came from behind, DS Crozier's from the front, and DS Buckley's drew alongside, blocking all avenues of escape. Gilroy ordered his driver to pull over to the opposite side of the road.

There was mayhem as four masked robbers spilled out into the street only to realise, too late, that the Flying Squad was there, waiting. A double-decker bus, marooned like a mournful red mammoth in the traffic jam created by the robbers and the police, trumpeted as its driver leaned on his horn. Pedestrians, astounded by the sudden activity, stood and watched; conditioned by a lifetime's diet of television violence, they seemed unable to separate fact from fiction. Somewhere, a woman screamed.

Flying Squad officers, wearing the funny baseball hats that identified them as armed police and, in theory, prevented them from being shot by their own, raced to tackle the robbers. Two of the villains fled into the offices, hotly pursued by Buckley and three DCs intent on preventing the raid from developing into a siege. One of the others immediately threw down his sawn-off shotgun as if to retain his hold on it might contaminate him in some way. Then he and his mate were seized and handcuffed.

The driver of the getaway vehicle, seeing his way blocked, opened the door of his car intent on escaping on foot. But as he turned, he found the barrel of a DC's revolver was almost in his mouth. 'Scale and polish?' asked the DC.

But it didn't go all that smoothly. It was at that point that a slight diversion occurred. The sort of cock-up without which no job like this seemed to be complete. A man came running out of the offices, straight towards DS Fletcher.

'Stop, you bastard,' shouted Fletcher. Even if DS Buckley had been careless enough to let him escape, there was no way that he was going to get past Fletcher. The running figure seemed to have no intention of stopping but as he drew level with Fletcher, he was arrested... literally. Fletcher slid his truncheon down the inside of his sleeve and grasping it so that about three inches protruded from his hand, jabbed the robber sharply in the solar plexus with it. Before he knew what had happened, the man, retching and spluttering, was face down over the bonnet of a police Jaguar, very conscious of the hard barrel of Fletcher's .38 Smith and Wesson pressing against his coccyx.

'Help! Police!'

'I am the bloody police,' said Fletcher, struggling to get his handcuffs out of his pocket. 'Who the hell are you?'

'I'm the manager. We're being robbed.'

'Yeah,' said Fletcher. 'We know.'

And suddenly it was all over.

The security van crew hadn't even had time to dismount.

*

Five disconsolate robbers sat on benches around the charge-room at Richmond police station. A jubilant Gilroy had reported the result to Fox who had been tempted to get into his car and rush down to join him.

'Incidentally, sir,' said Gilroy, 'we've found the wheelman from the Cobham job.'

'Yes?'

'Charlie Boakes, guv. Got him bang to rights.'

'In that case,' said Fox, 'I'll be down.'

'Yes, sir,' said Gilroy, and groaned. But not until he'd replaced the receiver.

*

'Well, well, well. Charlie Boakes.' Fox sat down on the chair opposite the wheelman and took out his cigarette case.

Boakes looked nastily at the detective. 'Do I know you?'

'Perhaps not. I'm Thomas Fox... of the Flying Squad, Charlie, but I know you. Let's look on it as the start of a long and fruitful relationship, shall we?'

'Do what?'

'What I mean,' said Fox, 'is that you're about to tell me everything I want to know. Starting with the Heathrow job.'

'Don't know nothing about no Heathrow job.' Boakes glared at Fox.

'But you were the driver, Charlie.'

'I said I don't know nothing about no Heathrow job.'

'And I've got a regiment of witnesses prepared to swear on a stack of bibles that you were there.' Fox leaned back and blew smoke towards the ceiling. 'Mind you...' He leaned forward again. 'What puzzles me is how you got from Cobham to Heathrow so quickly, but then they say you're a very good driver. Play your cards right and I'll put in a word for you with the Governor at Wandsworth. He's got a motor mower. He might even let you drive it if you're good.'

'I've got sod-all to say.'

'Now that's a shame, being the very intelligent chap you are. Let's face it, you've got to be intelligent to plan two jobs like Cobham and Heathrow — and to keep the heist from Heathrow all to yourself.'

'Who the bloody hell told you that?' Boakes sat up sharply.

'Silver Barnes as a matter of fact. Couldn't stop singing your praises.' Fox grinned. 'Well, that's overdoing it a bit. Couldn't stop singing is what I should have said.'

'That bloody Cobham job wasn't down to me. All right, I'll admit I was driving, but that was it. I got two grand for that.'

'And the rest,' said Fox derisively. He looked up at the barred windows of the interview room.

'Stand on me, Mr Fox. Two grand.'

'I hate to hear that, you know,' said Fox mildly. 'That's bloody terrible, that is. D'you know that Barnes and his three mates...' He paused and flicked his fingers.

Gilroy smiled. 'Harry Perkins, Dougie Grover and Bob Lambie, sir.'

'Of course.' It was all done for effect. Now Boakes would know that it was common knowledge. 'They netted about two hundred and fifty grand out of that job.' The lie sounded very convincing. 'They've seen you off, my son,' he said.

'I don't believe you.' Boakes glanced at Gilroy who nodded seriously, confirming the lie. He turned to face Fox again. 'Barnes told me they only got about twelve K out of that job.'

Fox nodded gravely. 'I have known Barnes to tell lies before,' he said.

'Well sod that,' said Boakes.

'My sentiments exactly,' said Fox. 'But it's all academic now, of course. We have the money and we have Barnes who, my friend, is willing to assist the police in exchange for a consideration. I should think about it, if I were you. We'll have another little chat later.'

*

'What's this consideration you were talking about, guv'nor?' asked Gilroy.

'That the police keep the money,' said Fox.

*

It was not often that Detective Chief Superintendent Fox of the Flying Squad visited any of the inmates of Brixton Prison, or any other prison for that matter, just in case it imbued them with an inflated sense of their own importance. It tended to make them cocky and truculent and give them an unwarranted standing among their fellows. And that was something that Tommy Fox wished to avoid at all costs. But there were occasions when he made an exception. And this was one of them. Mainly because he couldn't resist the temptation to see the expression on Silver Barnes' face when he told him that a woman called Ivy Barnes was somehow mixed up in the blaggings and the murder of the unknown woman whose body they had found at Cobham... in Donald Close's house. Fox believed that it was a good way of opening up the can of worms which now confronted him. A way to get shot of this murder enquiry which was bugging him, and which should have been none of his damned business anyway.

DC Swann, Fox's driver, was unhappy about his guv'nor going there too, but that was because the visit had interrupted an exciting — and for Swann profitable — game of cards in the Squad drivers' room. Consequently he muttered to himself for most of the journey.

'What's wrong with you, Swann?'

'Bloody traffic, guv.' Swann pulled out to overtake a bus on Brixton Hill, and swore. 'There are times when I wish I was a Traffic Division officer,' he said.

'Could be arranged,' said Fox, as Swann turned into Jebb Avenue.

*

'I've got nothing to say to you, Mr Fox,' said Silver Barnes when a prison officer brought him into the interview room.

'Why did you agree to see me, then?' Fox sat down, sideways on to the table, allowing one hand to play a silent tattoo on its top.

'Makes a break, don't it?'

'Well it so happens that you've got nothing to say that I don't know already.' Fox gazed at the high, barred windows with a bored expression on his face.

Barnes was mystified and curious to know why Fox hadn't sent one of his underlings. 'What you doing here, then?'

'I've come to talk to you, Silver.' Fox looked at Barnes and smiled, as though he was doing him a great favour. 'To tell you things.'

'Oh yeah?' Barnes felt uneasy and a little fearful. 'What things?'

'D'you remember Mr Gilroy telling you about a body we'd found at the slaughter where you and your assistants put the take from the Cobham job?' He paused. 'And the Heathrow job.'

'I told him, and I'm telling you, Mr Fox, we never had nothing to do with no Heathrow job.'

'Who did then?' Fox was beginning to think, after all, that Barnes and his team really had only done the Cobham job, and that some other team was marauding about the metropolis stealing money. And not the Richmond team, either. At least, they'd refused to hold their hands up to it. 'Search me,' said Barnes.

'We did... and the slaughter,' said Fox. 'Which brings me to my next point. Ivy Barnes.'

The name came at Barnes out of the blue, and he answered without thinking. 'What about her?' He instantly regretted it but it was too late. Fox had registered the reaction, and Barnes was left trying to limit the damage.

'Who is she? Your sister?'

Barnes hesitated only briefly before answering. 'Yeah.' He didn't like the way this conversation was going. 'What about her?' he asked again. 'You haven't nicked her, have you? She don't know nothing about any of this.'

'I'm afraid I've some bad news for you, Silver.' Fox sniffed eloquently.

Barnes frowned, suspiciously. 'What bad news?'

'It looks to us as though the body we found was Ivy's.'

Fox rested his chin on his hand and waited to see what reaction his lie would produce. It was an outside chance, of course, that the body was indeed that of Ivy, but the information from Australia tended to negate such a theory. But all the while the corpse in the mortuary at Esher was unidentified, the police had to keep their options open.

'You're having me on,' said Barnes eventually. There was no emotion in his voice, but it would be much later before Fox learned why.

'Been there about two or three weeks, the pathologist reckons... when we found it, that is.'

'What happened, Mr Fox?' The change in Barnes was quite marked. The aggressive villain had given place to one whose cunning was trying desperately to keep up with this policeman's ploy. He played for time. 'Who done her?' he asked after a while.

'I was hoping you might tell me, Silver.'

Barnes' fists were clenched on the table. 'I'll have to give that a bit of thought, Mr Fox,' he said.

Fox threw a cigarette on the table in front of Barnes who greedily lit it, puffing furiously so that the tip glowed fiercely.

'If you're thinking what I think you're thinking, Silver, forget it,' said Fox. 'There's no way you're going to be able to sort out whoever topped your kid sister, because you're going to be in here for a long time. Looking at your record, I reckon you're due about fourteen for this little lot.'

'Gawd'elp us, Mr Fox, don't say that. My brief reckons eight at most. That's if I don't get off.'

Fox laughed. 'Get off? You must be joking, my old son. We've got you bang to rights, and you know it.'

For a few seconds, Barnes smoked and gazed unseeing at the ceiling. Then he leaned forward. 'Can we make a deal, Mr Fox?' he asked earnestly.

Fox scoffed. 'A deal? What have you got to trade? You're not holding a very good hand.'

'Well, let's put it this way,' said Barnes. 'If I helps you out on this topping, will you see what you can do for me?'

'All depends. If I can hold the book in my right hand and honestly swear that you've assisted the police, well...' Fox deliberately paused.

'His name's Close. Donald Close.' Barnes' mental contortions had come to an end, overcome by the same greed that inspired all his actions. In this case, the greed of thinking — hoping — that even the Detective Chief Superintendent of the Flying Squad might be dragooned into helping him out of his present bit of grief.

'And who the hell's Donald Close when he's at home?' Fox's tone was scathing, dismissive. 'If you're trying to have me over, Silver, you'll find that you've made a mistake. A very nasty mistake.'

'You can stand on me, Mr Fox.' He paused for a second or two. 'He was in on it, the bastard.'

'Well, don't stop there.'

'Is this going to help me out?' Still Barnes couldn't resist the temptation to use anything to get himself out of trouble. And that apparently included the death of his sister.

'I'll let you know when you've finished telling me,' said Fox. He leaned forward threateningly. 'So don't spin me any fanny, Silver, or I'll put you away for so long that the Governor'll be keeping your old-age pension book for a good ten years before you see the light of day again.'

'Would I do a thing like that, Mr Fox?' The tone now was wheedling, the voice of a defeated toe-rag.

Fox almost felt sorry for him. Almost. 'Well you have tried before,' he said, lighting another cigarette.

'This bloke Close...' Barnes broke off to interrupt himself. 'Thought hisself a bit of a toff.'

'And wasn't he?'

Barnes laughed scornfully. 'Nah! He was a bleeding vicar, or something.'

The flat of Fox's hand smote the table top and Barnes moved back in sudden alarm. 'I've warned you once,' said Fox. 'Don't try and have me over.'

'It's the God's honest truth, Mr Fox. A bleeding vicar, he was. Used to wear his collar back to front.'

'Go on, then,' said Fox.

The detective's menacing attitude made Barnes feel jumpy. 'He was the bloke behind our jobs.'

'You're not propping him for the Thomas à Becket job, are you?' Fox could be very sarcastic when the mood took him.

'Who's he?' asked Barnes. 'Not a London topping, was it?'

'No,' said Fox. 'Canterbury. Kent Constabulary.'

'Oh, yeah,' said Barnes. 'Well I wouldn't know nothing about that, would I?'

'Get on with it,' said Fox. 'What d'you mean, he was behind your jobs?'

'Planned 'em and set 'em up.'

'A vicar set up your jobs?' Fox's facial expression was a masterpiece of acting, his tone of voice that of apparent outrage.

'They was hitched,' said Barnes in resigned tones.

'Who? Ivy and Close, you mean?' Fox looked as though he didn't believe a word of it.

'Yeah!' Barnes looked shifty. 'That was the trouble see. He was short of money. Dead short. And he'd bought this bloody great place down Cobham way. Well my skin... Ivy, she was a bit of a spender, she was, which didn't help, she was telling me that he'd got hisself in debt.

Couldn't afford it, like. Whacking great mortgage...' Barnes shook his head in wonderment at the plight of those who didn't just go out and take what they needed.

'Then it hit me. This drum what he'd got'd make a bleeding good slaughter.' Barnes opened his hands. 'Well, I mean, no one'd expect a vicar's pad to be used for a slaughter, would they, Mr Fox?' He stopped abruptly, his eyes narrowing. 'Come to think of it, how did you find it?'

'Your wheelman, Charlie Boakes, told us.' Fox lied unhesitatingly. 'You ought to have paid him more.'

'The bastard,' said Barnes.

'However,' said Fox in a bored tone of voice, 'you were telling me about the vicar.'

'Yeah, well he wasn't a vicar no more, not then, like. He got struck off, or whatever they calls it, a few years back. Got into a bit of bother. Done a bit of bird. Anyhow, when he comes out, he gets this drum, and carries on pretending to be a vicar. He was into the confidence game, by then. Very good at that by all accounts, according to Ivy.' Barnes shrugged. 'Anyhow, this looked like the perfect gaff. So we swans down and has a bit of a rabbit with this geezer. Well that was when he started putting us right. He told us our plans was all up the pictures, see, and why didn't we do it this way instead. Get more bread and take less risks. All that. Like I said, he'd got a head on him had this Donald bloke.'

'And you reckon that he topped Ivy?'

'I never said that.' Barnes folded his arms. 'But it's got to be down to him, ain't it?'

'And is that it, then?'

'I've told you everything I know, Mr Fox, so help me.' Barnes put his hand on his heart as if to endorse the veracity of what he had told Fox. 'Reckon you'll be able to do something for me?'

Fox stood up and rapped sharply on the door of the interview room. 'See you at the Bailey, Silver,' he said. 'Don't be late, it puts the judge in a bad mood.'

Chapter Six

Fox was not best pleased with the results of his visit to Brixton Prison. Barnes had added little to the mystery of the body found at Cobham, although it was interesting that he should have so readily put the finger on Donald Close. But Fox knew the criminal mind intimately and was convinced that most of Barnes' story was a pack of lies. He was either covering up for something, or was putting the boot in — or both. Barnes' mild reaction to the news that his sister may have been murdered — if she was his sister — was hardly what Fox had expected. There had been no weeping and wailing, no gnashing of teeth — and that was very odd. Villains were usually more demonstrative than most when tragedy befell their own — if some of the funerals Fox had been to were anything to go by — which was a bit of a laugh when one considered the cold indifference with which they inflicted pain and suffering on others.

There was no doubt that Close and Barnes were connected, probably engaged in the conspiracy to rob that Barnes had claimed, but the Barneses of this world did not inform on their co-conspirators. There had to be a reason. It might just be that Barnes was in custody and Close was not, or it might be that Close had the money which had not yet been recovered by the police. And Barnes knew that he had it. Barnes could not get out of prison to deal with the matter himself — whatever it was — nor was he likely to for some time to come, and his ready accusations against the unfrocked clergyman could well have been motivated by a desire to fix someone he was convinced had been responsible for his sister's death... or fix him for something entirely different. Although Fox refused to hold with the concept of a mastermind planning big jobs in splendid isolation and never getting his hands dirty, there was a chance that Close had welshed on his mates and Fox had just presented Barnes with a way to even the score.

'Perhaps we should tell the Australians what Silver Barnes said about Ivy being his sister and it being Close who topped her,' said Gilroy.

'Do leave off, Jack,' said Fox. 'What are you going to say? That we've found a body that we can't identify and that some villain with form as long as your arm's put it about that it's his sister?' Fox broke off and grinned. 'And that it was a clergyman who topped her sometime before she arrived in Australia? Christ, Jack, I should think they'd fall off their didgeridoos laughing at that.'

'Ex-clergyman.'

Fox shrugged. 'So what? There's no collateral for what Barnes said.'

'We've got a body,' said Gilroy, a little huffily.

'Yes, you have,' said Fox, 'but whose body? We don't know it's Ivy's. In fact, it's a racing certainty that it's not hers. Right now, we haven't got a clue whose it is.' Fox shook his head. 'I must say you're being a bit slow there, Jack.'

'Well I think we should at least tell them what we've got so far, guv'nor. Make them a bit more keen to find him.'

'The Aussies are much too busy,' said Fox dismissively. 'They're still looking for Ned Kelly.' Fox paused in thought for a moment. 'Do no harm, I suppose,' he said reluctantly. 'Only fair to keep 'em up to date. However, in the meantime, it might be useful if you were to make a few enquiries of an antecedent nature. See what you can find out.'

*

'Crosby!'

'Yes, sarge?'

'Give me a minute of your valuable time, mate.'

'Yes, sarge.' Senior Constable Crosby surveyed the pile of paper on his desk with a sigh of hopelessness, and then slammed shut the file he had been working on before walking through to the Fraud Squad sergeant's office.

'I've got a message here from our pommy friends.' The sergeant prodded a piece of paper with a thick forefinger. 'Y'remember that enquiry you did? About some bloody vicar. Bloke who came from Canada and shot through before we could get at him?'

Crosby ran a hand through his hair and then grinned. 'Oh, right.' What he remembered was the sexy Bobbie Howard. 'What about it, sarge?'

'According to this, they now think he might have murdered the sheila they found in his garden.' The sergeant leaned back, stretching his arms above his head and displaying the sweat patches under his armpits.

Crosby shrugged. 'What's that got to do with the Fraud Squad, sarge? I only did that job because it was a bank enquiry.'

The sergeant leaned forward. 'Nothing, mate,' he said, 'but it's got one hell of a lot to do with police work, so get out there and see if you can find out anything else about this bloke. After all, you started it off. I can't give it to anyone else now. Right?' Crosby sighed. 'Right, sarge.'

'Good on yer, mate,' said the sergeant, and grinned.

*

'Yes, I remember him.' Donald Close's former tutor studied the detective who now sat opposite him. 'A very dedicated young man...' He laid his hand on a leather-bound book on the table by his chair and smoothed the cover before looking up again. 'As befits one intent upon entering the church, of course.' The tutor smiled. 'What exactly is your interest in him, er... Inspector?'

'We found a body in his back garden.'

'Oh!' The tutor sat up a little and stared at Gilroy. 'In his back garden, you say?' He put slight emphasis on the word 'back' as if the finding of the body in the front garden would have put an entirely different construction on the affair.

'Back garden,' confirmed Gilroy and waited.

'Ah!' The tutor took time to digest this curious piece of information before speaking again. 'Well now, how can I help?' He broke off to cough distressingly.

The interview was a waste of time. Beyond learning of Donald Close's devotion to the river, there was little more light that the tutor could shed on the errant clergyman that might assist the police. Gilroy went back to Scotland Yard.

*

Having wasted half a day in Oxford, Gilroy decided it would be far more profitable to make further enquiries at St Catherine's House. If Close was married to Ivy Close, née Barnes, there would be a record. But according to the antecedent history on his criminal record, he had also been married to one Muriel Yates. In that case, there should be a record of Muriel Yates' death, or her divorce from Donald Close. But the marriage records might just tell them something useful... like the names of the witnesses. Perhaps.

*

There were records of both Close's marriages. The Reverend Donald Close had married one Muriel Yates in Middlesex according to the rites and ceremonies of the established church some seven years before he had married Ivy Barnes... in a register office. And that looked a touch like bigamy. In accordance with his instructions, Detective Constable March, who had found this intriguing piece of information, checked to see if the first marriage had been followed by a divorce, or the death of the clergyman's first wife. But there was no trace of either such event in the records of the General Register Office.

'Hadn't been divorced or widowed, I suppose?' asked Gilroy when March reported to him at Scotland Yard.

'No, sir.' DC March grinned.

'What were the names of the two witnesses? To the first marriage, I mean.'

March thumbed open his pocket book. 'A. Hunt and S. Goodall, sir.'

'And who are they? Got their addresses?'

'No, sir. They don't put any further pars on the certificate.' March was pleased that he had been so thorough.

DI Gilroy pondered that revelation for a moment and then stood up. 'Sod it!' he said.

*

Detectives of the Metropolitan Police are very good at finding people who, for some reason or another, do not wish to be found, and although the addresses of the witnesses to the Closes' marriage were not shown on the certificate, the addresses of the bride and groom were. That at least was a start.

Gilroy's team found an address. Not far from Pymmes Park in Edmonton, north London, there are a number of rather run-down terraced houses, one of which was the abode of Mrs Muriel Close. Why she did not live with the ex-Reverend Donald Close was something they hoped to discover. But there was no one at home.

Mrs Close's next-door neighbour was a positive mine of information — a real gem — the sort of informant that the police pray for but rarely find.

'Muriel? What's she done then?' The neighbour was called Halloran — *Mrs* Halloran — and Fletcher reckoned she was in her late fifties. Her hair was grey and rolled under in a fashion that had been popular in the late nineteen-forties but never since. She wore an overall that was like a sleeveless wrap-over dress with little flowers all over it. She folded her arms and stared truculently at DS Fletcher.

'She hasn't done anything... as far as we know,' said Fletcher. 'It's just that we think she might be able to help us with our enquiries.'

'Oh, yes!' said Mrs Halloran unbelievingly. 'Well we all know what that means, don't we?' She appeared to be addressing an invisible audience in her front garden.

'Well, do you know where she is?'

'Comes as no surprise,' continued Mrs Halloran. 'A right madam is our Muriel Close. A bit above herself, if you ask me.'

Fletcher hadn't asked her, and had the distinct impression that Mrs Halloran's half of the conversation had nothing to do with his own: like two parts of a scripted dialogue that had got out of sync. 'But do you know where she is?' he continued lamely.

'Always going off places. South of France, Spain, Morocco. So she says.' Mrs Halloran shook her head cynically. The expression on her face implied that if Mrs Close had ever got as far as Southend she would have done well. But it could have been envy.

'Is she in one of those places now, d'you know?'

'She said she was going to the South of France.'

'And did she?'

'Search me.'

Fletcher was thankful that that would be unnecessary. 'When did you last see her, then?'

Mrs Halloran gave that some thought. 'About a month ago, I suppose. Might have been longer. Went off in a taxi.'

'You saw her, did you?'

'I was putting the nets back up,' said Mrs Halloran. 'Wash them every week. The traffic makes 'em filthy. It's terrible down here now, what with them juggernauts. I don't know why you police don't do something about it.' She scowled at Fletcher. 'So you needn't think I'm always looking out of the window.' She shrugged. 'We mind our own business round here, you know,' she added defensively. 'All of us do.'

'Was there anyone with her?' asked Fletcher.

'No, she was on her own,' said Mrs Halloran a little too quickly. 'Probably meeting up with some fancy man, if you ask me. A dark one that.'

'What about her husband?'

Mrs Halloran scoffed. 'I should think he pushed off years ago,' she said. 'If my Liam had been married to the likes of her, he'd have been off, I can tell you.'

Fletcher immediately felt sympathy for Liam. 'If I leave you my phone number, perhaps you'd give me a ring when she returns,' he said. 'And I'd be grateful if you didn't mention our interest.'

Mrs Halloran tossed her head and immediately fingered her hair back into place. 'We're not gossips round here, either,' she said. 'None of us are.'

*

'I suppose we have to consider the possibility that the body we've got down at Esher is that of Mrs Muriel Close,' said Fox with a sigh. 'And it would appear that Close's marriage to Ivy is bigamous. All of which is a bloody nuisance,' he added.

'I've put out an ICPO circular,' said Gilroy, although, in common with Fox, he had little hope that it would achieve anything. At that time of year there were simply thousands of English people in the South of France, and although the French immigration system was supposed to keep track of tourists' movements, and where they were staying, it was such a formidable task that it usually took until Christmas to get the records sorted out. Just in time, in fact, for them to be destroyed to make room for next year's influx.

'That'll be no bloody good,' said Fox. 'Get a brief and spin her drum.'

*

The terse and esoteric instruction that Gilroy should obtain a search warrant and execute it on Mrs Muriel Close's house was carried out immediately.

DI Gilroy and three other officers, including DS Fletcher, arrived at the house at around midday, three days after Fletcher's first visit. He noticed a twitching of the curtains in the house next door as they pulled up outside, and nodded to Mrs Halloran who, quite by chance, appeared on the doorstep shortly afterwards to put out empty milk bottles.

Gilroy knocked on Muriel Close's door. Apart from the embarrassment of finding someone at home after you'd smashed the door down with a sledgehammer, it was much easier if the lawful occupier admitted you. But there was no reply. Which came as no surprise, certainly to Fletcher.

In his view there was no way that anyone could have got back into Mrs Close's house — even at dead of night — without Mrs Halloran knowing. The door was secured by a rim latch, and Fletcher sighed as he effected an entry with a credit card.

'What are we looking for, guv?' asked Fletcher, standing in the centre of the tiny sitting room.

'Anything,' said Gilroy. 'A good start would be an address book.'

Fletcher opened the drawer of a small bureau and raked around among the profusion of papers which spilled out of it. 'Like this, you mean?' He held up a cheap index book.

Gilroy took the book and glanced through it. 'Ah!' he said. 'There's a thing. Sylvia Goodall... and a phone number. If our luck's in, that's the S. Goodall on Muriel's marriage certificate.' He threw the book across to DC March. 'Rim a check on that number, my son, and then we'll pay a visit.' He thrust his hands into his trouser pockets. 'And now, Perce,' he said, 'I think we'll get a fingerprint team up here before we touch anything else. I've got a feeling in my bones that we're about to get lucky.'

*

'The fingerprint blokes have come up with an ident, sir,' said Gilroy. 'Well, a possible ident.'

Tommy Fox rested his chin on his folded hands and looked searchingly at Gilroy. 'Well, go on then, don't keep me in bloody suspense.'

'Most of the prints found in Muriel Close's house in Edmonton match those on the body we've got at Esher, sir. It rather looks as though it's her. Unless, of course, Ivy Close was in the habit of visiting Muriel Close and it's Ivy down at Esher.' Gilroy grinned.

Fox sank down into his chair and surveyed his DI from beneath lowered eyebrows. 'How come you lasted so long in something called Criminal Intelligence, Jack?'

*

The telephone number of Sylvia Goodall belonged to an address in Woodford, Essex, and Fletcher rang it and made an appointment to see her.

'Well?' asked Gilroy.

'She can't see us in the evening, guv. She works. Asked if it would be all right this afternoon.' Fletcher grinned. Most of the calls that detectives made were perforce in the early morning, turning over villains before they went to work — if they went to work — or in the evenings, seeing respectable witnesses after they got in from work.

'Well that's a turn-up,' said Gilroy. 'I'll let Mr Fox know, then we'll see what Ms Goodall has to say.'

*

Senior Constable Crosby had been a policeman for fifteen years and had thus developed a certain canniness, as well as a penchant for self-protection. One aspect of this precautionary behaviour was to conduct an investigation thoroughly, mainly for fear of bringing himself to the adverse notice of the chief inspector in charge of the division who might just be tempted to post him up-country. That was a fate which Senior Constable Crosby, firmly ensconced in a nice house on the fringes of South Yarra, did not relish.

The only thing he knew about Calvin or Close, or whatever his goddam name was, was what the bank manager here in Melbourne had told him: that Calvin had used the address of the bungalow on the outskirts of the city now occupied by Mrs Bobbie Howard. He telephoned Mrs Howard and made an appointment to see her again. Then he made one more call before slipping his .38 pistol into its holster and reluctantly putting on his jacket.

Crosby was surprised that Bobbie Howard was wearing the briefest of bikinis when she opened the door. Surprised because winter was approaching fast. The temperatures had started to drop and today it had gone below fifty for the first time. 'G'day, constable,' she said with a smile that was intended to be alluring. 'Nice to see you again.'

'G'day, Mrs Howard. Feeling the heat?' Crosby nodded towards her bikini.

'I told you, m'friends call me Bobbie. Come on in. Wanna beer?' She turned and walked through to the sitting room. 'I was upstairs on the sunbed when you telephoned,' she continued, speaking over her shoulder. 'Got to keep the tan up.' She turned to face him and smoothed a hand down her stomach. 'Mind you, I've put some clothes on since then.' She giggled and went into the kitchen, returning with two cans of beer. 'Don't mind a tinny, do you, if I remember rightly?'

'Thanks.' Crosby took the beer and tugged at the ring on the can.

'Make yourself at home.' Bobbie sat down on the sofa and crossed her legs. Then she patted the vacant seat beside her. 'Well now,' she continued, 'what can I do for you?'

'Not so much me as my colleague...' Crosby glanced out of the window. 'Who has just arrived,' he added.

'There's two of you?' Bobbie Howard did not look displeased at the prospect of having two detectives calling on her.

'Yeah. What we'd like to do, Mrs Howard, is have a look over your place to see if there are any fingerprints. This guy the poms reckon was living here, Calvin...'

The girl frowned. 'I said when you were here before, I never heard of him.'

'It seems that Scotland Yard think he might have murdered a woman... back in England.'

Bobbie Howard uncrossed her legs and leaned forward. 'Murdered a woman? Christ! You don't think he might come back here, do you?'

Crosby shrugged. 'I doubt it,' he said.

'Can't I have police protection? I've got a spare room here. Wouldn't be a problem, putting you up.'

Crosby grinned at her forwardness. 'I don't think that'll be necessary,' he said. 'If we had to provide you with a guard, he'd be outside, in uniform.'

'Oh! I was hoping he'd be nearer than that.' She laughed.

'That'll be my colleague now,' said Crosby as the doorbell rang.

'Oh sure.' Bobbie walked through to the hall and opened the front door.

The police officer who stood on the doorstep turned and stared at Bobbie Howard's bikini with an amused expression. 'I'm Woman Constable Shipley,' she said, 'from the Fingerprint Branch. Is Constable Crosby here?'

'Oh strewth!' said Bobbie.

Chapter Seven

'I think I shall come with you to see this Sylvia Goodall,' said Fox. 'Then Fletcher can get on with his enquiries.'

'Yes, sir.' Gilroy groaned inwardly.

'I suppose you think I'm interfering, just as it's getting interesting,' said Fox. He stood up and smoothed the jacket of his dark grey suit, flicking away a piece of fluff before making sure that the collar was seated properly. Then he spent a few moments adjusting his silk tie while glancing in the mirror to which his rank entitled him, next to the picture of the Queen... which his rank also entitled him to.

'Not at all, sir,' lied Gilroy.

*

Sylvia Goodall sat in an armchair and surveyed the two policemen sitting opposite her on the settee. 'I'm fascinated,' she said. 'Why should two policemen from Scotland Yard want to come and talk to little old me?'

Fox reckoned that she was about thirty-five years of age, and that they had been a pretty hard thirty-five years. She was wearing tight jeans, a sweater, and calf-length boots. Her hair, shoulder-length blonde, was dyed... badly — the black roots had already recaptured a good two inches of ground from the invader — and it was frizzy, as though it had been permed for the whole of its length and then forgotten about, in a style that many women thought was fashionable. To Fox it looked more like an explosion in a wire-wool factory. Despite all that, she possessed a coarse sexual allure.

'We understand that you were a witness at the wedding of Muriel Yates and the Reverend Donald Close, about seven years ago.'

Sylvia Goodall nodded slowly. 'Yes,' she said, a puzzled expression on her face.

'I imagine you know Mrs Close quite well.'

Sylvia Goodall laughed. 'Pretty well,' she said. 'She's my sister.' She looked from Fox to Gilroy and back again. 'What's this all about?' she asked.

'When did you last see her... your sister?'

Sylvia gave that a bit of thought. 'About a month ago, I suppose. To be honest we don't see much of each other — it's a sod of a journey from here to Edmonton — but we talk on the phone quite a lot.' She examined the chipped nail varnish on her fingernails but made no attempt to hide them from view.

'I see,' said Fox. 'When was the last time you spoke to her then?'

'Like I said, about a month ago. Just before she went on holiday. I did actually go and see her on that occasion. It's a bit of a problem, really. She works days and I work evenings... in a pub.' That came as no surprise to Fox. 'So we don't often have the chance.' She frowned. 'But you still haven't told me what this is all about.'

'I'm coming to that, Mrs Goodall, if you don't mind. We're by no means certain what we're dealing with yet.'

Sylvia reached down and took a packet of cigarettes from her handbag and proffered it to the two policemen.

'Thanks.' Fox offered his lighter. 'Where is your sister, Mrs Goodall? You say she's on holiday, but do you know where?' Sylvia laughed. 'She said she was going to the South of France... to get a bit of sun.'

'You sound as though you don't believe that.'

'I don't. She hasn't got two ha'pennies to bless herself with. Not that that's her fault, of course.'

'Really? What about her husband, Donald Close?'

'Huh!' Sylvia scoffed derisively. 'Don't you know about him?'

'No.'

'Clergyman! That's a laugh.'

Fox got the impression that if Sylvia had been a man, she would have spat in the fireplace. 'Well clergymen have never got much money, have they?'

'That one did. All of Muriel's.'

'Oh?'

'Our dad left us two girls quite well off. Very well off, in fact. He was into everything was our old man.' She smiled at the memory. 'Made a mint in the fifties and sixties. Had a market stall to start off with, but he had his fingers in so many pies... Not all of it strictly legal, either.' She shot a quick glance at Fox. 'I shouldn't be telling you that really, should I? Still, you can't touch him now. Been dead eight years.' Sylvia looked momentarily sad. 'What a bloody waste. Killed on the M1 driving his new Jaguar. Fifty, he was.' She shook her head. 'Anyway, I was amazed when it came to the will. Nigh on half a million he left between Mum, Muriel and me.'

Fox nodded. 'And shortly afterwards, the Reverend Donald Close appeared on the scene.'

Sylvia looked sharply at Fox. 'I think you know more than you're telling,' she said. 'Yes, he did appear on the scene, as you put it. He conducted the funeral service, didn't he?'

'How was the money split?' asked Gilroy, speaking for the first time.

'Three ways. A third to Mum, and a third each to me and Moo. Why?'

'I was wondering why she was living in such a run-down house in Edmonton,' said Gilroy. 'From what you say, I would have thought that she could have afforded better than that.'

'Yes, well you didn't let me finish, did you? Mum went off and got married again... to Dad's best friend, as a matter of fact.' She laughed cynically at that. 'They're living in Spain now. It's Mum's arthritis. The weather's no good for her here. We go over for a holiday now and then, but we don't see much of them. They never come over here.'

'And Muriel?' Fox took the questioning back again.

'This Close bloke saw her off for all her money and scarpered, didn't he?'

'Have you any idea where he is now?'

'No, and I don't want to know. If I ever get my hands on him, I'll cut his balls off, believe me.'

Fox thought she probably meant that and shuddered at the prospect. 'Did she come to you for help, at all?'

'What, for money, you mean?'

'Yes,' said Fox.

'No. But she wouldn't. Very independent is Moo. I offered, of course, but she wouldn't have it. Not that it would have done any good. My Frank reckoned that she'd made her bed and ought to lie on it.'

'So you inherited about a hundred and sixty grand each?' said Fox. Sylvia nodded. 'If you don't mind my asking then, why are you working in a pub?'

Sylvia smiled. 'We own it, love,' she said. 'I only work there because it's something to do. Otherwise I'd get bored stiff.'

'You said that your sister worked during the daytime,' said Fox.

'That's right.'

'Where?'

Sylvia thought for a moment or two. 'Shop assistant somewhere, I think. In Edmonton, I suppose.'

'But you don't reckon she's in the South of France?'

'I don't reckon she could afford it, not unless she's found another fella who'll pick up the tab.'

'Did she have a man friend that you know of?'

Sylvia shook her head. 'I don't think so, but she's a bit deep, is Moo. I doubt if she'd let on, even if she had. Keeps herself very much to herself. Wouldn't surprise me, mind you. Attractive girl is Moo... and refined too.' Sylvia stifled a yawn and laughed. 'Too many late nights,' she said. 'Now then, d'you mind telling me what this is all about?'

Fox studied Sylvia Goodall carefully, wondering whether she could withstand the shock of the full story, and decided that she probably could. 'We had occasion to search a house just outside Esher a short while ago,' he said. 'A house once occupied by Donald Close. We found a body there. I'm sorry to have to tell you that we think it may be your sister Muriel.'

For a few moments Sylvia studied Fox's face. 'Oh my God!' she said eventually. 'The poor stupid, silly little bitch.' She stared at the carpet for some time before looking up again. 'And you think that Close done for her?'

'We don't know, Mrs Goodall. But the fact of the matter is that we believe Close to be in Australia, and we can't trace your sister.'

'Oh my God!' said Mrs Goodall again. 'Well, all I can tell you is that when we spoke last — a month ago — she said she was having a holiday in the South of France. I just went along with it. Like I said, I didn't believe her, but if she wanted to pretend, just to keep her end up, well that's her business. I reckoned she was more likely off for a dirty fortnight. Well she's entitled, like. Who am I to interfere? I reckoned she was probably going to some sleazy hotel in Brighton with a bloke. Something like that, anyway. I'd have asked her where she was but I didn't take the call.'

'What call?' Fox shrouded his sudden interest.

'She rang the pub about a week ago, spoke to Frank.'

'Oh?'

'He didn't have time to chat, nor did I. He didn't tell me till after he'd put the phone down. Frank said she told him she was ringing from France, and was having a good time. That's what she told him. But it was a bad line, and he could hardly hear her.' Sylvia paused, reflecting. 'I wonder if she'd met up with Close again. The silly bitch always had a soft spot for that smooth-talking bastard, despite him having seen her off rotten.' Sylvia shook her head. 'Women,' she said. 'Sometimes I think we're our own worst enemies.'

'You said that Close took all her money. How did that happen?' Sylvia laughed. 'Came up with some great plan about pooling their resources and buying a big place somewhere in the country. Moo said he was going to give up the church and they were going into business together. Nursing home or something. Well it all sounded a bit iffy to me and, sure enough, when it came to it, he just disappeared. Left her with nothing but what she stood up in. Oh, she tried lawyers and that, but that was just throwing good money after bad. They said it was all quite legal, and that she'd signed it all over to him. Well she had, silly little cow. She should have asked Frank and me. We'd have told her. Quite honestly I never reckoned him as a clergyman at all. I mean, I know he done Dad's funeral, but... well funnier things have happened, haven't they? Anyway, I went round the public library and looked him up. There's a book in the reference that tells you...' She paused. 'Can't think what it's called. I had to ask the woman who works there to show me.' She laughed. 'That was Dad all over. Generous to a fault, but never saw no profit in spending it on our education.' '*Crockford's*,' said Gilroy, who was rapidly becoming an expert. Sylvia nodded. 'Yes,' she said, 'you're probably right, love.'

*

Fox carefully replaced the receiver and looked at Gilroy. 'The pathologist is absolutely certain that the body had been there for at least two weeks when we found it,' he said. 'So either it isn't Muriel Close, or this story about Frank Goodall taking a call from her is a bum steer.'

'Sylvia Goodall did say he told her it was a bad line, sir. Could it have been someone else, putting him on that it was Muriel?'

Fox laughed. 'Thank you, Jack, that's all we need. What would be the point?'

'Search me, guv. But when we're dealing with the likes of Barnes and his little team of robbers, there's no telling.'

'Like I said, thank you, Jack.'

'Incidentally, we've got another report from the Melbourne Police, guv. They found a few fingerprints in the bungalow where Close is supposed to have stayed.'

'Well they would, wouldn't they, Jack?' said Fox. 'You find fingerprints everywhere. But I suppose you mean that these have some significance...'

'Yes, sir. SO3 have checked them against Close's record —'

'And?'

'They're his, sir.'

'Terrific,' said Fox. 'What are they going to do now? They haven't found him, I suppose?'

'No, sir,' said Gilroy. 'They're too busy looking for Ned Kelly.'

'Well?'

'Nothing really, guv. As Mrs Goodall said, she worked in a shop in Edmonton. Took two weeks' holiday, five weeks ago, and they haven't seen or heard anything of her since. But apparently she was always taking time off. Seems they got fed up with her, so they've taken her off the payroll now. Reckon it happens all the time. People can't be bothered and just float off. That's the affluent society for you.' Gilroy shrugged.

'Didn't they make any enquiries?' asked Fox. 'Speak to the local nick? Anything like that?'

'No, sir.'

'What about her P45? That'd tell us if she'd got another job.'

'Not been issued, sir.'

'Bloody hell,' said Fox. 'What did the Inland Revenue say? They'd know if she'd taken another job.'

'They've got no record of new employment, sir,' said Gilroy.

'Christ!' said Fox. 'No wonder people get murdered.'

*

It is open to a prisoner on remand to refuse to be interviewed by police if that is his wish. One of the ways in which the British judicial system protects the interests of accused persons — to a far greater extent than it concerns itself with the interests of their victims — is to ensure that they are not bullied into making a confession by nasty policemen.

Thus, despite the fact that Silver Barnes was under no obligation to be interviewed by the police, there was no reluctance on his part to talk to Tommy Fox on the next occasion that the Flying Squad chief visited Brixton Prison. And the reason for that was quite simple. Silver Barnes was curious. In common with many villains with his amount of form, Silver Barnes was always hoping — usually in vain — that there might be good news, but as a general rule it was a desire to do some sounding out. To see what the police knew, preferably about the current case against them, and also that they might just pick up some information about another crime: a crime which had so far not been wholly attributed to the interviewee.

'What you found out, Mr Fox? Have you found that bleeding clergyman yet?' Barnes leaned over the table that separated him from the Detective Chief Superintendent.

'You've got bad breath this morning, Silver,' said Fox, moving back. 'You should try a decent mouthwash. The pharmaceutical department at Harrods has a very good range.'

'Very funny,' said Barnes, and then in a wheedling tone, asked: 'Have you got any snout, Mr Fox?'

Fox placed his cigarette case on the table and slowly pushed it towards Barnes with his forefinger.

'Cor! Thanks, Mr Fox.'

'One!' said Fox, rapidly retrieving the case. 'Now, Silver, you can begin by telling me just how involved Donald Close was with this blagging you and your merry team did down at Cobham.'

'We never did no job down Cobham,' said Barnes. It was an automatic reaction. 'My brief said I wasn't to — '

'Good-bye, Silver.' Fox stood up. 'Sorry you're not willing to assist me in discovering who topped your skin-and-blister...'

'No, hold on, Mr Fox. That ain't got nothing to do with Ivy.'

'How do you know? Are you investigating this murder, or am I?'

'Well I don't see how... Anyway, my brief said that the evidence of one...' Barnes faltered as his brow furrowed with an attack of acute concentration.

Fox nodded amiably. 'Your brief said that the evidence of one co-conspirator against another isn't worth a light unless it's corroborated.'

Barnes' face broke into a reluctant grin. 'Yeah, that's it,' he said and leaned back in his chair. Most villains had a good working knowledge of the criminal law — derived from being involved with it so often — and Barnes was no exception.

'Right,' said Fox, resuming his seat, 'let's start again, shall we? Was Close mixed up with that blagging?' Still Barnes looked apprehensive. 'Silver, I'm trying to find out whether he was still here at the time.'

'Well o' course he was still here.' Barnes spoke with evident reluctance.

'God Almighty!' said Fox. 'Look, Silver, you're bang to rights on that Cobham job. We nicked you recovering the proceeds from the slaughter, or has your brain gone completely? You're going down, old son, be under no illusions about that. And with your form, it'll be for a long time. What's more important is finding a taker for this body I've got on my hands.'

'Will they let me out for the funeral, Mr Fox?'

'Don't change the subject,' said Fox. 'Now, firstly, where did your sister Ivy live?'

Barnes looked puzzled. 'Well, where you nicked us, o' course.'

'And she lived there with Close, did she? As man and wife?'

'What you mean, as man and wife. They was man and wife, wasn't they?'

'No! Your holy brother-in-law wasn't your brother-in-law at all. He was already married before he went through a form of marriage with Ivy. He's certainly good for a charge of bigamy.'

Barnes opened his mouth and then shut it again. 'You mean he was screwing her under false pretences?'

Fox laughed. 'Don't tell me you're getting all moral in your old age.'

'No... I mean... well that's not on, Mr Fox. That's not bleeding on at all.'

'That's a novel concept coming from you, Silver.'

'Do what?'

'When did you last see Donald Close, and when did you last see your sister?' Fox had finally tired of playing games.

'About a month before the blagging, Mr Fox. Not that I know anything about that. I'll stand for the handling, but not the blagging.'

'Save it for the jury, Silver, will you? Right, a month, you say?' Barnes nodded. 'And what happened then? They went away presumably?'

'I s'pose so.'

'Where?'

'I don't know, Mr Fox. If I'd known that, I'd've told you last time you was here.'

Fox sighed. 'Did they often go away?'

'Dunno! I never lived there. Why don't you ask the neighbours?'

'Where can I find a photograph of Ivy, Silver?'

'Ain't there one in the drum?'

'No, there isn't. Have you got one? A wedding photograph for example.'

'Nah!' Barnes looked thoughtful. 'That Close finger wouldn't have none took of the wedding. Said it was registry office, and that they wanted it quiet. No publicity, like.'

'Yes, I'll bet he did,' said Fox. 'So you haven't got a photograph then?'

'Don't think so. You could have a look round my place in Clapham if you like.'

'We did. There weren't any photographs there.'

'Oh!' Barnes looked slightly offended, but was phlegmatic enough not to complain. He knew the law about that, too. 'Anyway, what d'you want a photo of Ivy for?'

'To assist in the identification of the body.'

'Is that all? Well I'll pop down and have a look if you like,' said Barnes with a grin.

'I get the impression that you're not too grief-stricken at the apparent death of your sister, Silver,' said Fox menacingly. 'Which leads me to conclude that you may know that it's not Ivy. In which case...'

'Hold on, Mr Fox.' An expression of naked fear settled on Barnes' face as though secure in the knowledge that it would be there for some time. 'I told you, and I told Mr Gilroy, I don't know nothing about that body. No more than what you told me.'

'Maybe,' said Fox. 'Maybe.' He carefully removed a shred of tobacco from the tip of his tongue. 'But as far as I'm concerned, Silver, you're still in the frame for this topping. Well in the frame, mister.'

Chapter Eight

'I'm sick and tired of the way this enquiry is pussy-footing around,' Fox said, gazing with distaste at the pile of statements and reports which were multiplying by the hour on a huge table in the incident room. 'It's time we sorted it out and got on with catching some decent criminals. They're taking the piss, Jack. Some bastard's put it about that we're tied up with this damned topping and, in the meantime, the villainry are marauding about all over London, knocking over building societies and sub-post offices and Christ knows what else. It's not good enough.'

DI Gilroy came to the conclusion that his detective chief superintendent was not in the best of moods this morning. 'Right, sir,' he said, which he thought was sufficiently non-committal not to attract any sort of sarcastic riposte. He was wrong.

'Right, is it? It's not bloody right, Jack. We've got to get going on this. I want it wrapped up by the end of the week.'

'We'll do our best, sir.' Gilroy sighed inwardly. Only a detective chief superintendent like Fox could come up with a requirement to solve a murder by the end of the week.

'Start with the travel agents in Edmonton. Make that the epicentre, as you might say, and work outwards. Work concentrically, Jack. Find out if this Muriel Close, née Yates, booked a holiday. And if she did, who she booked it with, and where she went. And then find out if she's still there.'

'I could try the French police, guv'nor.'

'Yes, you could, if you want to waste your bloody time,' said Fox. 'What the hell d'you think they'll be able to do?'

'But surely, the evidence of the fingerprints — at the Edmonton house and on the body — is conclusive enough to say that the victim is Muriel Close.'

'Of course it is, Jack.' Fox smiled urbanely. 'But when the Crown Prosecution Service' — Fox paused briefly to raise his eyes to the ceiling

— 'asks if we've made all those other enquiries, we can swear by Almighty God that we have. Got it?'

'Yes, sir.'

As Gilroy's hand reached the doorknob, Fox spoke again. 'And Jack...'

'Yes, sir?'

'Don't waste too much time on it.'

*

'Perce?'

'Yes, guv?' DS Fletcher looked up from his desk.

'Get a little team organised, telephoning every travel agent in Edmonton,' said Gilroy. 'Then work outwards, concentrically. Find out if Muriel Yates booked a holiday through them. If so, where, when, and when she's due back.'

'But surely, guv, the fingerprints — '

Gilroy held up a hand. 'If the Crown Prosecution Service asks if we've done it, Perce, we'd like to say yes. Just like the TSB. Got it?'

'Yes, guv.'

'And Perce...'

'Yes, guv?'

'Don't waste too much time on it.'

*

'It's just like looking for a needle in a haystack, guv,' said Gilroy. 'We've tried all the travel agents within about a ten-mile radius of Edmonton and got nowhere. But when you think about it, she could have booked a holiday from any agent anywhere. You can do it on the telephone these days. All you need is a credit card number. She could have rung up some agent in Edinburgh, for all we know.'

'Credit card,' said Fox reflectively. 'Why don't you get on to the leading credit card companies — most of them have got an ex-copper as security bloke — and find out if she had one. Tell you a lot, credit cards.'

'Yes, sir,' said Gilroy with a sigh. He wished he hadn't thought of it. 'On the other hand, she might just have got the train to Dover and got on a ferry. No booking, no nothing.'

Fox considered that for a moment, a frown on his face. 'You could be right, Jack. But then again, I shouldn't think there's much chance at this time of year. Usually fully booked, you see. Anyway, it's not a bad shout. Why don't you check the ferry companies as well?'

'Yes, sir,' said Gilroy. He resolved to stop thinking aloud.

*

Muriel Close had a Visa card, but she hadn't used it for over a month, and only then to buy some clothes in the West End, and she certainly hadn't used it to book a holiday.

'But she spent over two hundred pounds on clothes, guv,' said Gilroy. 'Seems a lot for someone who hasn't got any money.'

Fox nodded thoughtfully. 'Yes,' he said, 'it does.'

Gilroy got in with the answer before Fox's next question came. 'I spoke to the security bloke — chief investigator, he calls himself — and she spends about three hundred quid a month on her card... and clears it. Mainly on clothes, cosmetics, meals out, and quite a few weekends away at hotels — '

'Oh?' Fox sat up and took an interest. 'Where?'

'In the south, mainly. Well, always.' Gilroy thumbed open his pocket book. 'Hampshire, Sussex, Kent, even London.'

'Any of them more than once?'

Gilroy glanced down at his notes again. 'No,' he said. 'Doesn't look like it. There was one in Epsom though — '

'Which is not a million miles from Cobham,' said Fox softly.

'Exactly, sir.'

'Interesting,' said Fox. He grinned, and Gilroy recognised the expression. Fox always grinned when he'd got the scent of the hunt in his nostrils. 'I think we shall pay a visit, Jack.'

*

The hotel was just outside Epsom and, to quote from its brochure, had easy access to the M25.

'Very handy that,' said Fox. 'Junction Nine to Junction Ten, and you're in Cobham. Yes, very handy indeed.'

The manager of the hotel — in common with most of his profession — was not bursting with good humour at receiving a visit from the police, and ushered Fox and Gilroy quickly into his office, presumably from a fear that they might contaminate the guests.

'Mrs Muriel Close, you say?' Fox nodded, and the manager scribbled a few notes. 'I shan't keep you a moment, gentlemen,' he said, and left the office.

'Nice here, isn't it?' said Fox, gazing out of the window.

'She stayed here on the date you mentioned,' said the manager, returning with a computer printout.

'Yes,' said Fox patiently. 'We know that.'

'Ah!' said the manager. 'Then how can I help you?'

'Was there anyone with her?'

The manager looked askance at this proposition and referred to the printout again. 'It would appear not. At least, not that I can tell from the records.'

'Is there anyone on your staff who might remember her, then? Who could say whether she was with someone?'

'You mean you want to question the staff?' The manager looked decidedly unhappy.

'If necessary, yes.'

'The problem is that we have so many guests here, that I doubt if the staff would remember.'

'Meals?'

'I beg your pardon?'

'Did she take her meals in the hotel? Dinner, for example?'

The manager referred once again to the printout. 'Ah! Yes, she did... on both evenings that she was here.'

'Good,' said Fox, and held a hand out in Gilroy's direction. 'Photo, Jack.' Gilroy produced one that they had taken from the house in Edmonton. 'Perhaps we can have a word with the head waiter, restaurant manager, waiters, waitresses... whoever?' said Fox.

'Is this really necessary?' asked the manager, fiddling with the lapels of his morning suit.

Fox smiled tolerantly. 'When I am investigating a murder,' he said quietly, 'I do it my way.'

'Murder! Oh!' The manager looked taken aback. 'Whose murder, may I ask?'

'Hers, we think.' Fox tapped the photograph with his forefinger.

'Oh!' said the manager.

It was a waitress who added to the growing pile of information about Muriel Close. She was young, probably no more than nineteen, and clearly enjoyed being, albeit briefly, the centre of attention in a murder enquiry. 'Yes, I remember her,' she said, handing the photograph back to Gilroy. 'I served her one evening.'

'Was she alone or did she have someone with her?'

The young waitress giggled. 'No, she was with a vicar,' she said.

'What's funny about that?' asked Fox.

The girl shot a quick glance at the manager and blushed. 'I wondered if she was having a dirty weekend with a vicar,' she said. The manager frowned.

'But it wasn't a weekend.' Gilroy glanced at his notes.

'Oh, I know,' said the waitress. 'But it don't have to be a weekend... right...?' She giggled again, and the manager frowned again.

'What did he look like, this vicar?' asked Gilroy, and noted down what the girl said. It was not a good description, but descriptions seldom were. It could have fitted a hundred men. The only certain thing that the girl recalled was that Muriel Close's dinner companion was wearing a clerical collar, and nice though it would have been to jump to the conclusion that he was Donald Close, both Fox and Gilroy knew the danger of that. On the other hand, of course, they were doubtful if Muriel Close had got a thing about vicars. Especially after what they had heard from Muriel's sister Sylvia. Gilroy took a Criminal Record Office photograph of Donald Close from his pocket. 'Could that be him?' he asked.

The girl studied the photograph for some moments before handing it back. Then she nodded. 'It could be,' she said, 'but I'm not sure.'

'Interesting,' said Fox. 'If it was Donald Close, what in hell was Muriel doing having dinner with him when according to her sister, she didn't know where he was, and had an axe to grind because he'd made off with all her money?'

'There's more to this than meets the eye, sir,' said Gilroy.

'That,' said Fox, 'is a shrewd observation, even for a detective of your calibre.' He lit a cigarette and gazed reflectively at the smoke as it spiralled towards the ceiling of his office. 'When's this Henley caper?' he asked.

'Two weeks' time, sir.'

'I think we'll go.'

'We, sir?'

'Yes, Jack,' said Fox, turning his chair so that he faced his DI. 'We, the Flying Squad.'

'What, the lot?'

Fox grinned. 'Well, not quite. But if this Close finger is so mad keen on rowing, and has never been known to miss the Royal Regatta, I think we'll take a little team down there and see if we can't scoop him up.' He stood up and walked to the window. 'Boaters, Jack. We'll need boaters.'

'You're joking, guv.'

'No, I'm not.' Fox turned. 'If we're going to set up a surveillance at Henley, we've got to look the part. I've been studying the form, Jack. White flannels, blazers, club tie — and I don't want to see any CDD ties, either — and straw boaters. If you're well in, like a member of a boat club, then you can wear one of those hats that looks like a school cap. Otherwise, it's boaters.'

'Where the hell do we get boaters from?' asked Gilroy. 'I haven't seen one in years.'

'Obviously moving in the wrong circles, then. It's quite easy to get boaters. I should imagine that Herbert Johnson of Bond Street keeps a decent stock of the things. Ring up G Department, Jack, and see if we can persuade the Receiver to pay for them.' Gilroy had opened the door when Fox spoke again. 'I've just had an idea, Jack.' Gilroy took a deep breath. 'Have a word with Epsom nick. See if anything happened during the time that the estranged Mr and Mrs Close were staying at that hotel.'

'What sort of anything, guv?'

'Just anything, Jack, just anything.'

*

'You must be joking,' said Fred Willerby, who was the detective inspector at Epsom police station. 'It was a race week. They're all at it.' He waved a hand at the two crime books that rested on the corner of his desk. 'Only time we get really busy here,' he added. 'Every villain in Greater London and the Home Counties descends on us for the rich pickings.' He laughed cynically and scratched his ear. 'All these punters come down here in their Rolls-Royces and get seen off rotten. I tell you, Jack, they're all shrewd businessmen, but put a few racehorses out on the ground and they go all to pieces.' He stared sadly out of the window. 'It's greed, I suppose.'

'It's a hard life,' said Gilroy. 'Why don't you apply for a transfer to the Squad... for a rest?'

Willerby scoffed. 'You could be right,' he said and pushed the crime books in Gilroy's direction. 'Major crime and minor crime,' he said.

'You'll find some in each. We always have to put extra pages in at that time of the year. Anything in particular? We've got a wide selection.'

'Anything involving a clergyman, Fred?'

Willerby grinned. 'Excluding bustle-punching, I presume?' he said, reaching for the minor crime book. 'As a matter of fact there was something.' He thumbed through the pages. 'Yes, here we are.' He shook his head slowly and smiled. 'One of the oldest in the book, too. There's this mug staying at a local hotel — '

'Not the Royal, by any chance?'

Willerby glanced up. 'Yes, it was. How did you know that?'

'I'll tell you in a minute. Go on.'

'Well this mug is up on the course when he's approached by an attractive, well-dressed, well-spoken woman who insists that she knows him. She does, of course, but only because she's clocked him in the lounge of the hotel that morning. Anyway, she says something like, "You're Mr Smith from Wandsworth." Some sort of patter like that. Chummy says he isn't, but she laughs. Very insistent, she is. Anyway, to convince her, he produces an envelope addressed to himself and tells her that he's...' Willerby peered closely at the crime report. 'Mr James Forsyth and that he comes from Tavistock and he's up for the racing. At that, our heroine blushes coyly and apologises profusely. Hand to mouth and "What must you think of me?" et cetera.'

'So?'

'So she hotfoots it back to the hotel and imparts this information to her accomplice. The next thing that happens,' said Willerby, 'is that our Mr Forsyth is approached in the lounge of the hotel that evening by a clergyman — name of Calvin — who addresses him by name, claims to know him from Tavistock, mentions a few leading businessmen with whom he reckons he's on first-name terms — probably got them out of the phone book — and gets him to cash a cheque for a hundred quid.'

Gilroy shook his head in disbelief. 'I don't believe it. You mean he fell for it?'

'Oh but he did,' said Willerby, 'but only because it was a parson who asked him. And — I quote — you can always trust a clergyman, the man said.'

'But what about this clergyman's cheque card? Surely he could have cashed a cheque at the hotel? At least for fifty quid.'

'What, use his own money, you mean? Don't be silly, Jack.'

'I meant why didn't this bloke Forsyth ask that question.'

'He did,' said Willerby. 'Apparently the said clergyman told Forsyth that he'd inadvertently left his cheque card at home. You know as well as I do that there's no accounting for the idiocy of your average victim.' Willerby slammed the crime book shut. 'You were going to tell me how you knew it was the Royal.'

'And I can tell you who the clergyman was, Fred. Almost certainly a bloke called Donald Close. Got form for blackmail and a few con tricks... and also uses the name John Calvin.'

'Good,' said Willerby. 'If you can just tell me where I can find him, I can get at least one clear-up out of this mess.'

Gilroy laughed. 'In Australia, the last we heard, but the best you'll get for that little scam is a TIC.'

'Taken into consideration with what?'

'Conspiracy to rob. And, if we get lucky, murder.'

'Suits me,' said Willerby. 'I don't care how it's cleared up, so long as I get it off my books.'

'I'll let you know,' said Gilroy.

'Yeah. Thanks. Be lucky.'

*

'When you've got a moment, Jack, pop down to Woodford and see Frank Goodall. Find out a bit more about this phone call he was supposed to have received from Muriel. You remember, the bad-line job from France that Sylvia Goodall told us about. Get that cleared up.'

'Anything else, sir?' asked Gilroy, just managing to keep the sarcasm out of his voice.

'Yes.' Fox had the look of a man who had been poking about among the papers on his desk, searching for loose ends to tie up. 'These other hotels, Jack...'

'What other hotels, sir?'

'The ones that you got on the list from the credit card company.'

'What about them, sir?'

'Get them checked out, Jack. You never know. Might turn something up.'

*

It took Gilroy quite some time to convince the higher executive officer in the part of G Department that deals with what is called 'non-stock' items, that his enquiry about the acquisition of — and, more importantly, the payment for — straw boaters, was perfectly genuine. The chances of succeeding with the application were not improved when it was learned that the very cheapest boater cost close to thirty pounds. But on being advised that the items in question were needed for the serious matter of apprehending a person who could well be charged with conspiracy to rob — if not murder — the Receiver of the Metropolitan Police District eventually, and with an ill-concealed measure of reluctance, agreed to the purchase of four straw boaters. But there was a compromise. They would not be purchased from Bond Street, but from a small East End hatter who produced them much more cheaply for export.

Tommy Fox was phlegmatic. 'Can't win'em all,' he said.

Chapter Nine

It was the remains of the red dress that clinched it.

One of the truisms of a murder enquiry is that an unidentified body has to be identified before the enquiry can progress. But if the detective's only means of identifying a body is an item like a red dress, he will usually find that it was manufactured in bulk, sold through the largest retail chain in the country, paid for with cash, and is of a size that would fit 90 per cent of the female population. Detectives tend to describe this state of affairs as Sod's Law of Criminal Investigation. But that doesn't stop them trying. It can't. That's what they're paid for.

Gilroy, however, now had some firmer information upon which to base his enquiries. Namely, the credit card account. Along with the names and addresses of the hotels in which Muriel Close had stayed, this account also contained details of various establishments at which she had shopped. And that, in turn, pointed Gilroy in the direction of a boutique in north London.

The proprietress was a large but elegant lady, and was attired in a dress which was undoubtedly among the higher-priced of those of her range. She nodded when Gilroy produced the tattered remains of the red dress. It was not pretty — not any more — and still had traces of earth and putrefaction clinging to it. For the sake of propriety and common decency, Gilroy offered the owner the use of some plastic gloves. She donned a pair of spectacles that flew up at the comers like eccentric eyebrows — spectacles which were permanently attached to her by a gilt chain worn round the neck — and then sniffed. 'Yes,' she said, poking fastidiously at the garment, 'that's one of mine. Or was.' She pushed the dress away with a gesture that was meaningless other than to convey that she wished to have nothing further to do with it. 'Mrs Close,' she said curtly.

'You're quite certain?'

'Yes, of course.' The boutique lady looked mystified. 'Why don't you ask the customer herself?' she demanded haughtily.

'Love to,' said Gilroy cheerfully, 'but unfortunately Mrs Close is dead. She was found buried... in this.' He prodded the disintegrating dress. 'That's why it's in the state it's in.'

'Good heavens,' said the woman, taking a step back. 'How positively dreadful.' She pronounced it 'drettful', and Gilroy got the impression that she was more offended at the misuse of one of her dresses than at the fate of its wearer.

*

'Lovely,' said Fox, rubbing his hands together vigorously. 'That'll do for a start. Now we'll see what our merry band of villains has to say about that.'

'What they've got to say?'

'Yes,' said Fox. 'Until now, we were only half sure who the victim was. This, Jack, will give a certain edge to our enquiries. A certain impetus, wouldn't you say?'

*

The Goodalls' pub on the outskirts of Woodford was more like a fortress than a licensed hostelry. It was a huge block of grey concrete, and it had been built on the edge of a sprawling nineteen-twenties housing estate, to which had been added — just after the Second World War — a London overspill that covered the Essex countryside like a rash. The pub was probably a gold-mine; it was certainly crowded when Gilroy arrived and pushed his way to the bar.

'Yes, sir?' The Irish barman straightened the towelling mat on the mahogany surface of the bar.

'Guv'nor about?' asked Gilroy.

'You a rep?'

Gilroy grinned. 'What, at this time of night?'

'Hang on, I'll see.'

But it was Sylvia Goodall who appeared. After a moment's brief struggle trying to place a face she knew, she smiled. 'Oh, hallo,' she said. 'Any news?'

Gilroy nodded gravely. 'Yes,' he said, 'and it's not good.'

'Oh!' Sylvia Goodall glanced up and down the bar. 'You'd better come into the office,' she said. 'Go through there.' She pointed, and met Gilroy on the other side of a heavy oaken door marked 'Private'.

Gilroy followed her into a cramped room where there were piles of papers on a cluttered desk, and several open box-files spread around on two tables near the window, and on several of the chairs. She shook her head and started making enough room for the detective to sit down. 'I don't know why this place is always in such a state,' she said. 'What with VAT returns, invoices, orders and everything, we can't seem to keep up.' She waited until Gilroy was seated and then sat down facing him, her hands folded in her lap. 'Well?'

'I'm sorry to have to tell you that we are almost certain now that the body we found is that of your sister,' said Gilroy. 'The dress in which it was found has been identified by the owner of a shop in North London as one she sold to your sister.'

'Oh God!' said Sylvia and she pushed her hands up through her hair. 'I'll bet it was that bloody Donald Close,' she said. 'I'll put money on it.'

'Have you any reason for saying that?'

Sylvia laughed. It was a cynical bitter laugh. 'No reason at all. It's just that I don't trust him. Never have. How can you trust a man who nicks all your sister's money, for Christ's sake?'

'I sympathise,' said Gilroy, 'but it doesn't provide a good enough motive for murder, not unless there was something else going on that we don't know about.'

Sylvia nodded. 'Sean said you wanted to see Frank.'

'Sean?'

The barman.'

'Oh yes. I wanted to have a word with him about this phone call he said he got from your sister. The one that supposedly came from France.'

'Any particular reason?'

'Only that the call was made some time after your sister's death, and that doesn't make sense, of course.'

'You mean it wasn't her? Who would do a thing like that... and why?'

That's one of the things I'm hoping to find out,' said Gilroy.

'I think he's upstairs.' Sylvia shrugged. 'Watching television, I expect. You wouldn't think the pub was full of customers, would you?'

Frank Goodall was about five feet nine inches tall and heavily built. He was wearing a bright red waistcoat with brass buttons that made him look like the landlord of a Dickensian tavern, and his shirt-sleeves were rolled to just below his elbows. 'Syl said you wanted to see me.' There was hostility in his voice and Gilroy reckoned that either the local police had done him once or twice under the licensing laws or the CID expected free drinks.

'I'm Detective Inspector Gilroy of the Flying Squad.'

'Yeah, Syl said. What can I do for you?'

'It's about your sister-in-law, Mr Goodall.'

'What about her?'

'Did your wife tell you that we believe her to be a murder victim?'

Goodall nodded. 'Yeah, she did. I reckon it's that bastard Close. Clergyman be damned. Some Christian charity he's got.'

'Be that as it may,' said Gilroy, 'we have no proof that he's in any way responsible for her death.'

'Well I wouldn't mind betting that he's the one who'll go down for it eventually.'

'I wanted to talk to you about the telephone call you had from Mrs Close, Mr Goodall.' Gilroy had no intention of becoming involved in speculation about Muriel Close's killer. 'Can you put an exact date on it?'

'It was a Friday.' Goodall looked thoughtful. 'Must have been the Friday before last.'

'Time?'

'Er, I suppose it must have been about eight-ish. The pub was full. We had a couple of coaches in on top of everything else. Place was like a madhouse. It was me who answered the phone. It's in the passageway behind the saloon bar. You can hardly hear anything at the best of times, and the line was bloody awful.'

'What did she say?'

'Said she was in a bit of a rush, but would I let Syl know she was all right. Said she was in France.'

'Whereabouts?' asked Gilroy.

'She never said.'

'Had she rung before?'

'Not this time.'

'What d'you mean, not this time?' asked Gilroy.

'Not this holiday. She's rung before, when she's been away. Just to let Syl know she's all right. She didn't always ring. A bit scatter-brained was Muriel.'

'I got the impression from your wife, Mr Goodall, that she and Muriel were not particularly close.'

'Depends what you mean by close. They didn't see each other as often as Syl would have liked, but that was because Moo kept herself to herself, and anyway Edmonton and Woodford are a long way apart.' He paused for a moment. 'Well,' he added, 'not that far apart, but a rotten journey by road.'

'You said she was in a hurry.'

'Hurry?' Goodall frowned.

'Yes, you said she didn't have time to speak to her sister.'

Goodall grinned. 'Oh that. That's nothing. Always like that is Moo — was...' He looked momentarily sad as though unable to absorb the fact of her death. 'Moo was always in a tearing hurry. Always late. I used to tell her she'd be late for her own — ' He stopped suddenly, realising that to complete the sentence would be in bad taste. 'Why are you so interested in this phone call, then?'

'According to the pathologist's calculations, your sister-in-law was already dead when you received that call.'

'But that's bloody ridiculous...'

'You've obviously spoken to Muriel on the phone before,' said Gilroy. Goodall nodded. 'Can you be certain that it was her?'

Goodall half-smiled. 'As certain as I can be,' he said. 'As I said, it was a very bad line. It could have been someone else, I suppose, but what would have been the point?'

'If it wasn't Muriel, then someone clearly wanted you — and us — to think that she was still alive. If it was Muriel, then the body we found at Cobham is obviously not her. But if that's the case someone has gone to a lot of trouble to lead us into thinking that it's your sister-in-law.'

'Christ!' said Goodall. He looked earnestly at Gilroy. 'Make sure you get the bastard that did it, mate. Even if it's not Moo.'

Gilroy nodded. 'We usually do, Mr Goodall.'

*

'It makes no sense, guv'nor,' said Gilroy. 'Goodall gets a phone call purporting to come from Muriel Close a week after her death.' He paused. 'If the pathologist's got it right.'

'Pamela Hatcher doesn't make mistakes like that,' said Fox.

'So it wasn't Muriel Close who made that call, but someone pretending to be. In which case, who was it and why?'

'Someone who wanted Sylvia Goodall to believe that Muriel was still alive. On the other hand, as I suggested to Goodall, someone's gone to a great deal of trouble to make us think that that's Muriel Close's body.'

'But what about the fingerprints at Edmonton that match the body, Jack?'

'That's all they do, sir. So the body at Cobham left dabs all over a house in Edmonton. That still doesn't make it Muriel Close. We've not been able to identify the body with a visual. Even if we dragged Sylvia Goodall up to the mortuary, I doubt that she'd be able to say that those rotting remains were her sister.'

'Who would want to work a switch like that?' Fox gazed reflectively at his detective inspector.

'Close?' Gilroy grinned. 'And the woman he took to Australia really was Muriel. How's that for a theory?'

'And the body at Cobham?' asked Fox.

'Ivy Close, perhaps?'

'Who would want to do that?'

'How about Donald Close... or Silver Barnes... or each conspiring with the other?'

Fox gave Gilroy one of his best cynical looks. 'Very good, Jack,' he said. 'Very good.'

*

At three of the hotels the story was much the same as it had been at the Royal at Epsom where Close and Muriel had defrauded James Forsyth of Tavistock of one hundred pounds. DS Fletcher, who had got caught yet again for the routine enquiries that went with the case, did not bother to check at the local police stations to see if any crimes had been reported. It would have been a waste of valuable police man-hours which could be more profitably spent in solving the murder of the former clergyman's wife. It wouldn't have told them anything, except perhaps that Close and his wife — his real wife — had been up to their usual confidence tricks.

And so Fletcher continued. The next hotel was just off the A10, north of Cheshunt and beyond the boundary of the Metropolitan Police District. The enquiry followed the now familiar format: a check with the receptionist to confirm that Muriel Close had in fact stayed there, and then a word with assistant managers, restaurant and bar staff, and with night porters and linkmen if the hotel was grand enough to have them. So far, none had been.

'Yes,' said the waiter. 'I do remember her. Quite a good-looking woman, she was.'

Fletcher produced a photograph of Donald Close. 'And him?'

The waiter examined it closely and then shook his head. 'Couldn't say for sure,' he said. 'Might have been...' He made a see-sawing gesture with his hand. 'Then again... No. I couldn't honestly say. Have you spoken to May?'

'Who's May?'

'The waitress. She's — ah, there she is.' The waiter nodded towards an elderly grey-haired woman who had just emerged from the servery with three plates skilfully ranged up her left arm. 'She's a bit dodgy on her pins, but her brain still works.' He laughed. 'She might remember. I'll ask her to pop over.' Fletcher waited by the door. It was useful that there was a waitress as well as a waiter. In his experience, the male members of staff remembered the women, and the female staff recalled the men.

'Archie said you wanted to see me.' The waitress wiped her hands on a cloth and took the photograph of Muriel Close. 'Yes,' she said. 'I do remember her. Made a fuss about the duchesse potatoes. A bit of a madam, she was.'

'How about this man? Was he with her?' asked Fletcher handing her a photograph of Donald Close.

The waitress studied it carefully for some seconds. 'There was a man with her,' she said eventually, 'but he was nothing like this chap.'

'You're sure?'

'Absolutely.'

Fletcher put the photographs away in his pocket. 'Can you tell me what he did look like, then, this man who was with Mrs Close? How tall, for instance?'

'About your height, I should think. Maybe a bit shorter...' She paused. 'On the other hand, he may have been a little bit taller. Difficult to tell really, because he was sitting down.'

'Yes, I see. Colour of hair?'

'I think it was brown... dark, anyway.'

'Short, long, balding? Was he going grey?'

She appeared to give that some thought, but eventually she said, 'I don't really know.'

'Well how old was he?' asked Fletcher, knowing instinctively that he wasn't going to get very far with this description.

'About average,' said the waitress thoughtfully. 'Yes, about average age, I'd say.'

'Great,' said Fletcher. 'Well thank you very much, you've been very helpful.'

'That's all right,' said May.

*

'The object of this exercise,' said Fox, gazing round at the score of Flying Squad officers who were squeezed into the makeshift briefing room at Scotland Yard, 'is to apprehend one Donald Close. Close is the husband of our murder victim, Muriel Close. He has not been seen since the discovery of her body...' He paused. 'Nor, indeed, for some time before her death. Information is that he has never been known to miss a Henley Royal Regatta. Seems he's some sort of rowing nut.' There were a few laughs and Fox glared at his men, silencing them in an instant. 'He sometimes dresses himself up as a clergyman, but be warned. I don't want you nicking the first clergyman who comes in sight, and for those of you unfamiliar with the dress regulations of the Established Church, let me make it clear that those with purple dickies are bishops. I shall view very seriously anyone who nicks a bishop... unless he's got a good reason, naturally.' Fox lit a cigarette. 'If seen, Close should be arrested, but not interrogated. He is a suspect for murder, and anyone who makes a balls-up of nicking him and then questioning him will find himself — next Monday morning — accompanying those members of the privatised section of this outfit who go around putting wheel clamps on motor vehicles. Now this,' he continued, indicating a dark-suited man sitting at the side of the lectern, 'is Detective Inspector Hardy of the Thames Valley Police, who will be on hand in the police tent throughout the event. He will have a personal radio on our net, and is available to act as liaison officer and adviser for any queries about what goes on. Right now, he's going to give you a quick run-down on what this Regatta business is all about.'

'Right, gents, I'll tell you what it's all about,' said Hardy, in the manner of a policeman who was about to tell them what it was all about.

He walked across to a map pinned on a large board and studied it carefully. 'This is a map of the whole area, and shows where the hospitality tents are, where the enclosures are, and where the car parts are situated. And these areas...' He paused to tap noisily at various parts of the map with the half billiard cue he was using as a pointer. 'Are where your suspect is most likely to be.'

For the next ten minutes or so, Hardy talked about the Regatta, and the sort of arrangements that the police made to deal with it, before sitting down with a satisfied look on his face.

Fox stood up again and took a sheet of paper from his inside pocket. 'This is where you will be posted — at least for starters,' he said, and read out a list of twenty names. As each officer acknowledged his presence at the briefing, Fox indicated on the map the location at which they would be stationed. 'I shall be wearing a straw boater,' he continued, staring grimly at the assembled officers and defying anyone to smile. None did. 'As will Mr Gilroy, DS Fletcher and DS Crozier. The rest of you will be attired properly in white flannels, blue blazers and club ties, so that you can mould into the background.' He glared at the members of the Flying Squad who were sprawled around the briefing room. 'Any questions?'

'Are we going to be tooled-up for this one, guv?'

'No,' said Fox. 'Firearms will not be carried. We are operating in the Thames Valley Police area, and the Chief Constable will not allow any but his own officers to carry weapons. Not that it matters,' he added with a metaphorical side-swipe at DI Hardy. 'Close is only a tuppenny-ha'penny villain anyway.'

'You're going to look a bit flash in a boater, sarge,' said a DC to Fletcher as they left the briefing room.

'Just you watch it, my son,' said Fletcher, 'or I might be tempted to do something with it. And a boater's got sharp edges.'

Chapter Ten

On a good day, Henley Royal Regatta is the perfect place to be. If it's raining, it's not so funny. Fortunately for Tommy Fox and the twenty members of his team, it was fine and sunny. Striped awnings in red and white, and blue and white, stood out from the score of hospitality tents stretched along the Buckinghamshire side of the river, shielding their largely disinterested patrons from the blazing sun. The beech trees were in full red leaf, interspersed with horse chestnuts, weeping willows and flowering elderberry. From time to time, launches cruised up and down the river, full of laughing, blazer-clad men in school caps, and expensively dressed women pressing expensive straw hats on to their expensive hairdos. Most of them appeared, quite definitely, not to be umpires.

And all around, the air was filled with an everlasting volley of popping champagne corks firing a constant *feu-de-joie*. The idiot rich — and the sponsored — were at play.

The Flying Squad contingent had arrived early on the Wednesday morning and parked their various high-powered motor cars in an area secured for them by the Thames Valley Police. Easily accessible in case of emergency, and suitably discreet, these valuable parking spaces would have cost the average punter about ten pounds a car.

Fox was not happy at having to deploy so many men for five days — although he hoped that it wouldn't take that long — but could see no other way of catching Donald Close. Even then, there was a possibility — a very real possibility in the circumstances — that for once in his life, Close would voluntarily give Henley a miss. If they got lucky, the man might just show up on the first day, in which case they could arrest him and pull out. Fox, despite being there in person to supervise, was a little unhappy about having a marauding band of twenty Flying Squad officers roaming about in a place where there was an ample supply of alcohol, and an incredible number of extremely attractive ladies. Fox knew his men's weaknesses. All three of them. Fortunately, the third was absent: there was not a bookmaker in sight; a fact which, at first, utterly demoralised those detectives unfamiliar with river sports. The absence of professional turf accountants did not stop them, however, and quite a few side wagers were already being placed between the officers. Which came as no surprise to Fox, who had, on one occasion, seen two of his men having a fiver on which of the lifts at New Scotland Yard would arrive first.

As a social function, it was exactly right for Fox. Perching comfortably on his shooting stick under a horse chestnut on the Berkshire side of the river, he surveyed the scene from beneath the brim of the Receiver's boater which was tipped forward over his eyes. From time to time, he swept the opposite bank with his binoculars, carefully studying the numerous hospitality tents in his search for Donald Close and — a reflex action for a detective chief superintendent, this — making sure that his officers weren't womanising, drinking, or otherwise distracting themselves from their bounden duty.

'A beautiful day, isn't it?' The woman was slightly plump — nicely rounded was the term that sprung to Fox's mind — and wore a low-cut dress that left little to the imagination of a boobs-man like Fox. She wore a straw hat with the brim pinned back, and had long black hair that reached to her shoulder blades. 'D'you know who won the — ?' She stopped and consulted her programme. 'Ah, yes, Levski Spartak versus Baltimore?' She looked up and smiled. Champagne had taken the edge off her consonants.

'I beg your pardon?' Fox raised his boater.

It was then that the woman noticed the small radio receiver clipped into Fox's ear. 'Levski thing versus Baltimore,' she shouted at the top of her voice.

'Baltimore by a short head,' said Fox. 'Stewards' enquiry after allegations of bumping and boring on the rails, and excessive use of the whip.'

'Good heavens!' said the woman, and walked unsteadily away.

*

By the time Sunday came, Fox was in a decidedly bad mood. For four days he and his men had combed the enclosures, the hospitality tents, the bars and the little private parties that went on in and around the Regatta area, in their search for Donald Close alias John Calvin. It was a formidable task, not helped by the well-meaning but none the less false sightings that came occasionally from the uniformed officers on duty, all of whom had been supplied with photographs of the errant, unfrocked clergyman.

By about two o'clock, Fox was seriously considering calling it a day. But at the precise moment he decided to round up his troops and go home, a DC sidled up to him.

'DI Gilroy says he's got Close under surveillance, sir.'

'Is he sure?' Fox lit a cigarette.

'As sure as he can be, sir.'

'Where?'

'Down near the start. In fact right opposite Temple Island. That's what Mr Hardy said.'

'Is Mr Hardy down there, too?'

'Yes, sir.'

Fox strode rapidly towards the start, staying as close to the edge of the river as he could, but being obliged frequently to deviate because of tents and makeshift barriers. Several times he avoided guy ropes and tent-pegs at the last minute. 'Where the hell's he gone, Mr Hardy?' he asked the Thames Valley DI.

'Made off along the river sir. Brazen as you like. Ice-cream jacket and a clerical collar.'

'Some of my blokes with him?'

'Yes, sir.' Hardy paused. 'A DS Crozier, sir... I think.'

'Well thank God he hasn't put it over the air. And where's Jack Gilroy gone?'

Hardy shrugged. 'No idea, sir.' It wasn't really his problem. Then it came. A message confirming a positive sighting was broadcast to all the Flying Squad officers at the Regatta. Fox wasn't sure whether that was a good thing; policemen had a tendency to home in on the action despite instructions that they should stay where they were. But it was too late now.

It is in the nature of police radio broadcasts during a chase — whether on foot or in cars — that they are confused and rarely understood. None the less, Fox was able to get the drift.

'He's into a tent,' said a voice in Fox's ear-piece. 'No, out again. I don't think he's sussed us yet.'

Then another voice joined in. 'I'm right behind him now. He's definitely not on to us. He's stopped for a glass of champagne.' Fox addressed the transmitter secreted in his sleeve. 'Don't bloody ponce about, then,' he yelled. 'Nick the bastard.'

'Right, guv,' came a disembodied reply.

For some seconds there was silence, during which time Fox's temper got shorter and shorter. 'Well?' he shouted at his cuff, 'what's happening?'

'It's Fletcher here, guv. Our vicar's thumped Crozier and taken it on the toes.'

Fox silently vowed that he would thump Crozier too when he got hold of him. 'Where the hell are you, for Christ's sake?' he screamed into his transmitter. 'Anyone! Somebody speak to me.' By this time a little crowd of interested bystanders was watching the antics of the operational head of the Flying Squad who had clearly become deranged and was talking up his sleeve, literally. Exasperated, Fox pulled the receiver out of his ear and stuffed it into his pocket. 'Radio Three's got more listeners than me,' he said to no one in particular and made his way as quickly as possible to the point of the last sighting. Then he came across DS Fletcher. 'Where is he?'

Breathless, Fletcher pointed towards the road. 'Up and running, guv,' he said. 'Mr Gilroy in hot pursuit.'

'Sod it,' said Fox. 'Well don't stand there, get after him.' Fletcher sprinted away, only to see Close's escape facilitated by a point-duty policeman whose job in life was to hold up traffic and allow pedestrians to cross from the enclosure area to a cricket field that was making a huge profit out of being a car park.

Fletcher seized the officer's arm. 'You prat,' he said. 'That's Donald Close you've just waved across the road.'

For a moment, the PC looked blankly at DS Fletcher. 'You in the police?' he enquired eventually.

'Yes,' said Fletcher. 'Don't tell me you're thinking of joining.' Furious at the prospect of losing a capture when his suspect was almost within reach, Fox strode angrily to the entrance of a marquee. Then suddenly, Close was running towards him, fending people out of the way, and veering desperately in and out of the crowds. A table collapsed, leaving a screaming, laughing mêlée of arms and — in some cases shapely — legs.

A tormented voice complained of the wicked waste of a bottle of champagne, and Fox heard an effete young man suggesting that they must be making a film, a comment that caused his little party of adoring females to collapse in helpless laughter at such unbridled wit.

And so they came face to face. 'Close, I want you,' said Fox.

Close recognised Fox as a policeman, took a feinting step to the right and swung a punch. It was probably the worst thing he had ever done. Fox ducked beneath the flying fist and using his forearm like a horizontal flail, hit his quarry across the solar plexus. Close folded up and fell to his knees, gasping and spluttering.

Fox smiled down at the unfrocked clergyman and carefully stood on one of his hands. 'God bless you, my son,' he said. 'You're nicked...'

If there was one thing that Tommy Fox hated it was lodging a prisoner in another force's police station. He turned to DS Fletcher. 'Take the Reverend to Bow Street nick,' he said, 'and bang him up. And don't stand for any old madam from the custody sergeant.'

*

Bow Street Police Station does not exactly hum with activity on a summer's Sunday evening, and the arrival of the Detective Chief Superintendent of the Flying Squad was, to put it mildly, a bit of an event... and unexpected.

The station officer, a sergeant with wispy, balding, grey hair, sat behind his desk and pointedly ignored the tall well-dressed man standing at the counter, as is the custom of station officers trying to imply that they are overworked.

But not being a member of the long-suffering public, Tommy Fox had no intention of waiting upon the sergeant's pleasure. He slapped his warrant card on the counter with a resounding bang that caused the sergeant to jump, and then look up, and then frown. Fox's skilled eye recognised that the expression on the sergeant's face clearly indicated that he was toying with that section of the Metropolitan Police Act which dealt with disorderly conduct in a police station. 'Detective Chief Superintendent Fox of the Flying Squad,' he said. 'Open this damned door, will you?'

The sergeant immediately became servile. 'Yes, sir. Sorry, sir. I thought you were a member of the public,' he cried, leaping up from his desk and attacking the electric release button that allowed Fox and Gilroy to enter the private part of the front office.

'Get Donald Close up, will you?' Fox was not at all pleased at having to waste a Sunday evening talking to a prisoner. In the old days he would happily have let him stew until at least Monday morning. But now, the Police and Criminal Evidence Act put the pressure even on him.

Looking none the worse for wear, and still attired in his alpaca jacket and his clerical collar, Close seated himself at the table in the interview room and gazed at Fox with a sardonic expression of lofty superiority.

'I suppose you wish to extend these proceedings interminably by demanding the presence of a solicitor?' asked Fox. The implication — quite unfounded, of course — was that without having to await the arrival of a mouthpiece, Close would the sooner be walking out of the station, at worst on bail. And if that was what Close wished to infer, who was Fox to argue?

'The last time I had the benefit of the services of a member of the legal profession,' said Close, 'it cost me three hundred and fifty pounds. All I got for that was a plea in mitigation — which had little effect on the judge — and I reckon must have worked out at about five quid a word.' Close shook his head and smiled. 'I'm quite capable of taking care of myself, squire,' he added.

'I'm not a squire,' said Fox mildly, 'I'm a detective chief superintendent. And that,' he continued, indicating Gilroy, who was sitting in the corner with the Record of Interview book on his knees, 'is Detective Inspector Gilroy... also of the Flying Squad.'

'Oh!' Close adjusted his position slightly. The revelation that so senior a policeman was dealing with his case unnerved him, but not quite as much as the news that it was the Flying Squad that were interested in him. On the occasion of his last arrest, he had been dealt with by a mere detective sergeant from the local nick... a newly promoted sergeant at that.

'Right, shall we begin?' said Fox and, turning to Gilroy, added, 'Now would seem to be the time to switch on the tape-recorder, Jack.'

'Look,' said Close, 'I'm sorry about your chap. I didn't really mean to hit him. I just pushed him and he fell over.'

'That's what they all say,' said Fox, directing his remarks to Gilroy. Turning back to Close, he continued: 'But assault occasioning actual bodily harm is only one of the many things I want to talk to you about.'

Close didn't like the sound of that. He didn't much care for this detective either: much too confident for his liking. In Close's limited experience of the police, detectives tended to feel their way gently, because in most cases they hadn't got a shred of evidence. They fished... in the hope that their prisoner would, as the police say, cough. Nevertheless, Close managed to retain a certain air of injured innocence. 'I can't imagine what they could be.'

'Well, for a start, why are you all decked out as a vicar?' asked Fox in conversational tones.

'I am a clerk in holy orders.'

'No you're not. You got busted when you went down for blackmail. You're up to something, Donald, old friend.'

Close smiled. 'You'd be surprised how useful it is to wear a clerical collar,' he said. 'People are polite to you, and they afford you little privileges they wouldn't dream of according to laymen — and they trust you.'

'Trust you enough to cash a cheque for a ton in Epsom, you mean?' Fox gently pulled the lobe of his ear.

'I don't know what you're talking about, Chief Superintendent,' said Close, without any sign of the spasm of panic that had just attacked his stomach.

'But that's minor stuff really,' Fox went on. 'So for that matter is fraudulently obtaining a passport by means of a false statement. Which also involved a touch of forgery, if I remember correctly.' He glanced at Gilroy, an eyebrow raised. Gilroy nodded solemnly.

'I think you must have the wrong man in me,' said Close confidently.

'Oh! Who are you, then? John Calvin, perhaps?'

'All right.' Close laid his hands flat on the table, palms down. 'So I did fiddle a passport. What's that? Fifty-quid fine? That's no big deal.' Slowly, he drew his hands back off the table and folded them in his lap. Fox wondered if he was about to deliver a sermon on the subject of temptation. 'I was avoiding a bit of unpleasantness, to tell you the truth. Creditors, you know.' Close shrugged. 'I can't think why they were making such a fuss. They'll all get their money... eventually.'

Fox nodded as though satisfied with this explanation. 'All right,' he said, 'let's go back for a moment to the Royal Hotel at Epsom, and a certain Mr James Forsyth who, I may say, is somewhat aggrieved that he cashed a cheque for one hundred pounds for you, only to discover that it bounced all the way back to Tavistock marked "RD".' Fox sat back in his chair with a half smile on his face. Get out of that, you bastard, he thought.

Close did. 'Well, I don't see what the problem is there,' he said. 'It was a perfectly legitimate cheque, on a perfectly legitimate bank account. The fact that it didn't happen to have any funds in it at the time — although I firmly believed that it did have — was just downright unfortunate.'

'The account was in the name of the Reverend John Calvin,' said Fox.

'Yes indeed,' said Close.

'Well?'

'I hope that you're not implying that that's an offence, Chief Superintendent. If it is, then half the people in show business, many of whom have bank accounts in their stage names, are in quite serious trouble.'

'Is John Calvin your stage name, then?' asked Fox sarcastically.

Close smiled. 'Shouldn't you caution me before I answer that question?' he asked.

'Why? Have you committed some other offences? You've already admitted to ABH and obtaining a passport by means of a false statement, so we can forget about those. And your explanation of the unfortunate Mr Forsyth's one hundred pounds seems just about plausible enough to rule out any proceedings. Are you now saying, Donald, that you've been up to some other naughties?' Fox was quite pleased with the way the interview was going. He was deliberately leading Close along a path that gave the impression that his questioner — albeit a detective chief superintendent — was really a bit of a wally. Which was exactly what Close was thinking; after all, the fellow probably hadn't even been to university... either of them.

'Other offences?' Close contrived to look alarmed. 'Good heavens, no.'

'Good!' said Fox. 'Let's talk about your wife now then, shall we?'

'My wife?' A puzzled smile appeared on Close's face.

'Yes,' said Fox. 'Mrs Muriel Close, née Yates.'

Still Close looked puzzled. 'What about her?'

'She was involved in this business of Mr Forsyth's cheque, was she not?'

'I can't imagine what made you think that.'

'Very simple, Donald. She approached Mr James Forsyth on the racecourse at Epsom, insisting that he was someone she knew. Mr Forsyth eventually revealed who he really was and your wife apologised for what was clearly a case of mistaken identity. She then returned to the hotel and gave you the low-down so that you could have dear old Forsyth over for a hundred notes. Yes?'

'What an intriguing tale,' said Close. 'Certainly my wife was staying with me at the — ' He hesitated for a moment. 'Ah yes. The Royal. Yes, she was there, but I can assure you that she is not the sort of woman to accost strange men on racecourses.' Fox had to admire the man's reserve. The mention of Muriel should have rung alarm bells for Close. But only if he had murdered her. That left Fox with two options to choose from: either Close was a bloody good actor... or he wasn't the killer. 'When did you last see your wife, Donald? Before you went to Canada and Australia, that is?'

Close shook his head like a boxer who had received a particularly damaging punch. 'I really don't know what you're talking about,' he said. 'My wife accompanied me to both Canada and Australia. She didn't come to Henley today though. She really can't stand rowing. One of my great disappointments.' Close glanced at his wrist-watch. 'Incidentally,' he said, 'doesn't the law say something about me being entitled to a meal...?'

'Hungry, are you?'

'Just a bit,' said Close. 'And if there's somewhere private, I usually like to say matins about now.'

Chapter Eleven

'He's a cool bastard, I'll say that for him,' said Fox. After what to him was a frustrating interview, Fox had put Close back in his cell, determined to return the following morning and deal with the question of the dead body that had been found at the ex-clergyman's house. But it was apparent that some high-powered and rapid enquiries would have to be made in the meantime.

'I've sent a signal through to Melbourne, sir, to ask them if they can find anything that would indicate that Muriel Close was actually there with her husband.'

'Some hopes,' said Fox. 'I'm in no doubt that it's Muriel's body we've got. All that the Australians can come up with is that Close was staying in some bungalow on the outskirts of Melbourne, and that he had a bank account there that he closed. Seems pretty good at opening and shutting bank accounts, does Close.'

'Another thing, guv. We don't know where he's been living these last few days. We don't even know when he got back from Australia.'

'So make a few enquiries, Jack, there's a good fellow.'

'Yes, sir.' Gilroy always fell for it. He sighed and made his way back to his own office.

*

'I had an idea, guv,' said Gilroy.

'Oh, that's nice.' Fox was standing in front of the mirror adjusting his tie. It was a snip of a silk job that he had picked up on one of his regular forays through Angelos of Piccadilly. He turned to face Gilroy. 'What d'you think of the new whistle, Jack?' he asked, carefully smoothing the front of his jacket. 'Rather a nice number I picked up in Hackett's.'

'Yeah, very nice, guv. Must have cost you a few sovs.'

Fox tapped the side of his nose with his forefinger. 'Got to pay to get quality, Jack. Now, this idea you had...'

'I was going through Silver Barnes' CRO file, to get his previous convictions for the DPP's report — '

'Yes?'

'And, would you believe, he was in the same nick as our friend Close... at the same time?'

'Was he now?' Fox took the file from Gilroy and thumbed quickly through it. 'Well, there's a thing. D'you know, Jack, I've got this gut feeling that Master Barnes hasn't been entirely open and honest with us.' He shook his head sadly. 'How can you help these poor underprivileged wretches if they don't play fair with you?' He handed the file back to his DI. 'I think we shall have to have another little chat with Silver,' he said. 'But not before we've spoken to the Reverend Close again.'

*

While Fox had been busy interviewing the principals, DS Percy Fletcher had been pounding the pavements, conducting the mundane enquiries that are germane to any murder enquiry. DI Gilroy did not seem greatly interested — at least, not enough to ask questions — but after the visit to the hotel in Cheshunt, Fletcher thought it was time to report back. If for no other reason than to let Gilroy know that he was still at it.

'I reckon there were three couples over the side that night, guv,' said Fletcher, 'and two of them paid in cash — '

'Mr and Mrs Smiths were they?' asked Gilroy.

Fletcher grinned. 'Not any more. Much more imaginative these days. One couple was called Runciman and another Marsh. And each of them gave a duff address.'

Gilroy shook his head. 'And the other couple?'

'Not a couple, guv,' said Fletcher. 'A man... on his own. I reckon it was him who was with Muriel Close. She paid by credit card, of course, otherwise we wouldn't have known where to look. But the man called himself Armstrong. A. Armstrong. He paid cash, and his address doesn't exist, either.'

'Booked into a different room, I suppose?'

'Yes, guv, but on the same floor. Not that that was too difficult. There are only two accommodation floors in that hotel. It was a fifty-fifty chance anyway.'

'How many more have you got to do, Perce?'

'Seven, guv.'

'Keep at it,' said Gilroy.

*

Donald Close, having spent a night's sojourn in the cells at Bow Street Police Station, and being somewhat of an amateur strategist, decided to make a stand when he was brought into the interview room on Monday afternoon. 'I want to know what's happening,' he began truculently.

Fox nodded sympathetically. 'Know how you feel, old son,' he said. 'So do I.'

'Well, as I see it,' continued Close, 'you've either got to charge me with something or let me go.' He was standing in front of the table as if about to perform the sacraments.

'You've got a good point there,' said Fox. 'How does bigamy grab you?'

Close sat down suddenly.

Fox gazed at him calmly but said nothing.

Eventually Close collected himself. 'That was a bit of a misunderstanding, to tell you the truth.'

'Well, that makes a change... someone telling the truth.'

'No, you see I genuinely thought that my first wife was dead — '

'Did you now? And tell me, Donald, what steps did you take to verify that?'

'Well... I...'

'As I thought, sod-all,' said Fox brutally.

'As it happened, I was still on good terms with my first wife — '

'You just said you thought she was dead.'

'That was afterwards.'

Fox sighed. 'After what?'

'After I found out that she was still alive.'

Fox sat down in the chair facing Close, a resigned look on his face. 'I think you'd better begin at the beginning, Donald,' he said. 'And if it'll make you feel any better, anything you say will be given in evidence.'

For a moment or two, Close gazed up at the high, barred windows of the interview room before turning his attention once more to Fox. 'After the bit of trouble I got into — '

'You mean when you got four years' bird for blackmail?'

'Yes, but that was — '

'Don't tell me it was another misunderstanding,' said Fox, 'I couldn't stand it. Anyway, I know all about that. I've got a file that thick.' He held his thumb and forefinger three inches apart.

'The sad fact is, that despite what it says in the marriage service about for better, for worse, Muriel didn't come anywhere near the prison. I wrote... naturally —'

'Naturally,' murmured Fox.

'But got no reply. I made this rather rash assumption that she'd passed away.' Close looked reverently sad.

'And then up she popped. Just like that,' said Fox cheerfully.

'Yes, I'm afraid so.'

'And where is she now?'

'Who? Muriel?'

'Yes, Muriel.'

'I really don't know. You see —'

'Hold on,' said Fox. 'You said she came to Canada and Australia with you.'

'I did?' Close looked surprised.

Fox glanced across at Gilroy who rapidly turned back the pages of the interview book, looked up and nodded. 'Yes, you did,' continued Fox. 'I'm sure that Mr Gilroy will be happy to repeat your exact words.'

Gilroy cleared his throat. 'Mr Fox said, "Let's talk about your wife." You said, "My wife?" and Mr Fox said, "Yes. Mrs Muriel Close, née Yates."'

Close put his head on one side and smiled at Fox. 'Well, you said it, Chief Superintendent, not me.'

Fox swung round to face Gilroy. 'What did Close say then?' he asked.

Gilroy looked up from his book. 'Close said, "What about her?"'

'There you are then,' said Fox.

Close shook his head. 'I'm most terribly sorry,' he said. 'I really thought you were talking about my second wife, Ivy.'

'Your bigamous wife, you mean,' said Fox, determined not to let Close take the lead.

'If you say so, Chief Superintendent. But I honestly thought it was Ivy whose name you'd mentioned.' Close was sitting with his legs crossed, entirely unruffled by Fox's constant attempts to wear him down.

Fox paused to give the next part of his statement more effect. 'Ivy Barnes, sister of the Silver Barnes you were in prison with in Wandsworth, of course.'

A muscle twitched slightly on the side of Close's nose and he stared up at the fluorescent light tube above the table. 'Is that so?' he said, looking back at Fox. 'What an extraordinary coincidence.'

Fox felt like seizing Close's clerical collar and twisting it until it throttled him, but knew that he had still got a trump card to play. 'I ask you again, Close,' he said. 'When did you last see Muriel Close, your wife?'

'I must say you seem very interested in Muriel. I can assure you that she had nothing to do with that unfortunate business in Epsom — '

'Answer the question.' Fox's voice cut across Close's mild tones like a whiplash.

The disgraced clergyman sat back, a little startled. 'I — er — I suppose it must have been about the end of March.' A frown appeared on his face. 'But why all this interest in Muriel?'

Fox decided that the time had come. 'Because, Donald Close, she has been murdered and her body was found in the garden of your house in Cobham.'

Close was a good actor, and a cool operative, but even Fox had to admit that his reaction was a masterpiece of self-control. 'I don't believe you,' he said blandly.

'Oh, you'd better believe it, old son,' said Fox, 'because right now you're my Number One Suspect.'

*

'Would you Adam-and-Eve that bastard?' said Fox angrily.

'He's a smooth customer, all right,' said Gilroy. He and Fox were seated in the back of Fox's car, on their way to Brixton Prison, direct from Bow Street. Gilroy was uneasy. When Fox was riled, he tended to lash out in all directions.

'And where were you, Swann?' Fox spoke to the back of his driver's neck. 'I told you to wait for me at Bow Street.' Fox had had to make a phone call to the Yard and wait fifteen minutes for Swann to return with the car. 'Playing bloody crib again in the drivers' room, I suppose.'

Swann was imperturbable. 'Filling up with petrol, guv,' he said, and as an afterthought quoted a little-known paragraph from Metropolitan Police Transport Regulations: 'And getting the stones out, guv.'

'What's that supposed to mean?'

'Have to make sure there's no stones stuck in the tread of the tyres,' said Swann in a mournful tone of voice. 'Garage Sergeant plays merry hell, else.'

'Well next time you're late, I'll play merry hell,' said Fox. From which Gilroy deduced that Fox assumed himself to be in a good mood at the moment. That was bad news indeed.

Some forty-five minutes after leaving Donald Close at Bow Street, Fox and Gilroy were sitting in an interview room at Brixton Prison awaiting the arrival of Silver Barnes.

''Allo, Mr Fox. Nice to see you again.' Barnes strolled into the room and nodded to the prison officer who had accompanied him as though dismissing a butler. 'You got good news for me?'

'Sit down and cut the cackle,' said Fox. 'You and Close. Both in Wandsworth together then.'

'Ah! You know about that, then?'

'Yes, Silver, I know about that. So why didn't you tell me before, instead of giving me all this fanny about only meeting him through your sister Ivy?'

'I never thought it was revelant.'

'The word is relevant, Silver. And it's very relevant. In fact, if I was in a bad mood, I might also consider the question of obstructing police. But as you're probably going down for about fourteen, it won't make much difference.'

Barnes winced. 'Gawd! Don't keep saying that, Mr Fox.'

'Right then, you'd better start doing some nifty footwork with your mouth.'

For a moment or two, Barnes sat with a pensive look on his face, wondering just how much he would have to tell Fox to satisfy him. It was a dangerous ploy; the boss of the Heavy Mob was a man to be reckoned with. 'Yeah, well, I did meet him in Wandsworth, but the rest was true.'

'Explain!' growled Fox.

'Well, we like met up, see. And Donald was skint. So I said to him why don't he come in with me when we was through. We was both getting out about the same time, and — '

'What d'you mean by going in with you? Did you tell him you were into armed robbery?'

'Well, not exactly, Mr Fox.' There was a crooked grin on Barnes' face. 'I mean, he was a confidence man. Leastways, that's what he told me.'

'Well what's that got to do with blagging?' Fox knew that there were various disciplines of crime, and rarely did they overlap. He couldn't see a villain of Barnes' calibre trusting the smooth-talking Donald Close, whose idea of crime appeared to be dressing up as the clergyman he had once been and flying kites on honest citizens... as he had done with the unfortunate Mr James Forsyth of Tavistock.

'Like I said, Mr Fox, once we got talking, Donald was telling us about how we was going wrong — '

'I could have told you that,' said Fox.

'Anyhow, Don said as how he'd got this drum down Cobham, but he was going to have to flog it because he was boracic. Well I done a bit of thinking then — '

'Good Lord!' said Fox mildly.

'And I thought as how it'd make a good slaughter.' He spread his hands out, demonstrating objective candour. 'I mean, there's no harm telling you that now, is there? After all, I'm going straight when I've finished this little lot.'

Fox gave a polished performance of a man overcome by helpless laughter. 'Firstly, it won't be little, and secondly, the thought of you going out and doing an honest day's work just creases me.'

Barnes looked injured. 'Be fair, Mr Fox,' he said. 'I am trying to help.'

'So you are, Silver, so you are. Well get on with it.'

'Well it worked a treat — '

'You mean you used it as a slaughter for other jobs... apart from Cobham?'

Barnes stared at Fox. 'Are we talking TICs here, Mr Fox?' he asked plaintively.

'We might be. Not that it'll make a great deal of difference. If you get fourteen penn'orth for Cobham, I doubt if the learned judge'll tack any more on, however many other offences he takes into consideration. No, Silver, I'm interested in a murder job... as you well know.'

'Yeah, well.' Barnes licked his lips. 'Yeah, sure we used it for a couple of jobs, but Don was doing a nice little earner in conning at the same time.'

'How so?'

'Nice one, it was. Him and a mate — '

'Name?' demanded Fox.

Barnes shrugged. 'No idea, Mr Fox. But what he'd do was hang about in some place like the Savoy or the Ritz...' He paused in thought for a moment. 'I think he said he even done Claridges a couple of times. Anyhow, he'd hang about, by hisself like, having afternoon tea. Then his mate would come in and just as he was passing Don, who had usually sat hisself on the next table to some rich-looking Yank, his mate'd stop and say something like "Good afternoon, my lord."'

'Oh Jesus!' Fox sighed and looked at the ceiling.

'Well it was a sort of wind-up, see, so's the bloke what was sitting next to him'd think that Don was an English lord, see.'

'Yeah, go on.' Fox was well ahead of Barnes, but decided to let him continue just for the entertainment.

'Well, they'd have a bit of a rabbit, mentioning people like the Queen and the Prime Minister and that, like they and Don was the best of mates, see. Then Don's oppo would push off, and the Yank next door couldn't resist it. He'd start chatting to Don and the next thing you know... wallop!'

'Wallop?' Fox raised his eyebrows.

'Yeah. The next thing's this Yank'd get taken for a few grand. The usual old moody: shares or a good proposition in business. You know the score on that, Mr Fox, surely?'

Fox nodded. 'Yes, Silver, I know the score on that. I'm just surprised that there are still people about who fall for it.'

Barnes nodded sagely at the stupidity of the human race. 'It's greed, Mr Fox. That's what does it. Greed!'

'Good grief,' said Fox. 'You never cease to amaze me, Silver.'

'Oh yeah,' said Barnes loftily. 'And if it should happen to go wrong... you know, like if they was smart enough to find out where Don lived, and the punter come steaming down Cobham to get his money back.

Well, who should open the door? You've got it, Mr Fox. The Reverend Close. And of course, they'd never recognise him as the geezer what had'em over. He'd give 'em a load of bunny about what a diabolical plot it was, and how he ain't never heard of no lord and he was just an innocent clergyman like. Finish up practically crying on each other's shoulders.' Barnes paused for a moment and looked doubtful. 'Mind you, I told him. Don, I said, one day you're going to come a gutser, I said. But he wouldn't listen. Knew best, see. Always the same with them educated geezers. He just used to laugh. Reckoned he'd got another place across the river... up Edmonton way — '

Fox leaned across and seized Barnes' wrist. 'Where did you say?'

''Ere, hold on.'

'That's what I'm doing. Where did you say?' Fox leaned back and waited.

Barnes rubbed his wrist vigorously. 'Edmonton. Some cheap drum he reckoned he bought when we done a — ' He stopped suddenly.

Fox nodded. 'All right. It was his split from a blagging. Well, Silver, as we're going to put him up with you, you can give Mr Gilroy a few details of these little tickles you had between getting out the last time and getting nicked this.'

'You mean you've nicked him?'

'Mr Close is in custody, yes.'

Barnes grinned. 'You charged him with topping Ivy, have you?'

'No.'

'But I thought — '

'That's the one thing you didn't do, Silver. That's not your sister's body we found. It was Close's first wife. As well you know. And if I can put you in the frame for that, my son, I shan't hesitate. Unless you can give me a little more assistance.'

'What, grass, you mean?'

Fox shrugged. 'Call it what you like. But first and foremost, I want a picture of your sister Ivy... and I want it fast.'

'I ain't got one, Mr Fox, honest.' Barnes furrowed his brow in deep concentration. 'I know somewhere you might get one, though.'

'Keep going.'

'Well, before she met up with Close, she was doing a bit of acting. She was in one of them police series on the telly one time — '

'What as? A shoplifter?'

'Nah! As a policewoman,' said Barnes. 'And she had some of them pictures, for sending round to agents and that. You might be able to get hold of one of them.' Barnes scratched his head, releasing a shower of dandruff. 'She done three months in Australia, an' all,' he added.

'In the nick?'

'Be fair, Mr Fox. Nah, in some telly series.'

Chapter Twelve

'Get a leg man out, round the theatrical agents, Jack, and track down a photograph. Probably used an alias. I doubt if she called herself Ivy Barnes.'

'Probably find her stage name was something exotic and foreign,' said Gilroy morosely.

*

It took a week.

DS Percy Fletcher, relying heavily on his five years' previous experience in the CID at West End Central Police Station, worked his way round informants, dodgy doormen, strippers and ponces until he found what he was looking for.

The premises were much like all the others in the street, which in turn was much like all the other streets in that part of Soho. Photographs of naked women had been deprived of their luridness by pieces of paper pasted over the more provocative parts of their anatomy, but the message was just as clear as if they hadn't bothered. A large and oafish-looking man lurked in the shadow of the doorway. 'Continuous live show,' he said, as Fletcher approached. 'Most beautiful girls in London. All topless... and that's only for starters. Twenty quid,' he added menacingly as Fletcher made to enter.

'Well, well,' said Fletcher. 'Fred Briggs. What are you doing out so soon?'

The blue chin of the bouncer dropped a perceptible two inches. 'Gawd, Mr Fletcher, I never recognised you. It's free to you, guv'nor.'

'Don't insult my intelligence,' said Fletcher. 'Where does the creep who runs this place have his office?'

'Straight through the bar, Mr Fletcher. Door at the far end, marked "Private".'

'Good.' Fletcher paused. 'And if your finger goes anywhere near that bell behind the door, Fred, the next bell you push will be the one in Cell Two at West End Central. Got it?'

The bouncer spread his hands. 'Would I do a thing like that, Mr Fletcher?'

Fletcher strode through the tatty interior of the strip-joint and found the door to the office just as the owner was emerging. 'Ever hear of a bird called Ivy Close?' he asked by way of an opening.

'Who's asking?' The owner of the strip joint must have weighed at least twenty stones. The amount of cloth which had been used to make his suit would probably have made two for Fletcher... with waistcoats. He went by the doubtful name of Frankie Fanganari, although Fletcher knew from Frankie's criminal record that he had been named Albert Goldman at his birth in Wapping.

Fletcher removed his warrant card from his pocket and put it in front of Fanganari's face. 'Police, New Scotland Yard... Albert,' he said loudly.

Fanganari looked distressed. 'Er, better come in the office,' he said hurriedly. 'More private in there, like.' He led Fletcher into a small back room and closed the door. Then, emptying dregs of coffee out of a paper cup, he poured a liberal quantity of Scotch into it from a bottle he took from a drawer in his desk. 'Fancy a snort?' he asked.

Fletcher shook his head. 'Ivy Close, maiden name Barnes,' he said.

'Yeah! Called herself Gloria de Bonavista or some such crap.' Fanganari paused. 'Did you say Barnes?'

'That's right.'

'Nothing to do with Silver Barnes, I hope.'

'His sister.'

'Oh my oath!' said Fanganari. 'I never knew that.' A spontaneous outpouring of perspiration started to mingle with the natural grease of his face. It was an unedifying sight.

'Small world, isn't it?' said Fletcher conversationally. 'Got any pictures of her?'

'Should have. Hang on.' Fanganari walked across to a battered filing cabinet and flicked through the contents with his heavily ringed and podgy fingers. 'Here you are,' he said, plucking a folder out of the drawer. 'Cast your minces on them.'

Fletcher took the photographs and laid them on the desk. 'Gordon bloody Bennett,' he said. 'Just look at those bristols.'

Fanganari grinned. 'Ain't bad, are they? Used to go down a treat.'

'You mean they were pneumatic?'

'Do what?' Fanganari's face crinkled into a frown.

'Never mind.'

'These is better.' Fanganari produced two more photographs of Ivy Barnes in which she was completely unclothed.

'She was a stripper, then?'

Fanganari laughed. 'I can see how you got to be a detective,' he said. 'Yeah, she was a stripper, all right. She come here because her old man was short of money. So she said. Reckoned it was something to do with the mortgage.' He sniggered at that. 'I didn't give a monkey's why she was doing it. You get a lot of birds coming up West, falling over themselves to tear all their clothes off, just to make a bit of pocket-money... or their old man's in the nick... or he's pissed off and left 'em.' Fanganari shrugged. 'So what? Still, she wasn't bad at it. Sorry when I lost her.'

'And how long ago was that?'

''Bout six or eight months, I s'pose.'

'Where did she go, any idea?'

Fanganari shook his head. 'No,' he said. 'They come and go all the time. Half of 'em are on the game, anyway.'

'She claimed to have been an actress.'

'They all do round here. Tarts, most of 'em. Love to be on telly, but most never make it. Probably find she's hawking her mutton down the Edgware Road now. That's where most of 'em finish up.'

'And you're sure this is her?'

'Positive.'

'Good.' Fletcher picked up the photographs. 'I'll hang on to these.'

A look of sudden alarm crossed Fanganari's face. 'Here,' he said, 'you're not from the Clubs Squad, are you?'

Fletcher shook his head slowly. 'No, Flying Squad.'

'Oh Gawd,' said Fanganari. He produced a giant mauve handkerchief and started dabbing at the sweat that was now coursing down his face in increasing quantities. 'What's up, then?'

'Nothing really. Just a little topping we're trying to clear up.'

Fanganari pointed at the pictures. 'What, her?'

'Possibly,' said Fletcher. 'Difficult to tell really. The body was stinking to high heaven, falling apart and crawling with maggots when we found it. Most of the face was gone already. Makes identification a bit of a problem.'

'Oh my Gawd!' said Fanganari, and slapping his hand across his mouth ran through a door at the back of the office.

'Thanks for your help,' said Fletcher, but the only reply was a sound of retching.

*

'That's more like it,' said Fox, carefully surveying the photographs of Ivy Barnes, which Gilroy had laid on his desk. 'Now we're into territory I can understand.' He leaned his elbows on the desk, folded his hands and rested his chin on them. 'Tell you what, Jack. Nip down to Brixton and show these to Silver Barnes. Just to make sure that it is her.'

'He'll do his bloody pieces when he finds out she was a stripper — or, worse still, was on the game — and that it was Donald Close that sent her there, guv.'

Fox swung round in his chair and gazed out of the window. 'Yes, Jack, I should think he probably will,' he said. For a moment he studied two fire engines, blue lights winking, that had pulled up outside Caxton Hall. Then he swung back to face his DI. 'And I think that I shall come with you. I can't really resist seeing his face when you tell him.'

'Yes, sir,' said Gilroy with a resigned sigh.

*

To the surprise of Tommy Fox, Silver Barnes had not seemed at all put out to discover that Ivy had been appearing undraped before the lascivious eyes of the dregs of London's West End. In fact, he had been quite phlegmatic about it, expressing the view that if punters wished to pay good money to see Ivy with nothing on, that was her affair. After all, Barnes had said, she was a big girl now. Having seen Ivy's publicity photographs, it was a view with which Fox was not prepared to argue.

Even Gilroy's hint that Ivy might have taken to prostitution had merely produced a grunt. 'I ain't never paid for it yet,' Barnes had said, 'and if she can make a few shills out of putting herself about, well, that's business, ain't it?'

None of which put Fox in a better frame of mind. 'I don't like it, Jack,' he said. 'I've got a feeling. As a matter of fact, I've got several feelings. First, I reckon that Silver Barnes knows very well that it wasn't his sister that we found at Close's house, and secondly, that he knows who it really is, and third that he had something to do with it.'

DI Gilroy shrugged. 'You're probably right, sir. But what do we do about it?'

'We consider the evidence, Jack.' Fox yawned and reached out for his cigarette case. 'Point One, we have a body. Yes?' Gilroy nodded; he was never very enthusiastic about Fox's so-called brainstorming sessions. 'And Point Two, Messrs Close and Barnes have got something to do with it.'

'How do we know that?' asked Gilroy.

'Oh Jack, Jack...' Fox looked gloomily at his DI. 'We found the cadaver...' He paused for a moment to savour the word. 'We found the cadaver in a house previously occupied by one Donald Close — now in custody — and which was used by Silver Barnes and others — also in custody for divers offences — and no other party appears to have been involved. It's a racing certainty that the said cadaver is that of Muriel Close, née Yates, and therefore is not the body of Ivy Barnes, sometime Gloria de Bonavista, now using the name of Close as the result of a bigamous union.'

Gilroy stifled a sigh. 'Well, we know all that, guv.'

'Indeed we do, Jack.' Fox leaned forward earnestly. 'But it's not getting us any nearer to a result. However, Messrs Barnes, Close and their co-conspirators, do not know what we know. Therefore, in the fullness of time we will visit Barnes and Company and I shall put it to them that I am giving careful consideration to charging them all with her murder. In fact,' he continued, 'I might actually charge them on their next remand hearing.' For a moment he looked wistful. 'Haven't charged anyone at the back of the court for years,' he said. 'But first we'll put a similar proposition to Master Close. He's entitled after all.' Fox idly moved the cable of his telephone and looked pleased with himself.

'Entitled?' Gilroy gave Fox a quizzical look.

'Of course,' said Fox. 'It's his wife.'

'Are we certain enough of that to sustain a charge, guv?' Gilroy thought it a pertinent question.

Fox gazed out of the window. 'Doesn't really matter, Jack. If Close smiles, we'll know we've got the wrong body. And as far as Barnes is concerned, any old murder will do. I'll bet that Barnes has got at least one other topping up his sleeve that we know nothing about... but doesn't know that we know nothing about.' He smiled disarmingly.

*

Of the twelve hotels that Flying Squad officers checked against Muriel Close's credit card account, staff at two of them were adamant that Close was not the man who had been with her, but the descriptions they were able to give were sufficiently vague to encompass several million members of the male population of the United Kingdom. In short, they were no damned good at all. At four of the other hotels, staff could not be sure, when shown Donald Close's photograph, whether he had stayed there or not. The only real information to come out of the whole time-consuming exercise was that on at least two occasions, Muriel Close had stayed at an hotel with a man not her husband. On both those occasions the man had used the name A. Armstrong and the same false address.

'So what?' said Fox. 'Happens all the time.'

'Yes, sir, but the women they're screwing don't always get murdered,' observed Gilroy drily.

*

'I am of a mind to charge you with the murder of Muriel Close, née Yates, whose body was found in the garden of your property at Cobham,' said Fox in matter-of-fact tones as he lowered himself on to the hard wooden chair on the other side of the table from Donald Close.

For the first time since his arrest, Close appeared to be disconcerted. 'You mean it really was her?'

'I'd hardly be talking about charging you with her murder if it was someone else, now would I?' Fox smiled confidently.

'But — '

'But what, Donald?'

Close remained still, his hands clasped on the table in front of him and his head bowed. Then he looked up, a baleful expression on his face. 'Look, Chief Superintendent,' he said, 'I've pulled some strokes in my time...' He shrugged. 'I'm a con man, after all, but murder... not that.'

'You know, I suppose, that one of the security guards in the Cobham heist was shot and seriously wounded. In fact, he had to have a leg amputated. Damned nearly died.' Fox fixed Close with a steely gaze. He did not like robbers, and as far as he was concerned, by conspiring in the planning of the Cobham job and others like it — even though he wasn't there — Close might just as well have pulled the trigger himself. And he was pretty certain that the same view would be taken by the Old Bailey judge who eventually presided at Close's trial.

Close's face went white. 'I didn't know that,' he said. 'They didn't say anything about using guns.'

Fox shook his head wearily. He could just about believe that. The naive fool opposite him seemed to possess a story-book attitude to crime, as though he was the Saint or Bulldog Drummond. He had probably deluded himself sufficiently to think that he was taking from the rich to feed the poor. A sort of Robin Hood who'd defected to Christian Aid. 'Well, use guns they did, old lad,' he said, 'and on more than one occasion.' He lit a cigarette. 'And Silver Barnes, who I've got banged up in Brixton Prison, has put you firmly in the frame. Reckons that you were the brains behind it all.'

Close passed a hand across his forehead. 'But guns,' he repeated. 'They didn't say anything about guns.'

Fox grinned. 'And how, Donald,' he said, 'do you suppose that you'd persuade the crew of an armoured cash-in-transit van to part with their cargo of gelt without threatening them with guns? Where have you been? Don't you ever read the papers... watch television?'

'Will it help if I tell you about it?' Close looked up with a hopeful expression on his face.

Fox remained motionless, his face belying not a hint of what he was feeling. But he knew that the first fissure had appeared. The tiny tell-tale crack in Close's reserve. Well educated, he may be. A clergyman he once was. But it always came to this. Here was a villain, however he was dressed, whatever his background. When the chips were down, as they most certainly were now, the fight for the last seat in the lifeboat was on. But Fox was not a man accustomed to giving quarter. 'It's possible,' he said, but immediately crushed the ray of hope that appeared on Close's face by adding, 'but not probable.'

'What with Barnes and Muriel, I've got myself into a bit of trouble,' said Close, shaking his head wearily.

'That sounds like the understatement of the year,' said Fox, a firm believer in not giving comfort to the afflicted. 'However, if you assist the police, I may be able to make certain recommendations.'

'It was Muriel's fault.'

'I didn't for one moment imagine that it'd be yours,' said Fox with just a hint of sarcasm. 'Well, give it a run, Donald. What've you got to say?'

Close stared at the centre of the table, collecting his thoughts. Then he looked up. 'Well,' he admitted, 'I suppose it was my fault ... in a way. Clergymen don't get paid very much.'

'They're not alone in that,' said Fox.

'When I had the good fortune to marry Muriel, I discovered that she was quite a wealthy woman — '

'To the tune of about a hundred and sixty grand, you mean?'

'Oh, you know that.'

'I know lots of things, Donald. Do go on.'

'I have to admit that I was getting a bit fed up with the Church at that time. Felt that I was not fulfilling my vows. We all say that we are chosen by God, but I have to say that I think He sometimes makes mistakes.'

'Amen to that,' said Fox. 'And particularly in your case.'

'Anyway, I suggested to Muriel that we pooled our resources and go into a business venture together.'

'What sort of business venture?'

'A nursing home for old people, as a matter of fact.'

'Really?' Fox feigned great interest.

'And I — that is to say, we — bought the house at Cobham with a view to converting it.'

'You blokes are very good at conversions, so I hear,' said Fox drily.

'But then I ran into my little spot of bother. It was all a terrible misunderstanding really. The trouble is, I suppose, that when one has spent a lifetime in the Church one tends to be a little naive.'

Fox laughed. 'Well the bloke you tried to blackmail wasn't naive... and neither am I, mister, so don't try to have me over. That's all a load of moody. You pooled your resources all right. Muriel put in about a hundred and sixty K, and you put in about fourpence, I should think, and you certainly bought a house in Cobham. Unfortunately for Muriel, you forget to tell her the address before you decamped. And you conveniently omitted to tell her that the property was in your name... alone. Then, when you were in the nick, doing your well-deserved porridge, you met up with Silver Barnes. Having mortgaged the Cobham house up to the hilt to pay for your expensive life-style, and failing to recoup a few quid when you tried putting the arm on a certain parishioner of yours who was over the side, you found yourself in desperate need of funds. Consequently, when Silver Barnes made you an offer which involved the use of your drum as a slaughter, you found that it was an offer you couldn't refuse.' Fox glanced across at Gilroy, busily taking notes in the corner of the interview room, before turning back to Close. 'How am I doing, so far?'

Close nodded miserably. 'All right, I was a bit unkind to Muriel, but it wasn't criminal.' He stared at Fox, defying him to deny it.

Fox did. 'You're a bloody villain,' he said. 'There's no mistake about that, Donald. And if your late wife hadn't been daft enough to sign her money over to you, so that it could be wrapped up by some bloody lawyer's gobbledegook, she'd probably have been able to have you behind bars quicker than your adulterous parishioner did. However, I shall do what I can to make up for lost time because, just in case it's slipped your memory, I'm here to talk about a charge of murder.'

'Believe me, I know nothing about that. I didn't even know she was dead... not until you told me, the last time you were here. Then I didn't believe you.'

'Well you'd better believe me, old son. Now, I'll ask you the question I asked you the last time I was here. When did you last see Muriel?'

'In March.' Close spoke with resignation. 'I can't remember the exact date.'

'What were the circumstances of that meeting?' There was a longish pause during which Fox played a silent tattoo on the table-top with his fingers. 'Well?'

'After I came out of prison, I met up with Ivy — '

'Barnes' sister?'

Close looked surprised. 'I don't know where you got that from,' he said. 'She's not his sister. She's no relation. Actually' — he paused, looking guilty — 'he met her at a night club in the West End one night, and brought her home to Cobham. She lived with him for a while.'

'You didn't deny that she was Barnes' sister the last time I mentioned her,' said Fox angrily. This was yet another twist in the story, but he silently vowed that he and Barnes were going to do some serious talking.

'Really?' Close raised his eyebrows. 'I must have missed that,' he said.

'Get on with it,' Fox growled.

'Well,' continued Close, 'she was all the things that Muriel wasn't —'

'Poor, you mean?'

'No, not that. It had nothing to do with money.'

Fox laughed. 'There are two things that men go off the rails over,' he said. 'One is money, and the other is the other.' 'What?'

'Sex, Donald. Sex. You know what I'm bloody talking about.'

'Oh! Yes, I'm afraid so.'

'Yes, well you'd have been all right there,' said Fox with an abrasive laugh. 'She was a professional, after all.'

'What d'you mean?'

'I mean that she was a stripper... and a prostitute.'

Close looked suitably shocked. 'I don't believe it.'

Fox looked grave. 'D'you know, Donald, I'm beginning to believe that you really are naive.' He didn't, of course. What he did know was that Close was an accomplished con-man, and made the necessary allowances for it. But Fox was interested to see where Close's yarn would take him next. 'Yes, she was at it. On the game. Probably still is. Incidentally, where is she now?'

'I'm afraid I don't know.'

'Don't know or not saying? Believe me, Donald, if you're being awkward, it won't help your case. I'm still thinking about charging you with your wife's murder.'

'I told you, I didn't even know she was dead.'

'Well don't let me interrupt your little story. You said that you last saw your wife — your real wife — in March. What was that all about?'

'We'd planned a little job together.'

'Another old folks' home, was it?' Fox grinned sarcastically.

Close paused as if uncertain what to say next, knowing that every time he opened his mouth, he was probably incriminating himself further. But at the end of it all was this nasty policeman's threat to charge him with murdering his wife. And that was something he wished to avoid. 'No, as a matter of fact, we'd arranged a little plan to relieve someone of some money.' Close hung his head, aware that every sentence was revealing more of his criminal past.

'Ah!' said Fox, with certain satisfaction. 'Are you now telling me that your wife Muriel was your accomplice in these scams you were perpetrating?'

Close nodded miserably. 'It was the only way I could think of to get her money back for her. I felt badly about that.'

'What you felt badly about was that she'd found you. Tell me, how did that happen? A bit careless of a skilled old lag like you, Donald.'

'It wasn't long after I'd come out of prison. It was a bit of a misfortune really — '

'Seems that most of your life's work has been a bit of a misfortune. So what happened?'

'I bumped into her in the street. She was very angry.'

'So are most people who've been swindled out of a hundred and sixty grand, Donald. It's one of the facts of life.'

'I said that I'd do my best to make it up to her. I went home with her to her house in Edmonton.'

'Why on earth did you do that? Why didn't you do a runner? It's what you usually do.'

'She threatened to make a scene, call the police. Well I couldn't have that, not having just come out of prison... and I was wearing a clerical collar — '

'To which you were not entitled.'

'Perhaps not,' said Close, 'but it's not a crime. I once heard about a group of policemen going into a pub dressed as vicars and — '

'I've no doubt that you and Ivy would know all about a vicars-and-whores party, if that's what you're talking about,' said Fox, 'but just get on with the story, will you?'

'Anyway, I went back to Edmonton with her — it was an awful little house — and we talked about her problem.'

'Sort of Christian counselling, I suppose?'

Close smiled. 'Not quite. But I said that I was practically broke — '

'You didn't tell her about the house at Cobham, then?'

'I couldn't very well. Anyway, it was mortgaged, and I didn't think that she'd approve of Barnes and Company.'

'I shouldn't think many people do,' said Fox.

'Then, to my amazement, she suggested that we did a few little jobs together.'

'Confidence tricks, you mean?'

'Yes. Apparently she'd been going it alone. Working the South of France. Rich widowers... that sort of thing.'

Fox laughed. 'Her old man was bent as well, so Muriel's sister Sylvia said.'

'Oh, you've seen her, have you? She's an absolute bitch, that one.'

'Yes,' said Fox, 'she speaks very highly of you, too.'

'The upshot was that we did quite well. Until Ivy put her oar in, that is.'

'Oh dear! In what way?'

'Wanted me to marry her.'

'What for?'

'Security, she said.' Close looked depressed.

'That's a laugh,' said Fox. 'And so you committed bigamy.'

'Yes, I'm afraid I did.'

Fox shook his head. 'What the hell for? I don't understand that.'

'She persuaded me that I was doing myself no good, sticking with Silver... and she was fed up with him too. She said that we were both worthy of better things and that we ought to get away from it all. Emigrate. I must say that I thought she was right. I could see myself finishing up in prison again if things went on the way they were going. And I wanted to get shot of Muriel. I was only putting up with her because she was virtually blackmailing me. Ivy seemed to have come up with the answer. Get married and go to Canada.'

'And you did.'

'Yes.'

'But then you went to Australia. Why?'

'Didn't like Canada.'

'Why?' asked Fox. 'Mounties breathing down your neck, were they?'

Close looked hurt. 'Not at all,' he said.

'And you didn't like Australia either, I presume.'

'No, Australia was fine.'

'What are you doing back here, then?'

Close gazed steadily at Fox for some seconds. 'You may find this difficult to believe...'

'Try me.'

'But I've never missed a Henley Regatta in my life... apart from — '

'Apart from when you were in the nick.' Fox grinned.

'Exactly. And that proved to be my downfall.' Close looked sad. 'How did you know where to find me, incidentally?'

'It's called detective work,' said Fox. 'By the way,' he added, with all the subtlety of a hand-grenade, 'when did you make Muriel pregnant?'

'What?' For the first time since his arrest, Close appeared genuinely astonished. 'That's nothing to do with me. She must have been — '

Fox laughed. 'Makes a change for you to be had over, my old son,' he said.

*

'You know the trouble with this enquiry, don't you, Jack?' said Fox. 'Everyone we speak to is a bloody liar.'

Chapter Thirteen

The revelation that Ivy Barnes was not Silver Barnes' sister did not please Tommy Fox. Not because it was vital information and pertinent to his murder enquiry — it was probably neither of those things — but because he had an ingrained dislike of being had over by a member of the criminal fraternity. He had returned to Scotland Yard from Bow Street, following his interview with Donald Close, and had been sitting at his desk fretting about it until, finally, he boiled over.

'That does it,' said Fox. 'That bloody does it. Get Swann.' And then, ignoring the fact that he had just given DI Gilroy that instruction, he strode to the door of his office and bellowed down the corridor. 'Get Swann... on the front. Five minutes.' He stomped back to his desk and picked up his cigarette case. 'I'll have that bastard, Jack, so help me. Bloody toe-rags, think they can have me over. I'll sort that bugger, you see if I don't.' Gilroy had no doubt about his chiefs intentions, nor his ability to carry them to fruition. But it made him nervous. Not because Fox, when riled, was a dangerous man, but because he was likely to do something that might prove to be an embarrassment to the investigation when exposed to the clinical examination of defence counsel. And then, Gilroy knew, everyone would be bobbing and weaving to try and sort out the mess. 'Will it do any good, sir?'

'It won't do Barnes any good, that's for sure,' said Fox. 'Incidentally, I've found a criminal record file for Ivy Barnes, sir,' said Gilroy, once they were seated in the back of Fox's car.

'That's very industrious of you,' said Fox. 'And if I may ask an impertinent question, what took you so bloody long?'

'It's not in her name, sir,' said Gilroy. 'So I got Crozier to do a trawl through the toms register. Shot in the dark, really.'

'Oh!' Fox nodded sympathetically. 'That would explain it. Perhaps, Jack, in your own good time, you'd tell me what name it is in?'

'Fisk, sir. Ivy Fisk. Aged thirty-one. Form for tomming, theft as a servant, and one or two con tricks.'

'So? She used a duff name the first time she was nicked... and kept on using it.'

'Not quite, sir. You see, Fisk is her maiden name. From what Close was saying — about her having been shacked up with Silver Barnes - I should think that she adopted his name until she split with him and hopped into the Reverend gentleman's bed.'

Fox laughed. 'It's beginning to come together, Jack. I should think that Silver Barnes was well pissed off when the bold Donald not only had his bird off him but took it on the toes as well. They're the two things that upset a villain: having his bird nicked, and having to do bird when the bloke who's nicked her has done a runner.' Fox chuckled. 'I rather like that,' he said.

*

Fox's mood had not been improved by the length of time it had taken Swann to carve his way through the evening rush-hour, and by the time they reached the prison, he was probably in a worse temper than when he had left Scotland Yard.

Barnes had almost got to the point where he looked forward to the occasional visit from Tommy Fox, regarding it as a little break in the routine. Today put paid to that.

Fox was standing under one of the barred windows, his back to the wall, when Barnes was brought into the interview room by a prison officer.

''Allo, Mr Fox. Nice to see you again.'

'You're up before the beak on Thursday, for a remand hearing,' said Fox, ignoring the introductory courtesies, 'upon which occasion, I am of a mind to charge you with the wilful murder of one Muriel Close, née Yates. You and your mates.'

'Here, hold up, Mr Fox,' said Barnes, the smile vanishing from his face as the cold hand of fear gripped his bowels and gave them a nasty twist.

'This Ivy Barnes, later Close, brackets bigamous, we've been talking about — '

'What about her?'

'Is not your bloody sister at all.'

'Oh!' Barnes sat down heavily on the rigid chair behind the table. 'You know about that, then.'

'Yes I do, and no thanks to you, you lying git.' Fox glanced at Gilroy. 'I hope you're not writing this down, Jack.'

'Writing down what, sir?' asked Gilroy innocently. Although not always condoning his chiefs methods, he was well accustomed to them.

'What's it all about then?' Fox glared angrily at the contrite Barnes.

'Well I never thought it made no difference, Mr Fox. I mean to say, what's it matter?'

'Not a lot, I suppose, except that we had a little chat, not too long ago, when you intimated that you were prepared to assist the police in exchange for a consideration. Well, if you want to piss on your chips, Silver, that's your problem.'

'But what difference does it make?' Barnes voice had assumed a wheedling tone.

'If it makes no difference, why didn't you tell me in the first place? Thought you'd be clever, did you? Have the boss of the Squad over. Ho, ho, ho! Well, have I got news for you, mister. Anyone who thinks he can see off Thomas Fox of the Flying Squad is making a desperately bad mistake. And I should have thought that you'd have known that, Silver.' Fox walked slowly across the room and sat down opposite Barnes. He lit a cigarette and left the case lying open on the table. But be didn't offer it to Barnes. 'So start talking.'

*

'D'you remember, Jack, when we went to see Sylvia Goodall, she said something about her husband Frank trying to help Muriel get her money back?'

'Vaguely,' said Gilroy.

'And presumably Frank Goodall tried to find Close. But we never asked him whether he'd had any success.'

'Is there any point? After all, we've got Close in custody.'

'I don't know,' said Fox. 'Won't hurt to have a word with him. See what he knows.'

*

Frank Goodall couldn't help. He told Gilroy that he had been to his solicitor who had told him that an enquiry agent might find Close, but that finding him wouldn't necessarily mean that Muriel would get her money back. The solicitor had gone on to say that, from what Goodall had told him, there was nothing illegal about what Close had done. It seemed that Muriel had signed her money over to Close quite legitimately, and Close had disappeared. Goodall had made a few enquiries of his own — mainly through the publicans' network — but had drawn a blank. His view was that Muriel had eventually found Close on her own and that when faced with an ultimatum, he had murdered her. Gilroy thought that that might be the case, but on the evidence so far available it would be impossible to prove. And set against Goodall's theory was Close's claim that he had met Muriel and that together they had committed crime.

Fox tossed the statement to one side. 'Not worth the paper it's written on, Jack. Why did it take so long?'

'He wasn't there the first time I rang, guv,' said Gilroy. 'Bloody nuisance. He didn't get back until yesterday.'

'Where'd he been, then?'

'Nipped over to France apparently. A bunch of the local publicans have a knees-up every once in a while and they go over there on the piss.'

'Take their wives, do they?'

'Not if they can get away with not taking them, guv,' said Gilroy with a grin.

'No,' said Fox, 'probably not.' He swung from side to side in his chair for a second or two. 'Tell you what, Jack. See if he was away from home on the two dates that we know for certain that Muriel Close was staying at a hotel with the man Armstrong. Percy Fletcher's got the pars.'

'What's the point in that, guv?'

'Just a hunch, Jack, just a hunch.'

*

The two dates in question were seven weeks apart.

'These two dates, Mr Goodall,' said Gilroy. He laid a piece of paper on the desk in the cramped office of the Goodalls' public house.

'What about them?'

'D'you happen to know whether your sister-in-law was away from home on those two dates? Abroad, I mean.'

'What's so special about those, then?' Goodall drew the paper a little closer and adjusted his glasses.

'She reported her credit card stolen a week or two before her death,' said Gilroy. He had carefully rehearsed his story before travelling out to

Woodford. 'It's probably just a simple case of fraud, but we want to get it out of the way. Just another loose end that needs to be tied up.'

'Well I don't know, for God's sake. She didn't always tell us where she was going. Sometimes she'd ring — like the time you asked about — but not always. Quite honestly, we never knew whether she was in England or abroad. Home or away, as you might say.' He chuckled at that.

Sylvia Goodall leaned across and read the dates on the slip of paper before turning back a few pages in the desk diary. 'I usually put it in here, if she ever bothered to tell us where she was going. Sometimes she'd ring up and let us know that she'd be away for a fortnight, but more often than not we wouldn't hear for weeks. I'd ring up and just get her answerphone. I used to say to her, look you really ought to tell us where you are, in case anything happened. But she wouldn't listen.' She opened the diary and flattened it down the binding with her hand. 'No,' she said, 'there's nothing in here.' She laughed. 'And it's no good asking him, either.' She nodded towards her husband. 'He was away too. Boozing in France.'

Frank Goodall pulled the diary across the desk and glanced down at it. 'I thought there was something familiar about that date,' he said. He flipped back a few more pages. 'And I was away on that date, too.' He looked up at Gilroy and laughed. 'Honest, officer,' he said, 'I didn't nick her plastic.'

Gilroy laughed, too. 'I shouldn't think you'd need to, Mr Goodall,' he said.

*

Silver Barnes, Harry Perkins, and their two co-conspirators, Lambie and Grover, had been brought from Brixton Prison for their remand hearing and were sitting in a disconsolate group in the male detention room at Bow Street Magistrates Court.

Fox and Gilroy had arrived early and explained to the court inspector what was required of him. Consequently, before their brief appearance in court, each member of the quartet was charged with the wilful murder of Muriel Close, the charge was read over to him and he was cautioned. The answer each made to this charge was such as to indicate his complete and utter innocence. Fox was unimpressed. When that little ceremony was over, Fox and Gilroy crossed the yard to Bow Street Police Station and charged Close with the murder of his wife, and with bigamy. His answers, like those of the villainous four across the way, protested his innocence of Muriel's murder. To the charge of bigamy, he made no reply. Just for good measure, Fox advised him that he was very likely to be charged with conspiring with Barnes and company to commit robbery. Close shrugged. After the first two charges, he had reached the stage where mere quantity seemed not to make very much difference to his future plans.

'I reckon they'll have formed a choir within twenty-four hours,' said Fox cheerfully in the car on their way back to the Yard. 'Be singing like mad before the sun comes up, I wouldn't wonder.' He leaned back in his seat. 'Swann,' he said, 'you're exceeding the speed limit.'

*

When Fox arrived at the office the next morning, there was a message from Brixton Prison on his desk. It said that remand-prisoner Lambie wished to speak to the officer in charge of the Muriel Close killing... urgently.

'Shall I get Swann to get the car up, sir?' asked Gilroy. 'Certainly not,' said Fox. 'Let the bastard sweat until tomorrow. Then you can go.'

*

'And what did Mr Lambie have to say for himself, Jack?'
'Says he didn't do it, guv.'
'Well now, that is a surprise, isn't it? But did he have anything of value to say?'
'No.'
'Oh?' Fox looked annoyed. 'D'you mean that he got you all the way down to Brixton just to tell you that?'
'Not exactly, sir. He said that he had information to give, but that he'd only give it to you. He said he didn't know me, but he knew he could trust the head of the Flying Squad.'

Fox pulled at the cuff of his jacket and flicked at a piece of fluff. 'Yes,' he said, 'well even some criminals have got taste, you know. Right, well we'd better go and see the little bugger, I suppose.' Fox yawned and stood up.

*

Robert Lambie was in his early thirties and had spent most of his adult years in prison. He had a small, wizened face that wore a permanently foxy scowl and peered at the world suspiciously — as well it might — for it was a world that had not done Robert Lambie too many favours. But to be fair, he hadn't done much for the world, either. There was little doubt that he was one of life's losers.

'You have something to say, I understand,' said Fox. He carefully laid out his cigarette case and lighter on the table and flicked a few specks of dust off the chair with his handkerchief before sitting down.

'Yes, Mr Fox, I — '

Fox, fully aware of the common law presumption of innocence, held up a staying hand. 'Robert Lambie,' he said portentously, 'you are not obliged to say anything unless you wish to do so, but anything you do say will be taken down in writing and may be put in evidence.'

Stunned by this forensic recital, Lambie coughed nervously. 'Well I know that, guv'nor,' he said.

Fox looked over his shoulder at Gilroy. 'Get him to sign that before he goes any further, Jack.'

Gilroy walked across to the table and laying the book on it, handed Lambie a government issue ball-point pen. Lambie took it and made a scrawl which was the nearest he could get to signing his name.

'Right,' continued Fox, 'am I to understand that you wish to make a statement?'

'Well o' course I do. That's why I asked you to come down here.'

'Yes, well so long as you understand that you are facing a charge of murder — '

'But I never done it,' said Lambie. 'I told him I never done it.' He pointed an accusing finger at Gilroy.

Fox nodded sympathetically. 'Unhappily, Robert, a plain denial of the commission of a crime does not automatically absolve one of a conviction therefor.'

Lambie shook his head. 'I don't know what the bleeding hell you're going on about, Mr Fox, straight.'

'Strange word to hear coming from your lips, Robert,' said Fox. 'However, we'll get on, shall we?' He leaned forward so that his face was close to Lambie's. 'There is another caution, Robert,' he said.

'Oh?' Lambie frowned. He had only ever heard the one.

'Yes. Let me caution you against wasting my time. That could be very serious.'

'I seen her,' said Lambie, determined to get to the nub of the matter, and terrified that he would be convicted of a crime he had not committed.

'You saw who?'

'The woman what got topped.'

'By whom I take it you mean Mrs Muriel Close with whose murder you stand charged?'

'I told you I never done it,' said Lambie desperately.

Fox ostentatiously drew back the cuff of his Thomas Pink shirt and glanced at his wrist-watch. 'I do not have all day, Robert,' he said.

'No. Well, it was the night after the blagging. On the day we done the job we stashed all the loot down Cobham and went back to London. The next night we went back to split it up. I parked the car round the back and followed the others in. Well, when I got in the house, I saw Silver dragging a body out of the back door — '

'The body of a woman, I presume?'

'Aye, that's right. Her in a red dress. Well I thought that Silver had done for her, and he seemed a bit panicky. Well, you would, wouldn't you?'

'I imagine so,' said Fox.

'Well I didn't ask no questions, and Silver said to get a shovel and start digging. So that's what we done. But I never killed her, Mr Fox, so help me. I never touched a hair of yon woman's head. I reckon it's down to Silver.'

'What did Silver have to say about it? Anything?'

'Aye. He reckoned it was down to Close... and Ivy.'

'What made him say that?'

Lambie shrugged. 'I don't know, Mr Fox. Silver's the boss.' Fox smiled benignly. 'What a beautifully plausible tale you tell, Robert,' he said. 'My colleague here, Mr Gilroy, will now take down in great detail all that you have just told me, and you will sign it. Understood?'

'Shouldn't I ask for my solicitor, Mr Fox?'

'That'll be nowhere near enough, Robert,' said Fox. 'You'll need at least a silk and two juniors to dig you out of this lot.'

For over an hour, Gilroy wrote down Lambie's every word, and at the end of it Lambie signed his name.

*

'Now,' said Fox, 'we are getting somewhere.' He placed the typewritten copy of Lambie's statement squarely in the centre of his blotter and gazed at it. 'What I want you to do now, Jack,' he continued, 'is to serve a copy of this statement on Messrs Barnes, Perkins, Grover and Close.' He tapped the document with his forefinger. 'As is their legal right. And we'll see what they have to say about that.'

Perkins, Grover and Close merely shrugged when they received their copy — it was, after all, nothing to do with them — but Silver Barnes became extremely agitated. He swore vengeance on Robert Lambie but otherwise declined to make a rebutting statement.

'Now what do we do, sir?' asked Gilroy.

'I think the time has come to send a photograph of the lovely Ivy to our friends and colleagues in Australia,' said Fox.

Chapter Fourteen

'Well stone me sideways,' said Senior Constable Crosby of the State of Victoria Police. 'Would you just have a go at that.' He spread the photographs of Ivy Barnes out on his desk and peered closely at them. 'The old poms have certainly come up with a bonza shout for photographing female crims.'

Another detective walked across and leaned over Crosby's shoulder. 'Strewth, mate,' he said. 'Get a load of them tits.' Tommy Fox had seen no reason why the Metropolitan Police should not share the delights of Ivy Barnes' undraped flesh with their colleagues down under and had authorised the sending of her publicity pictures — as well as the one on her criminal record file — to Melbourne. But it wasn't just an act of charity; a CRO photograph is often a notoriously poor likeness.

It is one of the less publicised laws of nature that male detectives, given the opportunity of examining the photograph of an attractive nude woman, will look at the face of the subject last of all. Which is exactly what Senior Constable Crosby did. It was, therefore, some seconds before his gaze moved up the glossy print on his desk. When it did he swallowed hard. 'Christ!' he said. 'It's Bobbie Howard.' And his brain moved rapidly into top gear. Working with the speed of a highly sophisticated computer it examined all the reasons that his superior officers might have for censuring him for neglect of duty until, finally and with a sigh of relief, he decided that he was not culpable. He leaped from his chair, seized his revolver from the top drawer of his desk and sped into the sergeant's office.

*

'It would seem,' said Fox, tossing the Interpol message on to his desk, 'that our Australian friends arrived too late. To employ an apt cliché, Jack, the bird had flown.'

'And presumably, guv'nor, they have no idea where she has flown to.'

'Whence she has flown, Jack,' corrected Fox. 'No, regrettably they have not.' He picked up the message form again. 'Are these Australian chaps on the telephone, Jack?' he asked.

'I imagine so, sir.'

'Good,' said Fox. 'Give'em a bell. We'll set traps.'

*

Unbeknown to Senior Constable Crosby, the new occupant of the bungalow in which Donald Close and Ivy had spent a few brief conjugal days in Melbourne was a newspaperman. He had listened with interest as the detective had explained his problem, but like Bobbie Howard, alias Ivy, he was a short-term renter and had been unable to offer any help as to the present whereabouts of the last tenant. But when the police left, he had rung his newspaper and given them the story. Consequently, when Ivy read the papers the next day, she had upped and left her new temporary abode. Fortunately for her self-respect, the Australians are far more prudish than the British and they did not print any of her publicity photographs which they could doubtless have obtained from Frankie Fanganari in London had they known of their — or his — existence.

The other photograph, taken from Ivy's criminal record, had been circulated by the Australian police to those officers concerned with observing the travelling public at ports and airports. They had also been advised of Fox's instruction, issued once he knew that Ivy was on the road again, that she should not be arrested if it appeared that she was on her way to England. Consequently when she took an internal flight to Sydney and from there a Qantas Boeing 747 to London, the Sydney police telephoned Scotland Yard, and Special Branch officers at Heathrow Airport were able to alert the surveillance team which had been awaiting her arrival.

But the address of the flat in Ruislip to which she went did not appear in any of the police records that related to her, and an examination of the electoral roll indicated that the sole resident was a Sonia Farrow.

*

'What do we do now, sir?' asked Gilroy.

'You're a bloody detective inspector,' said Fox rattily. 'Use your initiative. Think of something.'

'I think we should interview her in the presence of her solicitor,' said Gilroy. 'And serve her with a copy of Lambie's statement.'

'There's no bloody point in that,' said Fox. 'Lambie is in custody, accused of conspiring with others, but not with Ivy. I don't see why we should take the word of some ratbag who just feels like slagging off a fine young woman like her... not yet anyway. Anyway, it's only hearsay. Lambie told us what Silver allegedly said about Close and Ivy being responsible, and that's of no more use than the rest of his bloody statement. Get hold of DS Fletcher. I think we should make some quiet enquiries.' Fox stretched his arms above his head. 'And a few hours in registry might not be wasted, Jack,' he added.

*

Fox gave Fletcher the latest information about Ivy Barnes — or whatever her real name was — finishing up by telling him that she now appeared to be Sonia Farrow and was residing in Ruislip, something which, in itself, Fox found very strange. 'Perce,' he said, 'get out and beat on the ground. See what comes up.'

*

The loping figure of DS Fletcher peered round Fox's door. 'Got a minute, guv?' he asked.

'What is it, Perce?'

The complete body of Fletcher came into view. Beneath his left arm was a stack of files about a foot thick. 'This Sonia Farrow, guv. I've been doing a bit of poking around.'

'Good, good. Come in, Perce.'

Fletcher entered the room and deposited his paper burden on a side table.

Fox regarded the files gloomily. 'Is that all to do with the Barnes woman?'

'No, guv.' Fletcher grinned. 'Not directly. Most of it's about an insurance fraud. Explosion job.'

'Explosion?'

'Yes, guv. Most unfortunate. Gas explosion. All his stock went up... and his books of account. The insurance company weren't at all happy... refused to pay out. Geezer who ran it was called Elvis Farrow, though.'

'Farrow?'

Fletcher nodded amiably. 'Sometime husband of Sonia Farrow, alias Ivy Barnes, alias Bobbie — '

Fox held up a hand. 'I think I've got the drift, Perce. Tell me the story... as briefly as possible.' He pointed at a chair and Fletcher sat down.

'Right.' Fletcher licked his thumb and slid the top file off the pile. 'This deals with a complaint of bigamy. Starts off with an anonymous letter to the Commissioner. The writer says that as a public-spirited, law-abiding citizen, et cetera, she — ' Fletcher broke off. 'I suppose it's a bloody woman, guv.' He sniffed. 'It's usually a woman that puts the boot in. Anyhow... the writer felt it to be a public duty to draw the attention of police to the fact that one Sonia Farrow recently...' Fletcher looked up. 'This was six months ago, guv.' He glanced back at the file. 'Recently got married to a finger called Donald Close, but that the said Sonia Farrow was already married to another... and so was Donald Close.'

'Oh my Gawd!' said Fox. 'Does it name Elvis Farrow in the letter?'

'Yes, guv, but it's not signed. The letter I mean.'

'No,' said Fox drily, 'the writers of anonymous letters don't usually sign them. What happened?'

Fletcher shook his head. 'Not a lot, guv. Pushed out to the local nick, and some DC made a few enquiries, but there was no Sonia Farrow at the address given. No Elvis, either.'

'Was it put in the Crime Book?'

'Doesn't look like it,' said Fletcher. 'This DC went round to the register office, according to this...' He tapped the docket. 'And there's a copy of the entry on file. But all it says is that Elvis Farrow, bachelor, married Sonia Fisk, spinster — '

'Fisk? Did you say Fisk?'

'Yes, guv.'

'She's used that name before — '

'It's her real name,' said Fletcher. 'Leastways, there's an entry at St Catherine's House in the name of Ivy Fisk.'Bout the same age. It's the one we came up with when we did the last check.'

'Did you — ?'

'Check the deaths?' Fletcher grinned. 'Yes, guv. No trace. The DC more or less wrote it off as a malicious complaint.'

'Ah!' said Fox and swivelled from side to side on his chair, and then, after a while, 'Ah!'

'This bloke Elvis Farrow had a shop selling records which he got on credit.'

'Everybody does these days,' said Fox.

'But he was greedy,' continued Fletcher. 'Not only does the shop blow up, but according to the fire brigade, there weren't any records in it anyway. The DI who investigated it reckoned that Elvis had had the records away before the tragic accident, and knocked 'em out cheap. Then he tried to claim the insurance.' Fletcher sighed. 'Like I said, the fire brigade report not only said there were no records, but that there were at least three seats of explosion. The gas board had a gander, too, but they stated that there was no seepage of product...' Fletcher looked up and grinned.

'What the hell does that mean?' asked Fox.

'Means there wasn't a gas leak. And that was probably on account of there being no gas connected to the premises.'

'Seems reasonable,' said Fox. 'And what did Mr Elvis Farrow have to say about all that, Perce?'

'Not a lot. The DI interviewed him, but said he'd got nothing to say and refused to make a statement.'

'Sounds like *The Independent*,' said Fox drily. 'What happened?'

'Copped two years porridge and did a runner after his release. Hasn't been heard of since.'

'How long had he been in business, then? When he was nicked.' Fletcher flicked over a few pages. 'Couple of years, it says here.'

'He'd hit bad times,' said Fox, 'that's what that was all about.' He looked thoughtful for a moment or two. 'How long after his marriage did all this happen, Perce?'

'Six months, guv.'

Fox nodded his head slowly. 'Things are beginning to come together, Perce,' he said. 'They are definitely coming together.'

*

'I suppose there's always the possibility that Goodall was over the side with his sister-in-law,' said Fox. 'Judging by her picture, she was much better looking than Sylvia.'

'Depends what you want,' said Gilroy. 'There's a certain animal magnetism about Sylvia, but there's no doubt, I should think, that Muriel was the classier bird. She certainly seemed to spend more on clothes than Sylvia does.'

'Yes.' Fox drew the word out pensively. 'Make a few discreet enquiries, Jack. Just a thought, that's all.'

*

There are rare occasions when detectives have moments of great inspiration. It is not something that they advertise for fear of being likened to their fictional counterparts, the vast majority of whom do little else but have great inspirations. But solving crime is like solving crosswords: sometimes you have to have a bit of luck.

Fox considered the case of Elvis Farrow for quite some time. Someone who sells all his stock and says that he has lost it in a gas explosion — in a shop without gas — in order to claim the insurance, was undoubtedly a criminal. He therefore possessed a criminal mind, and despite the frequent claims of criminals that they are going to go straight, it rarely happens. Being an expert on the workings of the criminal mind it was not difficult for Fox to imagine that once a man had run a record shop and been a villain, the likelihood was that he would be running a record shop again... and still be a villain.

'Jack,' said Fox, 'I think that a little chat with Ivy might be in order. See if we can get her going. Oh,' he added as Gilroy reached the door, 'and make sure there's an obo on her drum before we get there. Wouldn't like to frighten her away... not without knowing where she's going.'

*

It was Ivy Barnes who answered the door.

'Sonia Farrow, is it?' asked Fox.

'It might be,' said Ivy. 'Depends what you're selling.' She was wearing jeans and a check shirt, and her long brown hair was tied back.

'We're police officers,' said Fox.

'Oh,' she said, 'then I suppose you'd better come in.'

'Why are you calling yourself Sonia Farrow?' asked Fox, following the girl into the sitting room.

'It's my name... if it's any of your business.'

'I see. You're not by any chance the same Sonia Farrow who married one Elvis Farrow about four years ago, are you?' Fox wrinkled his nose.

Ivy kicked off her sandals and crossed her legs. 'What exactly do you want?' she asked.

'A few answers would be a great help,' said Fox.

Ivy studied Fox for some moments and then glanced briefly at Gilroy. Then she looked back at Fox. 'I'm saying nothing unless my solicitor is present.'

Fox shrugged. 'Please yourself,' he said. 'I'm just trying to save you a bit of money.'

'Very decent of you,' said Ivy. 'Is this part of the new image of the police I've been reading so much about in the papers recently?'

'Donald Close...'

Ivy's eyes narrowed very slightly. 'Who?' she said.

'Donald Close. The Reverend Donald Close.'

Ivy shook her head. 'I'm sorry,' she said. 'Am I supposed to know him? Frankly, I haven't been to church for years.'

'He's in custody, charged with the murder of his wife Muriel,' said Fox. Ivy sat forward, the look on her face a combination of concern and intensity. 'And,' continued Fox, 'so is one Alfred Barnes, better known to us of the Flying Squad as Silver.'

They left it at that. Ivy, who had now added another alias to the files, that of Sonia Farrow, refused to say anything. She sat and listened politely, but denied all knowledge of her bigamous husband Donald Close, or of Silver Barnes with whom she had once lived. But the latest revelation, that she had married Elvis Farrow at some time, tended to make the whole business far more complicated. But Fox was not too concerned about the bigamy. He could have arrested her for that, there and then, but he knew fine that from then on she wouldn't say anything — not that she'd said much so far — and once in custody, wouldn't be able to lead them anywhere. And that didn't suit Fox. He was, after all, still trying to get to the bottom of a case of murder, and he was hoping that his visit might just provoke her into doing something rash. What, precisely, he had no idea.

*

There were two teams of three, one team in each car. In the boot of each car was a folding bicycle. They had learned the hard way, these surveillance officers. If the target is on foot, it's easy; in a car, it's easy. Well, not easy, but easier. But if the quarry is on a bicycle, the observation team is in trouble... unless they too have got a bicycle. So there was a bicycle in the boot.

They didn't have long to wait after Tommy Fox's visit to Ivy Barnes. The same evening in fact.

At seventeen thirty-two hours — that's how it was recorded in the log — Ivy emerged from her Ruislip flat. She was wearing a close-fitting all-in-one suit that looked like an up-market set of dungarees. It was a surveillance officer's gift: bright orange, tucked into white boots that came half-way up her calves. One of the observation team suggested that the weather was much too hot for boots, but they agreed — in short bursts of radio transmission — that they were glad she'd worn them. They made her look sexy. But more to the point, any officer who lost a target dressed as distinctively as Ivy deserved to be struck off the list of qualified surveillance officers.

It's a long way from Ruislip to Croydon, and anyone going there has got to have a damned good reason; no one goes to Croydon unless they've absolutely got to, particularly if they have to go by public transport.

Ivy Barnes walked to South Ruislip tube station and caught a train. She changed to the Victoria Line at Oxford Circus and rode to Victoria where she got on a train to East Croydon. All the way, she was followed by the surveillance officers, skilfully changing the rotation of their cover, so that sometimes she was followed by a chap in blazer and flannels, then one in jeans and a sweater, or by a girl in a mackintosh. But she never once looked behind her. No one ever does.

In Croydon, a short walk from the station, she knocked at the front door of a semi-detached, dowdy-looking house, and was admitted by a man who clasped her briefly and kissed her on the cheek. The detective who watched this little cameo described the man as being in his mid-forties, with thinning hair and a pair of wire-rimmed half-glasses on the end of his nose. He was wearing a green cardigan. Ivy Barnes was inside the house for a period of one hour and forty-seven minutes. Then she came out and went home. To complete the operation, a check on the voters' list revealed that the occupant of the house was a man called Edward Frazer.

'Now isn't that interesting?' said Fox when this information was passed to him. 'She certainly puts herself about does our Ivy. Find out who this finger was that she was all lovey-dovey with on a doorstep in Croydon, Jack.' Fox looked gloomily out of his office window. 'It's all getting too complicated for me. Whatever happened to honest crime?'

Chapter Fifteen

Commander Murdo McGregor bitched and moaned, but eventually agreed to assign yet another surveillance team, this time to the house in Croydon that Ivy had visited. They didn't have long to wait. The very next morning, in fact. The Croydon resident was followed to work. Work proved to be a small record shop... also in Croydon. Further enquiries revealed that the shop was owned and run by one Edward Frazer whose name appeared on the electoral register for the house from which he had been followed. But once the surveillance team had examined the photograph of Elvis Farrow in the criminal record file now reposing on Tommy Fox's desk, they positively identified Edward Frazer and Elvis Farrow as being one and the same.

'Presumably,' said Fox in the car on the way to Croydon, 'so that he didn't have to change the initials on his pyjamas.'

Farrow was forty-five years of age according to the file that dealt with the mysterious explosion at his previous premises. He was a short, podgy man with a few long strands of hair carefully combed across his head in an unsuccessful attempt to cover the bald expanse that now glistened beneath the fluorescent fights of the shop, and he wore a pair of bent, wire-framed half-glasses that clung precariously to the end of his nose. To complete this unappealing picture, an ill-fitting, faded green cardigan was held together over his pot-belly by two buttons. The remaining buttons were apparently unequal to the strain.

'Mr Frazer?'

'That is I.'

'Splendid,' said Fox warmly and produced his warrant card. 'The name is Fox — Thomas Fox — and I am a police officer.'

'Oh!'

'Yes,' said Fox, 'I thought that's what you'd say. Now then, Mr Frazer, or Farrow, or whatever you call yourself. You and I need to have a little chat.'

'What about?' Farrow did not seem at all enamoured of the idea. 'I've done nothing wrong.'

'Apart from trying to defraud an insurance company you mean?'

'I did time for that. It's over, finished. You've no right to bring that up again. I do have my civil rights, you know.'

'Are you saying that you're unwilling to assist the police, then?' Fox smiled benignly.

Farrow gave a resigned sigh and glanced at his watch. 'As a matter of fact, I was just closing, so — '

'Yes,' said Fox, 'that's why we came at this hour.'

'I'll just slip the catch and put the "Closed" sign up — '

'My colleague's just done all that,' said Fox. 'Now, then.'

'It was all a mistake... about the explosion — ' Farrow began. 'Isn't it always?' said Fox sympathetically. 'But I'm not much interested in that. I'd rather talk to you about your wife.'

'My wife?' Farrow looked apprehensive.

'Yes. You do remember her, don't you? Name of Sonia Fisk.'

'Oh yes,' said Farrow bitterly. 'I remember her, all right.' 'Good. Tell me about her.'

'What d'you want to know? We got married, and she took off with all my money. That's it.'

'How did you allow that to happen?'

'She blackmailed me, that's how.'

'What about?' Fox stared keenly at Farrow but for some seconds got no response. 'I'm waiting, Mr Farrow.'

'Some years ago, I got into a bit of trouble.'

'Oh?' Fox raised his eyebrows. He was certain Fletcher had said that Farrow had only the one previous conviction. 'You mean the insurance fraud?'

Farrow looked round nervously, as though afraid of being overheard, and adjusted his spectacles. 'No, not that. I was a clergyman,' he said, and then stopped.

Fox nodded wisely. 'Little boys or little girls?' he enquired.

Farrow looked down at the ledger on the desk in front of him, toying with the corner of a page. Then he looked up, a frown on his face. 'It was young girls,' he said crossly, as though the suggestion that he might have interfered with little boys in some way impugned his character or his manhood.

'Don't tell me. The choir?' said Fox. Farrow nodded miserably. 'What happened? Did you get arrested?'

'No. It was all hushed up.' He glared at Fox defensively. They were over the age of consent,' he added.

'How much over the age of consent?' Fox glanced at Gilroy to make sure he was making notes. He was quite prepared to arrest Farrow here and now if he got an admission, whatever it might do to his murder enquiry. He had a thing about nauseating middle-aged men who interfered with little girls. And he usually started off by giving them a good smacking.

'Seventeen or eighteen, they were.'

'They? How many were there?'

'Four.'

'Christ!' said Fox. 'So you got the sack, I suppose.'

'I was advised to resign my living, yes, and I went into the record business.'

'Tell me about Sonia.'

'It was about a year after that bit of bother, and I'd set up in business. Doing very well, too. I thought all my troubles were behind me. Then Sonia came into the shop one day and bought some records.' Farrow looked closely at the ledger and then slammed it shut with greater violence than the task demanded. 'She came in two or three times as a matter of fact, and it was quite obvious that she... well, she fancied me, is the modem expression, I think.'

Fox looked up at the ceiling, wondering why odious creeps like Farrow so often attracted women. 'And?'

'We got married.'

'Just like that?'

'Not exactly. It followed the usual pattern. I took her out to dinner once or twice, and — '

Fox suddenly laughed. 'Then she told you she was pregnant.'

Farrow looked up in surprise. 'How did you know that?' he asked.

'There's a lot of it about,' said Fox. 'What happened then?'

'Well it turned out to be a false alarm.'

'There's a surprise.'

'Anyway, she seemed to know all about my bit of bother, and threatened to make trouble if I didn't give her all she wanted.'

'Sex, you mean?' asked Fox. He was joking.

'Oh no! There wasn't any more of that.'

'No, I'll bet there wasn't,' said Fox, gazing at Farrow's pale and sweaty face. 'What sort of trouble, then?'

'She threatened to let people know that I'd been sacked for having games with young girls. And she said that if that became known, I'd lose all my trade, because women wouldn't come in here, and they wouldn't let their kids come in, either. She said she'd put it about that I'd raped these girls, and that I couldn't deny it because there was no record anywhere. She said that people would know that I hadn't resigned my living for nothing. No smoke without fire, is what she said.'

'How apposite,' murmured Fox. 'So what happened?'

'She took me for every penny I had and then disappeared. I never saw her again.'

'So you hit on this marvellous scheme of blowing up your shop and claiming the insurance, having sold all the stock first?'

Farrow nodded. 'Yes. It wasn't very clever, I suppose. But there had been two or three gas explosions at about that time, and I thought — '

'But you forgot that you didn't have gas connected to the premises.'

Farrow nodded, the nod of one who had only become wise after the event. 'Yes,' he said, 'that was one of the things I didn't think of.'

Fox stood up and walked to the door. 'There were quite a few things you didn't think of,' he said. 'Like going to the police when you were being blackmailed by your wife...' He stepped out on to the pavement, slamming the shop door behind him, and took a deep breath of fresh air.

Farrow opened his ledger and smiled. It wasn't too difficult to fool the police.

*

Gilroy picked the pub nearest to the one owned by the Goodalls to start his enquiries into Frank Goodall's movements. There was a chance that he would get nowhere — as a detective he was accustomed to such disappointments — but he was lucky this time. The publican there, Tom Gash, told Gilroy that he and six others, local licensees and their friends, had been to Calais on the two dates, and went on to list those who had been in the party. When he reached the fifth member of the party, he stopped.

'Two more?' asked Gilroy.

'Oh, there was me.' Gash laughed.

'And Frank Goodall?'

'Yes, of course. Never misses, Frank. How did you know his name?'

'I've got a list of all the local publicans,' said Gilroy blandly. 'I'm working my way through them. You were the first. Where did you go, once you arrived in Calais?'

'God knows.' Gash grinned. 'We started off with a meal at a cafe not far from the port. It's one we usually stay at, and then we went on a pub-crawl. Well, cafe-crawl I suppose you'd call it over there.'

'What times were you over there, on the second of those two dates?'

'We caught the afternoon boat on the Tuesday and came back on the three o'clock boat the following day. Got back to Dover about half four, I suppose. Very much the worse for wear. I don't know why the hell we do it. Anyway, what's this all about?'

'Enquiry from the French police,' said Gilroy. 'There was a robbery in Calais apparently and they're seeking witnesses. It was just down from where you were staying...' He paused as if trying to remember.

'Café de la Paix,' said Gash.

'That's it.' Gilroy laughed. 'Now for the good bit,' he said. 'The robbery took place about half an hour after you arrived back in Dover.' He stood up. 'Sorry to have wasted your time, Mr Gash, but that's the French all over.'

Gash laughed. 'Forget it,' he said. 'Have a drink before you go.'

*

'What is it about Ivy Barnes, or whatever her damned name is, that makes her go for clergymen, Jack?'

'Easy, sir. They're very often naive, and if they've been unfrocked, as Farrow and Close were, it's in all the papers. It's like coppers. If a bloke spent five minutes as a special constable twenty years before he gets nicked, it's "Ex-policeman charged". They can't resist it. Same with clergymen. Especially if it's little boys... or, as in the case of Farrow, little girls. All that Ivy's got to do is read the papers. It's all there.'

'But Farrow said he'd resigned, not that he was unfrocked. And they weren't exactly little girls. I doubt whether any of that would have been in the Press.'

Gilroy shrugged. 'Well she found out somehow, that's for sure.'

'So far, we've got her down for one bigamous marriage,' said Fox. 'Assuming, of course, that Elvis Farrow was her first and legitimate husband, she then went through a form of marriage with Donald Close. What we don't know is whether Farrow was her first, or how many others there might have been. And we've no way of finding out. Not if she used duff names all the time.'

'What are the chances of them all being bent clergymen, guv?' Fox shrugged. 'Your guess is as good as mine,' he said, 'but I suppose she might have widened the field a bit. Scoutmasters, perhaps. Schoolteachers. When you start casting about, Jack, the list of wickedness among the so-called trustworthy is endless. But what's the point? I'm not going to waste my time chasing around after blokes who've been seen off by some smart tart who's found a way of financing herself without working too hard. Not a job for the Flying Squad. I'm only keen to get to the bottom of this bloody murder enquiry we've been lumbered with. As far as the bigamies are concerned, we can parcel that lot up and dump them on the desk of the Commander SO1 Branch. That's right up his street.'

'If he'll accept them,' said Gilroy.

'He will,' said Fox, 'once our commander's had a word with the DAC. The job of the Flying Squad,' he continued loftily, 'is to catch mobile robbers, not to ponce around trying to sort out bloody bigamies. That's for desk detectives. And there are hundreds of them sitting round in SO1 Branch just sweating on a lovely juicy bigamy.' He shook his head sadly. 'It's the sort of thing that gets you through a promotion board, Jack. "What have you been doing, Chief Inspector?" the assistant commissioner will ask. "I've solved four hundred bigamies, sir... all by myself." "Splendid work. Go away and be a superintendent."' Fox scowled. 'Better still,' he added, 'wear a funny hat and devise a new traffic system that'll cock up the West End. Sure way to the top, that is.'

'Yes, sir.' Gilroy had no intention of getting involved in that argument. Fox's scathing views of what he called the woodentops were well known... and very boring. 'We still haven't got anything firm on the murder, sir. Unless you count Lambie's statement.'

'Load of rubbish,' said Fox. 'And no good on its own anyway.

He puts the finger on Barnes, but hasn't got any proof. Didn't really see anything. No, Jack, all he was trying to do was get out from under.

Just because we charged him with the murder, he thought he'd get his two-penn'orth in first. It won't wash.'

'Well, what are we going to do about Ivy Barnes, sir? Have her in?'

'No. At least, not yet. All we've got against her is a bigamy — '

'And the blackmail, sir.'

'You are joking, Jack. Can you see Farrow getting up in court, giving evidence that he'd been having it off with his choirgirls, and as a result the bishop or whoever told him to put his papers in? No chance, Jack.'

'So we let her run?'

'Until we've got something worthwhile, yes. The moment we arrest her, she'll clam up, and we'll be stuck. No, Jack, we'll let her run for a bit, like I said. See what she gets up to.'

*

The *inspecteur* of the Police Judiciaire in Calais upon whose desk Gilroy's enquiry landed, made quick work of it. Within twenty-four hours, Gilroy was reading the reply. And having done so, he went into Fox's office.

'Interesting, guv'nor,' he said. 'Gash, the publican I went to see, told me that his little party of licensed tipplers always stayed at the Café de la Paix in Calais. He gave me a list of the party that went over on the two dates that the mysterious Armstrong stayed at the same hotels as Muriel Close.'

'And?' Fox looked interested.

'And Frank Goodall wasn't among them. Wherever he was, he wasn't in Calais on those two dates.'

'So why did Gash lie?'

'I don't know,' said Gilroy, 'but I intend to find out. It's cards-on-the-table time, I think.'

*

'Silver Barnes wants to talk to you, sir.' The incident room sergeant handed Fox a message flimsy. 'Sounds a bit desperate. According to the screw at Brixton, he wants to make a clean breast of it.'

Fox scoffed. 'That'll be the day.'

The sergeant laughed. 'Yeah! You're dead right there, guv. I asked the screw if we were talking about the same Silver Barnes.'

*

'I hope you're not wasting my time,' said Fox, 'because quite frankly, I'm getting sick to the back teeth of you.'

'Straight, Mr Fox, I want to tell you about it.' Dwarfed by an immense prison officer, Barnes stood by the door, a shabby little figure, with his hands held out, palms uppermost. He seemed to have lost weight. Fox hoped it was the worry.

'You're still under caution,' said Fox. 'Sit down.' He glanced at his Tissot wrist-watch. 'I don't have much time.' Barnes sidled towards the table and carefully placed himself on the hard wooden chair. 'Well, get on with it.' Fox yawned.

'It's about the body, Mr Fox.'

'What body?' Fox gazed at the ceiling, a look of consuming disinterest on his face.

'The one what you found down the slaughter.'

'Right. Go on.'

'Don's missus, it was.'

'Yes, I know. It's her murder you're charged with.'

'And that wouldn't have happened if bleeding Lambie had kept his trap shut, an' all.'

'Lambie's statement was made after I charged you with murder,' said Fox. 'None the less, Silver, you should pick your business partners more carefully. However, you'll have plenty of time to reflect on that.' He looked pensively at the wall beyond Barnes' left shoulder before realigning his gaze on the robber's bristly and fox-like face. 'Life, minimum thirty, I should think. The general public's getting a bit pissed off with murdering bastards like you. So much so that even the judges are noticing.' Fox lit a cigarette. 'And that's saying a mouthful.'

'I never done it, Mr Fox, honest.'

'So you keep telling me, Silver, old son, just as I keep telling you that it needs more than a simple denial of the facts. Who's your brief?'

Barnes' face wrinkled as his brain appeared to start working. 'Can't remember his name,' he said. 'S'matter of fact I was thinking of giving him the push.'

'I should think that's favourite. Throw yourself on the mercy of the court.'

'When we went back down the slaughter to shift the gear — '

'The money you stole with violence, you mean.' Fox paused, a sudden look of interest on his face. 'What d'you mean, to shift the gear?'

'Yeah, well!' Barnes struggled on, a sour look on his face. He knew he was putting his head in the noose but he could see no alternative. Sometimes you had to give something to get something: a policy that went very much against his nature. 'Me, Harry Perkins, Lambie and Grover, see. We went back down there the next day, to like share it out, see. And when we got down there, we found this body in the lounge. Very unnerving, it was, Mr Fox.'

'You have my sympathy, Silver. Not the sort of thing you want to have to deal with at the end of a hard day's work.'

'And there was no sign of Don. And he should have been there, waiting. Looking after the gear, see.'

'Can't trust anybody these days,' said Fox. 'Just can't get decent staff. So what did you do? Apart from panic.'

'It wasn't funny, Mr Fox.'

'I'm not laughing.'

'We never even knew who she was, this bird.'

'Really?' Fox sounded doubtful. Very doubtful.

'Honest, Mr Fox. Never set eyes on her before, so 'elp me.'

'What did you do then?'

'I told the others to get digging in the garden, so's we could get rid of the body. If we hadn't, it would've cocked everything up.'

'I can imagine that,' murmured Fox.

'We reckoned it'd be best to lie low for a bit, see. But then that silly sod Perkins put the heave-ho on that, talking to your DI down the boozer in Stockwell. A right prat is Harry Perkins. Don't know why I ever got mixed up with him.'

'Why d'you think that Lambie put the finger on you, then?'

Barnes laughed, a humourless, grating laugh. 'Wanted to get out from under, didn't he? Thought he'd put it down to me, see. Score a few points with the filth.' Fox frowned. 'Oh! Begging your pardon, Mr Fox,' added Barnes.

'I should bloody think so,' said Fox. 'And you're now trying to tell me it wasn't down to you, I suppose?'

'Stand on me, Mr Fox. That ain't my style. You should know that.'

Fox shook his head slowly. 'But I don't know it, do I, Silver?

You're a double-dyed villain, and you didn't hesitate for a moment when it came to shooting that security guard.'

'That wasn't down to me neither. That was bloody Lambie. I told him to go easy on the shooters.'

'Oh he did, Silver. Only fired once... both barrels, mind you. But I don't believe you. You're all going down for armed robbery, all five of you.'

'Five?'

'Yes. You, Perkins, Lambie and Grover... and Close.'

Barnes nodded gravely. 'Yeah, I suppose so,' he said.

'Mmm!' Fox nodded amiably. 'All very interesting, Silver, but I don't believe a bloody word of it.'

'But — '

'Because, among other things, when I suggested that the body in question was Ivy's you agreed with me. And furthermore, you told me that she was your sister. Now I learn that you and she were shacked up together. What you're trying to do is work one off on Donald Close because he took her off you, and work one off on Lambie because he fingered you... quite rightly too, I should think.'

'But, Mr Fox — '

'So give me one good reason why I should believe what you're telling me now.' Fox sat back and folded his arms, a triumphant smile on his face.

'But it's true, Mr Fox.'

'That's what you said last time, Silver, but try to see it from my point of view. I've got five robbers of varying shades locked up, and I'm charging them all with murder. As far as I'm concerned, you can fight it out between you at the Bailey — or your counsel can, and that'll be a very expensive pastime.'

'I haven't got any money,' said Barnes sullenly. 'It'll have to be Legal Aid.'

'Tell me something I don't know,' said Fox.

Barnes sat with his chin on his chest for a moment or two and then looked up. 'I s'pose I'd better tell you the rest of it, then.'

'What a good idea.'

'I knew about Ivy being married to some finger called Farrow, but not till after.'

'Not till after what?'

'It was this club, see, up West. I was up there with a few of the lads, celebrating — '

'Another successful blagging, was it?'

Barnes looked forlorn. 'No, nothing like that. Anyhow, this bird, Ivy — well she was calling herself Gloria something — come on, see, and done a strip. Bleedin' gorgeous, she was. Well when she'd finished, she done a walk round the tables, just wearing a garter. You know like they do, so's the punters can stick money under'em. Well, we'd had a nice little tickle — '

'Which job was that?'

'No, down the races. We'd done Kempton — '

'Many a true word spoken in jest,' said Fox mildly.

'And I was a bit flush, so I bunged her half a ton.'

'You mean you put a fifty-pound note under the lady's garter?'

'I just said that. Yeah! And I asked her if she'd like some champagne.'

'You really were lashing out, weren't you?'

'Anyhow, she said as how she wouldn't mind, but reckoned she'd have to go and put some clothes on first.'

'You can't win 'em all, Silver.'

'Anyhow, one thing led to another, and we got sort of pally.'

Fox nodded. 'Please don't go into the sordid details,' he said.

'Well, I thought she was on offer like.' Barnes paused, searching for the right words. 'Anyhow, to cut a long story short, she agreed to come and shack up with me. But, God's honest truth, Mr Fox, I never knew she was married already. I mean, you don't go round asking for trouble, do you?'

'You could have fooled me, Silver... quite easily,' said Fox. 'So you set up home together, did you?'

'Well, sort of. She shacked up with me at Clapham for a bit. It was what you might call convenient for the West End, 'cos she still had her career.' Barnes ignored Fox's derisive laugh.

'All this about her appearing on television and in Australia was a load of moody, then? She was just a stripper.'

Barnes shrugged. 'That's what she told me, Mr Fox. I never seen her on telly, mind you. And I don't know nothing about Australia. Could have been true. I mean to say, she was Australian.'

'Is that what she told you?'

'Yeah. Reckoned she was born in Melbourne. She had an Oz accent anyhow.'

'Well she's a lying bitch,' said Fox. 'She was born in Wandsworth.' But it was obvious that she was sufficient of an actress to be able to fool the Melbourne police in her guise as the Australian Bobbie Howard. There was also the possibility that the husband she told Constable Crosby was in Adelaide really existed, and might even pre-date Elvis Farrow. But Fox had no intention of getting involved in all that. All he wanted, right now, was to solve a murder and get back to dealing with ordinary villains, not unfrocked clergymen, insurance fraudsmen and bigamists. 'And what about Donald Close?' continued Fox. 'You said that he was missing when you got to the slaughter the day after the Cobham heist.'

'Yeah, that's right,' said Barnes. 'And I never seen him again, nor Ivy... ungrateful little cow.'

'Where was she when you went out to do that job?'

'In bed, asleep, down Clapham. But she'd gone when I got back after the job. But then she would have been. She used to go to work about three. But she never come home that night, and I never seen her again.'

'But you knew that she'd been through a form of marriage with Close?'

'Yeah!' Barnes shook his head sadly. 'That bastard Close has seen me off. I reckon they've had me over, the pair of them.'

Fox smiled. It was pretty certain that Close had been had over too, if Ivy had continued to sleep occasionally with Barnes in Clapham after her so-called marriage to the ex-clergyman. He glanced at Gilroy, writing furiously in the corner of the room, before turning back to Barnes. 'Now let me get this straight. You and the other three did the job and stashed the haul at the slaughter at Donald Close's place at Cobham. You went back the next day and expected to find Close there, but he'd done a runner. All you found was the body of Muriel Close?'

Barnes nodded. 'If you say so, Mr Fox,' he said miserably. 'Like I said, I never knew who she was. Never seen her before.' He shook his head. 'Nasty shock, that was, I can tell you.'

'And when you eventually got back to your drum at Clapham, Ivy had gone, apparently to work, but never came back. And you didn't see either of them again.'

'That's about the up-and-down of it, Mr Fox.'

Fox looked long and hard at Barnes. This time it had better be the truth, Silver,' he said.

'Does that get me off the hook for the topping job, Mr Fox?'

Fox smiled benignly. 'Don't be ridiculous, Silver,' he said, and stood up.

Chapter Sixteen

'Now, Jack,' said Fox, stifling a yawn as the prison officer departed with an unhappy Barnes, 'let's have another go at the Reverend.'

Ten minutes later, a different prison officer produced Donald Close, who having been charged with the murder of his wife Muriel, divers offences arising out of the armed robbery at Cobham, and bigamy, had also been remanded in custody to Brixton Prison to await his trial.

'The day after the heist at Cobham, when you were supposed to be waiting at your place, you went missing. But the body of your wife was there. Where did you go and why?' Fox had made up his mind that he was not going to mess about any more. The murder of Muriel Close, which in Fox's view he shouldn't have been saddled with in the first place, was taking up far too much of his time. He had decided that he was going to shake the tree a bit and see what fell out.

'I don't think that I should — '

'You want to be tried for murder then, is that it? Suits me. Take your chance with the jury. It's no skin off my nose.'

'I didn't kill anyone.'

'Then what the hell are you poncing about for? Now, I'll ask you again. Where did you go, and why?'

'Out.'

'What's that supposed to mean?'

'I'd been up to London.'

'What for?'

Close hesitated. 'I had to see a man about a little deal I'd got going.'

'A confidence trick, I suppose. Another of your little scams?'

Close realised that any admission he made now would merely be taken into consideration with the other more serious charges he was facing. 'Yes,' he said. 'When I got back, Ivy was there. So was Muriel... but she was dead. Ivy said there'd been an accident — '

'What sort of accident?'

'She said there'd been a fight and that Muriel had fallen awkwardly and... well...'

'Did Ivy say that she had been involved in this fight?'

'No, not exactly.'

'I thought you said, at one of our earlier interviews, that Muriel didn't know about the house at Cobham.'

'No, she didn't. I'd no idea how she'd found me, but apparently she had arrived while I was out. Ivy was there and something had happened.'

'What happened next?'

'Well, Ivy said it would look bad for me. That it was my house, my wife, and that the police would automatically think that I'd killed her. I must admit that I panicked a bit.'

'Yes,' said Fox, 'I can imagine that. So what did you do?'

'Upped and ran,' said Close.

'Yes,' said Fox. 'I can imagine that, too. Where did you go?'

'To Canada. It was Ivy's idea. We'd agreed it some time before, but she said that we couldn't possibly stay in England now and that anyway we both deserved to start a new life. She was fed up with her acting career, said she wasn't getting anywhere, and that she wanted to get out of England.'

'You were already married to her, of course. I use the term loosely. It was bigamous: each of you then had a living spouse.'

Close nodded. 'I know. But it seemed the only thing to do. I know it was dishonest, but I didn't care any more. I'd had enough. Muriel's murder decided it.'

'Did it not occur to you that Ivy may have been the one who'd killed her?'

'Yes. But I understood what she meant about the police suspecting me because Muriel was my wife, so it made sense to go anyway. I tried not to think that Ivy might have been a murderess, but she'd said it was an accident and I believed her. I wanted to believe her.'

'Did you ask her if she'd killed Muriel?'

'Yes, I did eventually.'

'And?'

'She denied it. She said that she'd come back to the house. She was expecting Alfred — '

'Alfred?'

'Alfred Barnes.'

'Oh yes. Silver. Yes, go on.'

'But that when she arrived, the house was empty, apart from Muriel.'

Fox laughed as he stood up. 'That's the nicest story I've heard in years, Donald,' he said. 'You'll be telling me next that Muriel disturbed a burglar and it was he who'd topped her. Pull the other one, old son.' He paused at the door to the interview room. 'See you at the Old Bailey,' he said.

*

'Well, guv'nor, what d'you think?' asked Gilroy when Close had been taken back to his cell.

'Get on the eau de Cologne to Fletcher, Jack. Tell him to get up to Ruislip as fast as his little legs'll carry him and arrest Ivy Barnes.'

*

Rosie Webster was one of the few women detective constables on the Flying Squad. No one argued with her, police officers or criminals, male or female. She had cropped blonde hair, was six feet tall, weighed fourteen stones and had a figure upon which, had he been five hundred years younger, Sandro Botticelli would undoubtedly have cast a loving gaze. She used expensive cosmetics, a discreet and equally expensive perfume and her fingernails were always impeccably varnished in scarlet. Her only concession to being on duty was to remove her earrings, which, if they were to be pulled off in a fight — always a possibility — could cause injury to her ear lobes. Despite her size, she was all woman, and the only officer ever to suggest that she might be a lesbian was offered the chance to find out how wrong he was. Unfortunately for that officer's reputation and self-esteem, the offer was made in the centre of The Tank, as the bar on the ground floor of New Scotland Yard is known, which was very crowded at the time. No one had ever doubted her femininity since.

It was no surprise, therefore, that when DS Percy Fletcher received a telephone call telling him to go to Ruislip and arrest Ivy Barnes, he directed WDC Webster to accompany him.

The flat was on the first floor. Fletcher rang the doorbell but there was no immediate response. 'She's playing hard to get,' he said. 'According to the obo team, she's at home.'

'Then we'll just have to flush her out,' said Rosie, and leaning across in front of Fletcher she placed her thumb firmly on the bell-push... and kept it there.

The front door was wrenched open and Ivy Barnes stared truculently at the two detectives. She was wearing a thigh-length terry bathrobe and had a towel wound round her head. 'All right, all right,' she said. 'I was in the shower.' She looked at Rosie and then shifted her glance back to Fletcher. 'Well,' she demanded, 'what d'you want?'

'We're police officers,' said Fletcher. 'Flying Squad. Sonia Farrow, is it?'

'Thought I'd be seeing you lot again somehow,' said the girl and, leaving the door ajar, strode through into the living room and started to dry her hair.

Fletcher closed the door and followed her. 'Sonia Farrow, otherwise known as Ivy Close or Ivy Barnes or Fisk, or half a dozen other aliases no doubt, I'm arresting you in connection with the murder of Muriel Close, née Yates,' he said.

Ivy stopped towelling her hair for a moment. 'Never heard of her,' she said. 'Anyway, what d'you mean, in connection with?'

'All right,' said Fletcher, 'arresting you *for* committing the murder, if that makes you feel any better. Anyway, you're coming to the station with us.'

'You got a warrant?'

'Don't need one,' said Rosie, gazing round the sitting room. 'It's what the law calls an arrestable offence.'

'Well I can't come like this.' Ivy waved a hand down her bathrobe.

'You'd better put some clothes on then,' said Rosie.

Ivy started to walk towards the bedroom but stopped when she realised that Rosie was following her. 'You a dyke then? Naked women turn you on, do they?' she asked.

Rosie laughed. 'If you think you're hopping out of the window and down the drainpipe, you can think again,' she said. 'You can come like that if you want to. Makes no difference to me, but it'll probably liven up the day for the lads at the nick.'

'Sod you!' said Ivy.

It took nearly an hour to drive the thirteen miles to Bow Street, and when they arrived, Fletcher's first task was to phone the Yard and tell Fox that Ivy Barnes was in custody.

'Good,' said Fox. 'Lock her up and let her sweat.'

*

'Mr Gash, when I came to see you recently, you told me that Frank Goodall was with you when you went to France,' said Gilroy.

'Yes, probably.'

'He wasn't.'

'Wasn't he?' Gash looked surprised. 'Does it matter? You said that the robbery happened after we left Calais anyway.'

'That's right. However, we don't tell everybody everything when we're making enquiries.' Gilroy leaned forward confidentially. 'So why did you say that he was with you?'

'Well, he usually is,' said Gash.

'But he wasn't with you on either of the two occasions I mentioned.'

'No.'

'Then why did you say he was?' There was a sharpness in Gilroy's voice that made Gash uneasy.

'Is this confidential, Inspector?'

'Depends. But for the moment, yes.'

'He's got a bird,' said Gash. 'He sees her sometimes when we go across to France. We always say that he was with us in case it gets back to his missus.'

'Terrific,' said Gilroy angrily.

'It's human nature, isn't it?' Gash grinned nervously. 'Been happening since the world began. I mean, it's not a crime, is it?'

'No,' said Gilroy, 'but wasting my time is. And if the fact that I've been talking to you about this matter should get back to Goodall, that's what you'll get done for. Wasting police time.' Gilroy knew that such a charge wouldn't stick, but Gash didn't know that it wouldn't.

'You needn't worry about that,' said Gash. 'I've met his missus and I don't want any bother with her.'

*

'Arrange for Mr Goodall to call at Scotland Yard,' said Fox. 'And tell him that it will be in his best interests not to tell his wife where he's going. He should be able to think of an excuse. He could tell her he's going to Calais.'

*

Frank Goodall looked nervously around the entrance hall of New Scotland Yard. It was bustling with activity. Several small groups of people were engrossed in deep conversation, and a couple of very senior officers — if the amount of silver on their uniforms was anything to go by — were staring aimlessly out of the huge plate-glass windows at a rain-drenched Dacre Street, waiting for their cars to appear.

Goodall walked up to the desk. 'I have an appointment to see Detective Chief Superintendent Fox,' he said.

'Which department?' The girl did not look up, but started thumbing through a black book.

'Er... Flying Squad, I think.'

'Just one moment.' The girl made a phone call and then glanced at Goodall. 'Take a seat,' she said. 'Someone will be down.'

It was Gilroy. 'Mr Goodall, thank you for coming in.'

Goodall grunted; he reckoned that he hadn't had much choice. Gilroy escorted him into one of the interview rooms off the corridor that led to the Yard's Press Bureau and invited him to take a seat.

'What's it about?' asked Goodall, but he had a nasty feeling that he knew already.

'Mr Fox will be with us in a moment,' said Gilroy by way of an answer.

'Thomas Fox... of the Flying Squad.' Fox entered the room a few moments later and held out his hand; Goodall noticed that it was a firm grip. 'Do sit down,' continued Fox and he took a chair on the opposite side of the table from Goodall. 'It was good of you to come in, Mr Goodall,' he said, 'but there are one or two things that don't make a lot of sense.'

'Oh?' Goodall felt inhibited by this confident detective, immaculate in a well-cut, dark blue suit.

'When Mr Gilroy came to see you, he mentioned a couple of dates,' said Fox, indicating the DI with a wave of his hand.

'Dates on which you said that you had been to France with a party of local publicans...'

'Yes?' Goodall didn't like the sound of this.

'You didn't go to France with that party,' said Fox bluntly. 'Where were you?'

'Er...' Goodall ran his tongue round his lips. 'Can I have a look at my diary?'

Fox smiled. 'By all means, Mr Goodall.'

Goodall produced a small pocket diary and started turning the pages. 'I'm sure that I — '

'Shall we stop messing about, Mr Goodall?' said Fox. 'Or do you prefer to be called Armstrong?'

'Oh!' Goodall dropped the diary on the table and allowed his hands to fall into his lap. 'You know about that, do you?'

Fox nodded. 'Yes, Mr Goodall, we do.' It had been a chance, but one that he had reckoned worth taking. It was what he called a racing certainty, and human failings were, after all, his stock-in-trade.

'It started after Donald Close took off with Muriel's money,' said Goodall. 'I offered to help her find him... and the money.'

'Did you have any luck?' asked Fox.

'No. He'd disappeared without trace. I suppose I should have got her to come and see you people, but the solicitor said that we'd probably be wasting our time... and yours.' He grinned ruefully.

'Might have worked,' said Fox. 'We're very good at finding people, but unless there was evidence of a crime...' He left the sentence unfinished. 'So you and Muriel started an affair?'

'Yes, it was... Well, one thing led to another.'

'Why the hotels? Muriel was living on her own at Edmonton.'

Goodall looked at Fox. 'Have you seen her house at Edmonton?' he asked. 'Not exactly the place for a romantic tryst, is it?'

'A what?' Fox laughed.

'Well, you know what I mean. If you're going over the side, you've got to do it properly. Apart from anything else, she had a nosy neighbour.'

'So whenever your drinking mates went across to France, you were having Muriel over in some grotty hotel?'

Goodall frowned. 'Well, that's one way of putting it,' he said.

'And her pregnancy was a natural outcome of that liaison, I suppose.'

Goodall looked startled. 'Her pregnancy?'

'Yes,' said Fox. 'She was three months' pregnant when she was murdered.'

'The bitch,' said Goodall. 'D'you mean she was two-timing me?'

Fox smiled. 'Sounds like a case of the pot calling the kettle black,' he said. 'Why is it that men always feel free to cheat on their wives, but if a woman does it to them it's all wrong?'

'I'd never thought of it like that,' said Goodall. For a second or two he looked contrite.

'Do you know of any other men that she might have been seeing?' asked Fox, a slight edge to his voice. He knew of plenty of men — a lot of policemen included — who committed adultery on a regular basis, but he had little time for any of them.

'Of course not.'

'In the circumstances,' said Fox, 'seeing that you've already lied to the police once, I'm sure that you won't mind accounting for your movements on the fourth of April this year.'

Goodall seemed puzzled. 'What's so special about the fourth of April?' he asked.

'It's the day upon which Muriel Close was murdered.' Fox withdrew a cigarette from his case and lit it, all without taking his eyes off Goodall.

Goodall leaned forward, reaching for his diary. 'May I?' Fox nodded and Goodall started looking through the small leather-bound book. 'Of course, Manchester,' he said triumphantly.

'Oh? What were you doing in Manchester?'

'Cup-tie replay,' said Goodall. 'Everton and United.'

'Football fan, are you?'

Goodall nodded. 'Saw the cup final, too.'

'Were you with anyone else... when you went to Manchester?'

'Why?'

'Well, Mr Goodall, anyone can say that they've been somewhere, but I need more than that.'

Goodall leaned back in his chair and gazed reflectively at the policeman. 'Are you suggesting that I may have had something to do with Muriel's death?' he asked.

'No. But when I investigate a murder, Mr Goodall, I have to do it thoroughly. The principle is that when you have eliminated everything you can, what's left has got to be the answer. I'm not sure who said that — probably Sherlock Holmes — but that's the way it is.'

'Well I went to Manchester to see the cup-tie replay. I didn't go with anyone else, but there were thousands of other people there.' Goodall spoke a little truculently.

'I see. How did you travel?'

'By train... from Euston.'

'And what time would that have been?'

'I caught the three o'clock. It takes about two and a half hours.'

'But that would get you there at about half past five, surely?' Fox raised an eyebrow.

'Yes. It was an evening match. Kick-off at seven. They often hold replays in the evenings.'

'And you returned home when? That night, or did you stay over?'

'No,' said Goodall. 'Came back straight after the match. Made it a late night, but what the hell!'

Fox stood up. 'Thank you, Mr Goodall. Sorry to have brought you all the way up here, but I'm sure you understand.' He smiled. 'And your secret's safe with me.'

'Is that all?' Goodall sounded surprised.

'Yes. Why? Can you think of anything else?'

'Er... no.' Goodall grinned. 'You didn't ask who won,' he added, his confidence returning.

'I know who won. A bloody fluke it was too,' said Fox.

'Well, guv'nor?' said Gilroy when he'd seen Goodall off the premises.

Fox laughed. 'I wouldn't give much for his chances if Sylvia ever catches him at it,' he said. 'But check his story out, Jack. Never know your luck.'

*

It was Fox's decision to put an observation team on Elvis Farrow's shop that threw another spanner into the works. Although the arrest of Ivy Barnes had released one of his surveillance teams, Commander Murdo McGregor had not been happy at redeploying it to mount a static observation that was likely only to add snippets of evidence to Fox's bigamy job rather than to advance his murder investigation. None the less, the commander grudgingly assigned four officers for a week with the caveat that he would withdraw them if nothing came of it. Fortunately for Fox something did come of it... on the fifth day.

But, ironically, it had nothing to do with either Fox or Commander McGregor's team of watchers.

A youth emerged from Farrow's record shop leaving the door open behind him. He was dressed in dirty jeans which, in the prevailing fashion, had gaping and carefully torn holes in the knees, below which — and serving no useful function — were sewn two short lengths of chain. Painted on the back of his leather bomber jacket was a rough depiction of a clenched fist. Inevitably, there was a brass earring in his left ear. His hair, dyed a rusty blonde, was shaved high above his ears, but apart from that slavish devotion to the mode of the day, appeared not to have made the acquaintance of a comb for some considerable time... if ever. Oblivious to his surroundings, he ambled across the busy road outside Farrow's shop, straight into the path of a patrolling police car. The driver braked to a standstill within feet of the wandering youth who merely waved and made to go on his way, apparently unaware that he had escaped great danger only as a result of the high standards set by the Police Driving School at Hendon.

The wireless operator leaped from the car with uncharacteristic speed and agility and laid hands on the errant pedestrian fifty yards down the road, on the opposite side from Farrow's shop. 'What's your game?' he enquired.

'Do what?' said the youth.

'What d'you think you're doing, throwing yourself in front of police cars? If you'd dented the front of that it would have cost you a few quid, I can tell you.'

'Do what?' asked the youth again, and stared blankly at the constable.

'You been drinking?' The PC moved closer to the youth and sniffed. In the old days, one only expected drunks at lunchtime and in the evenings. But now, they roamed about at all hours... and this was a quarter past nine in the morning.

The police car had moved up the road and now pulled into the kerb. The driver joined his colleague and inspected the youth. 'Drugs!' he said casually. 'Turn your pockets out.'

Hesitantly, the youth started to remove the contents of his jeans and held up for inspection a filthy handkerchief, a bunch of keys and a few coins. 'And the back pockets,' said the wireless operator. Reluctantly, the youth produced a packet of white powder. 'Thought so,' added the operator. 'Where did you get that from?'

'Can't remember.'

'Right, you're nicked on suspicion of possessing a controlled substance.'

'Do what?' said the youth again.

'You heard,' said the driver.

At that point, one of the DCs involved in the static operation, somewhat alarmed at the turn of events, moved up behind the driver of the area car. 'Have a word, guv?' he said.

The driver turned as the DC produced his warrant card. 'What's up, mate?'

The DC drew the driver out of the youth's hearing. 'What you got?'

'Possession of drugs. Looks like cocaine. Why?'

'Could be connected,' said the DC mysteriously. Where you taking him?'

'Croydon.'

'Right,' said the DC. 'I'll see you there. Don't bail him, will you? I think the Flying Squad might have an interest.'

Chapter Seventeen

Tommy Fox stared at the message form. 'I don't bloody believe it,' he said to the DC who had brought it in. 'Get hold of Mr Gilroy, urgently.'

Seconds later, Gilroy walked into the office. 'Something up, guv?'

'Read that,' said Fox, handing the form across his desk.

Gilroy skimmed through the brief message and laid it on Fox's desk with a shrug. 'So?' he said. 'Just because some yobbo comes out of Farrow's shop with a packet of cocaine doesn't mean he didn't have it when he went in.'

'I'll put money on Farrow being a supplier,' said Fox, emphasising his point by gently tapping the message form with his forefinger. 'He's a bent bastard for a start. Secondly, what a lovely set-up. There you've got a bloke who's selling all this crap that passes for music to a clientele that looks like the cast of *The Rocky Horror Show*. It's a bloody good cover, Jack. You've got to admit it.'

'If it's true, guv.'

'Of course it's true.' Fox spoke dismissively as though any other explanation was unworthy of consideration.

'Well what are we going to do about it? Talk to Farrow?'

'Not yet, Jack. First we're going to talk to Ivy, who Percy Fletcher has obligingly got binned up at Bow Street nick. Then we'll have a little chat with Master Farrow. But not until you've had a chat with this drug-crazed lout down at Croydon.'

*

'Where did you get this from, then?' asked Gilroy by way of an opening.

'Wouldn't you like to know?' said the youth, whose name was Wayne Crick, a combination of initials which his parents should have taken into account at his birth in order to reduce the ridicule to which he had been subjected in his nineteen short years.

'Yes, I would,' said Gilroy. 'That's why I'm asking.'

'I've got nothing to say,' said Crick.

'That's very silly,' said Gilroy. 'You're going to have it all on your own, are you? Brave fellow. A lot of thanks you'll get for that.' Gilroy shook his head.

'Do what?' asked Crick.

'How much did you pay for that packet of talcum powder, then, Wayne?'

Crick looked suspiciously at the DI. 'Do what?' he asked again.

Gilroy shrugged. 'It's your money... I suppose. Or are you on the DSS?'

'What d'you mean, talcum powder?' The prospect that he had paid good money — even if it was someone else's — for talcum powder began to dawn on Crick and it was obvious that it did not please him. Gilroy smiled but said nothing. He knew it was the real thing, but this was a delicate matter. There was a long silence. 'The geezer in the record shop,' said Crick eventually.

'Right.' Gilroy stood up so quickly that Crick moved back sharply, believing that he was about to become one of the point-nought-one per cent of persons who claim to be assaulted in a police station. 'You will now make a written statement to that effect... and sign it.'

Detective Sergeant Percy Fletcher, who had been present throughout this short exchange, produced a statement form as if by magic, and started writing. Sixty-five minutes and twelve corrections later, Crick had effectively condemned Elvis Farrow to a very distressing interview.

*

'That's nice, Jack,' said Fox, dropping the typewritten copy of Crick's statement on to his desk. 'Nice bit of work that.' He stood up. 'Get hold of Rosie Webster.'

'A chance'd be a fine thing,' said Gilroy, a wistful look in his eye.

From her pouting face and truculent attitude, it appeared that Ivy Barnes was not in the slightest cowed by her incarceration at Bow Street Police Station, but, for all that, she shot an apprehensive glance at Rosie Webster when she and Tommy Fox entered the interview room.

'The situation is this,' said Fox as though he were opening a briefing to selected officers on the restructuring of the force. 'We found the dead body of Muriel Close, née Yates, at the Cobham home of Donald Close to whom you were bigamously married. She had been killed feloniously. And in my view it's down to you, or to Donald Close, or to Alfred

Barnes... or even to Elvis Farrow.' Fox gazed at the girl opposite, a relaxed expression on his face, and gave her time to digest his opening gambit. 'At the moment,' he continued, leaning forward again with contrived earnestness, 'I have enough evidence to sustain a charge of conspiracy to murder against all of you.' He hadn't — not quite — but when Tommy Fox said it, it sounded convincing.

'I don't know anything about it.' Ivy's Australian twang was suddenly quite strong.

Fox stood up. 'And you can cut that out as well,' he said. 'I know you were born in Wandsworth.'

'I'm not making any statements,' said Ivy, lapsing into her native south London accent.

'All right, then,' he said, and walked out of the room, out of the station and into the pub on the opposite side of Bow Street where Jack Gilroy had already ordered him a large Scotch.

Rosie Webster walked gracefully across the room and sat down in the chair vacated by Fox. She crossed her legs and straightened her skirt before opening her handbag and taking out a packet of cigarettes and a gold lighter which she placed on the table. 'Well, you threw that chance away, didn't you?' she said. 'Cigarette?'

'Don't mind if I do.'

Rosie pushed the cigarettes towards the girl opposite her and watched while she lit one.

Ivy puffed smoke towards the ceiling. 'I don't know what you mean,' she said.

'Quite simple, really,' said Rosie. 'Conspiracy to murder carries the same penalty as the substantive offence. So you, my girl, are facing up to about thirty years on the inside. Still, it won't affect your career...'

'Eh?' Ivy moved her position slightly.

Rosie shook her head. 'Believe me, when the girls in Holloway set eyes on you, you'll find that you're doing a strip twice nightly with matinees on Wednesdays and Saturdays. And that'll only be the beginning. Love a bit of slap and tickle, that lot.'

'What d'you mean?'

'I mean,' said Rosie, 'that some of the inmates of Holloway'll have you for breakfast... literally. There aren't any men in there, you know.'

Ivy's face paled, leaving just two high-spots of colour on her cheeks. Suddenly her make-up looked as cheap as it was. 'I'm not a bloody lezzy, for Christ's sake,' she said as the significance of Rosie's remarks hit home.

'No,' said Rosie, slowly extracting a cigarette from its packet, 'not at the moment, anyway.' She thumbed her lighter. 'But you'll soon get the hang of it. The dikes of Holloway Prison will just love a shapely young lady like you.' She held Ivy's gaze for a moment or two and then smiled.

'Look,' Ivy said, 'I never knew nothing about it, honest I never. It was there, the body.'

'What d'you mean, it was there?'

'Oh Christ!' Ivy turned sideways and stubbed out her cigarette with a violence that shifted the tin lid that substituted for an ashtray. 'I suppose I'd better tell you the whole thing.'

'I think that might be helpful,' said Rosie, 'but just hold on a second.' She stood up and walked to the door of the interview room. 'Skip.'

The station officer turned. 'Yeah?'

'Skip, be a darling and send me a CID officer, will you?'

The station officer, uncertain of Rosie's rank, but persuaded by her impressive appearance, lifted the handset of his telephone.

A minute or so later, a young, fresh-faced DC entered the interview room. 'Someone in here want a CID officer?' he asked.

Rosie slowly appraised the youthful detective. 'Yes,' she said. 'Are you such an officer?'

'Yes. DC Downs.'

'Well I'm blessed,' said Rosie. 'I'm WDC Webster, Flying Squad.' She pointed at a recording machine on a side table. 'Can you operate that thing?' she asked.

'Yes, of course. But anyone would have switched that on for you.'

'Well turn it on and come and sit down, but don't interfere.

You're just here to act as a witness to a very important statement that this young lady is about to make.' Dismissing DC Downs from her mind, she turned back to Ivy. 'Right,' she said, 'everything you say from now on will be recorded. At the end of this interview, that officer there will hand you a copy of the recording and I shall keep the other. Got it?' She smiled sweetly.

DC Downs walked across to Rosie and whispered in her ear. 'Shouldn't you caution her?' he asked.

Rosie stood up and seizing his upper arm in a vice-like grip, steered the young detective towards the far corner of the room. 'If and when the prisoner makes a statement that indicates to me that she is the author of the crime I am investigating, then — and only then — will I caution her.'

'Well — I' DC Downs found himself staring at Rosie's cleavage.

'In the unlikely event that you ever become a DS on the Squad,' continued Rosie relentlessly, looking down at the young DC, 'you can tell me what to do. But not until. In the meantime, sit down and listen. You might learn something.' She returned to her chair opposite Ivy. 'Right,' she said, 'let's get on with it.'

'I was at this strip club see,' said Ivy, 'and I'd done my thing one night and I was doing the rounds with my garter — '

'Would you like to explain that?'

'Yeah, well I was just left with my garter, see, and I was collecting.'

'Ah, yes,' said Rosie, 'I think I get the picture. You were walking round the room, stark naked except for a garter, inviting the gentlemen present to make a contribution. Is that it?'

Ivy nodded. 'Yeah, that's it. Well, Alfie Barnes was there with a crowd of his mates. They was really living it up. Champagne and all that, and Alfie stuck a fifty in my garter — '

'Fifty-penny piece?'

'Nah! A fifty-quid note, of course.'

'Good Lord,' said Rosie, 'there are times when I think I'm wasted in the police. What happened then?'

'He asked me to join him and his mates, so I did.'

'Still wearing your garter?'

'Nah, course not. I went and got dressed first. Anyway they was having a good time and they was going on to some other place and they asked me along an' all.'

'So you went?'

'Yeah. An' I finished up down Alfie's place in Cobham. Least, I thought it was his, but then I found out later that it belonged to Donald.'

'Donald who?' Rosie knew but wanted it on the tape.

'Donald Close. It got a bit complicated, because Alfie reckoned I was his bird like, but I fancied Donald. A real gent, he was. Know what I mean? Always opened doors for me and stood up when I come in the room, just like I was a real lady.'

'So you changed sides?'

'Yeah, but we never let on, least not straight off, but then Alfie began to realise that me and Donald had got this thing going and more or less okayed it. He'd got some other bird by this time anyway. Donald was a bit fed up with everything and wanted to emigrate to... Australia. An' one night he says to me, what about you coming an' all, Ivy? Well I was getting pissed off with stripping an' that. It ain't much fun, having all them men staring at you when you ain't got nothing on, and knowing that all they really wanted to do was screw you... and worse. So I says yes. An' we got married. Ever so nice it was. Very quiet. Register office.'

'What about his first wife, Muriel? Did he mention her at all?'

Ivy looked down at the table. 'Not till he had to,' she said.

'Well?'

For a moment or two, Ivy stared at the WDC, obviously wondering whether to tell her the whole story. Then she shrugged. 'We knew Alfie and the others was going to pull this job down Cobham, and we reckoned we'd have it off and clear out to Australia. Don had got it all worked out. He bought tickets for Canada, so's Alfie'd think that's where we'd gone, but he got tickets for Australia an' all. He's ever so clever, is Don. He'd worked out all about the bank accounts, so's anyone looking for us would think we was in Canada. What was going to happen was that the night of the heist down Cobham, after Alfie had left the money and cleared off back to the Smoke, me and Don would go straight to the airport and be off, see.'

'But it didn't work out quite like that, I suppose?'

'No, it never. Well, not quite. 'Cos of the body see.'

'I wondered when we were coming to that,' said Rosie, pushing another cigarette in Ivy's direction.

'I was supposed to wait in a pub in Esher for a phone call from Don and then go straight to the house, but he never rung. I didn't know what was happening so I went out there and let myself in. Don was in the sitting room, white as a sheet, and this woman was lying on the floor. I thought she'd fainted or something, but Don said she was dead and it was his wife. Well, you could've knocked me down with a feather. I never knew he had no wife. So I says, you'd better do a bit of explaining, I says. Anyhow, he told me all about her and how she was after him for his money, but he never knew that she knew where he lived. He says that he got a phone call from some geezer asking him to meet him in a pub that night. That's why he never rung me. But no one turned up and when he got back, there was his missus. Done in... on the floor. His proper missus like. Well she was. I s'pose I am now... proper, I mean.'

Rosie shook her head. 'You're not, I'm afraid. You went through a form of marriage with him before his first wife died.' She decided not to mention Ivy's own bigamous marriage to Farrow in case it interrupted the flow about the more important matter of the murder.

Ivy shrugged. 'Oh well,' she said. 'Some you win, some you lose. Anyhow, I says to Don that everyone would think he done her, on account of it being his wife and his house like, and we'd better scarper anyway, like we'd planned. Well, I mean to say, we had a better reason now, didn't we? Don wanted to get rid of the body first, but I says to him that we hadn't got time, because of the flight, and when Alfie come back he'd have to do something. Couldn't just leave her there, and anyway, he probably knows more about getting rid of dead bodies than what Don did. I mean, he's all right for doing it proper, Don I mean — funerals an' that — but not that sort of burying. Anyway he sees the sense of that and we took off.'

'Is that it?'

'Yeah. We went to Oz. I helped him fiddle a passport for hisself, and he signed one for me, and off we went.'

'But then he left you out there?'

'Yeah, but he was coming back, he said. Reckoned he had a bit of business to finish off, and he wanted to go down Henley... see the boat race, or something.'

'The Henley Royal Regatta, I think you mean,' said Rosie.

'Yeah, well, whatever.'

'And what about Farrow?'

'Oh, that was something else.'

'Yes,' said Rosie, 'I know it was something else. What, exactly?'

Ivy pointed at Rosie's cigarettes and the WDS nodded. 'D'you think it might go easier for me, me helping you an' that?'

'Go easier? In what way?'

'Well, I was into drug-smuggling.'

Rosie nodded. 'I can't give you any guarantees, but I must tell you, at this stage, that anything further you say will be given in evidence.'

'Yeah, I s'pose so,' said Ivy phlegmatically. 'Well, when I was working Amsterdam — '

'What d'you mean, working Amsterdam?'

'On the game, of course. Rich pickings over there, I can tell you... all them businessmen. But as I was going to and fro, I thought it wouldn't hurt to bring a bit of snow back from time to time. I bunged it to Elvis and he knocked it out in his shop.' 'How did you come to meet Elvis?'

Ivy considered the question thoughtfully for some moments. 'D'you know about him?' she asked.

'A bit.'

'Yeah, well, I heard about him from some of the girls on the game. Strange tastes, he had. Still...' She shrugged. 'If they're willing to pay... so what? Anyhow, I heard this whisper as how he was a clergyman, see, so I thought, I'll put the arm on him a bit, I thought. But I never had to as it happened. He had to resign. Got caught out in the organ loft with four naked girls from out the choir.' Ivy smiled. 'Bit of a giggle, when you think about,'cos none of them complained. Probably never had anything like it in their lives before. Anyhow, couldn't have that, amateurs taking the bread out of the mouths of professionals. So I went down his record shop, after he'd resigned and set up like, and had a few words, see.'

*

Two hours later, Rosie Webster returned to New Scotland Yard and walked into Fox's office. She laid the tape cassette on his desk and smiled. 'I think you'll find that that answers a lot of the questions, sir,' she said.

Fox picked up the tape and gazed at it. 'Get Mr Gilroy in here,' he said.

The three of them sat listening to Ivy Barnes' revelations and at the end of the recording Fox sat back with a satisfied smile on his face. 'Well done, Rosie,' he said. 'What did you threaten her with?'

'Me? Threaten her, sir? How could you say such a thing? You won't find any threats on there.' She pointed at the tape and smiled sweetly.

*

Fox settled into the front seat of his grey Ford Granada and adjusted the back of the seat slightly. Gilroy made himself comfortable in the back, wondering yet again why it was that his detective chief superintendent had to come out on a job and interfere. It was a mystery to Gilroy why Fox couldn't do what most other officers of his rank did: stay in the office and play with the paperwork. DC Swann, Fox's driver, muttered to himself as he started the powerful car. Swann always muttered.

'That obo team is still on at Farrow's, I hope,' said Fox.

'Yes, sir.'

'Good. What time is it?'

'Quarter past two, sir,' said Gilroy, pointedly leaning forward and looking over Fox's shoulder at the clock on the dashboard.

'Good. Swann, get a move on, will you?'

'There's a speed limit, guv.'

'Don't argue, Swann, just get on with it.'

They pulled up outside Farrow's shop and got out. The other car, containing DS Fletcher and WDC Webster was not far behind, but Fox strode across the pavement and tried the door of the record shop. It was locked. 'Where the hell is he?' Fox enquired of no one in particular.

'Perhaps he's not back from lunch, sir,' said Gilroy.

Fox turned to Fletcher and Webster as they arrived and got out of their car. 'The bugger's not here, Perce,' he said. 'D'you know where the obo post is?'

'Not offhand, guv, no,' said Fletcher.

'Well get on the air and find out, and don't hang about.'

Fletcher slipped back into the front seat of his car and picked up the handset of his radio. After a few moments of cryptic conversation, he emerged once more. 'Other side of the road, over the shoe shop, guv.'

Fox groaned. 'Nip up there, Perce. See what they know. And it had better be good,' he added.

But Farrow suddenly appeared, walking briskly along the pavement.

'Hold it, Perce,' shouted Fox, but Farrow, rapidly taking stock of the situation — and not liking what he saw — turned and ran.

'Bloody hell!' said Fox. 'Get after the bastard. Go on!' He waved at the other three officers who promptly set off in pursuit of Farrow. Fox got back into his car. 'Down there, Swann. Follow them,' he said. 'Why the hell does everyone in this job have to run away on foot?' Fox shook his head wearily. 'On television, they always do it in cars.'

The Ford Granada surged forward, catching up with the running figures of Gilroy, Fletcher and Webster about sixty yards down the road. But then Farrow, remarkably agile and fast for his weight, ran across the road, narrowly avoiding a Post Office van, and cut down a side turning.

'He's making for the Whitgift Centre, guv,' said Swann mildly.

'I can see that, you prat,' said Fox. 'Keep going round the block, and see if we can catch him coming out the other side.'

'Got a better idea, sir,' said Swann, and he switched on the headlights and the siren. He turned the car into the street which Farrow had taken, just missing a rare road-sweeper. At the far end, he swung left and then drove on to the pavement and down a narrow alleyway that led into the heart of the shopping precinct.

'What the hell are you doing, Swann, you idiot?'

'This is where he is, guv,' said Swann, hunching forward over the wheel. 'And this is where we'll catch him.'

'Stop the bloody car,' said Fox. 'You'll never get it down there.' Swann, disappointed, braked to a standstill and Fox leaped out. 'Now get round the other side and catch him coming out.'

Swann, clearly upset at not being allowed to have his own way, reversed into the roadway and accelerated away.

The Whitgift Centre was crowded with people, and Fox looked around. Some way away there appeared to be a commotion and Fox saw that the canopy of the AA kiosk had been brought down, its two poles laying at odd angles across the front of the caravan. An AA patrolman was attempting to disentangle himself from the wreckage. Fox worked it out in an instant. 'Which way did they go?' he asked.

'Don't ask me, guv'nor,' said the disgruntled patrolman. 'I was too busy trying to get out of this lot.' He sniffed loudly.

''Ere, you in charge?' he shouted at Fox's disappearing back, having belatedly worked out that Fox might be the very person to talk to on the subject of compensation.

They all met up by the subway that led out into Wellesley Road.

'Well?' demanded Fox. 'Where the hell is he?'

Gilroy spread his hands. 'Lost him, guv,' he said, leaning against a wall and trying desperately to recover his breath.

'Bloody marvellous,' said Fox. 'The cream of the Flying Squad and you can't catch a middle-aged cripple like Farrow.' He scoffed in disgust and looked round. 'I wonder where bloody Swann's got to.'

Fox led the disconsolate little team up the steps into Wellesley Road where fortunately — particularly for Swann — the Chief Superintendent's Granada was parked.

'D'you see him?' Fox poked his head through the window of the car.

'No, guv, not a sign.'

'Probably gone home, sir,' said Gilroy helpfully.

'You must be joking,' said Fox, 'but I suppose we'd better have a look.'

They drove round the block and dropped Fletcher and Webster off by their car, and then drove on to Farrow's house not far from East Croydon station. There was, as the police are wont to say, no answer to repeated knockings.

'Right!' Fox made a decision. 'You and Rosie hang on here,' he said to DS Fletcher, 'and get on the air to DI Evans and his team. I don't care where they are, but I want them here, now. Tell them to get a couple of W's on the way and spin this drum until it rattles. Then go round and do his dew-drop. And you two can stay and help.' Fox, having thus directed that warrants be obtained and searches of the house and shop be undertaken, got back into his car and slammed the door. He was not in a good mood.

*

'Circulate Farrow to all forces and all ports, Jack,' said Fox when they were back at the Yard. 'I want England closed!' he added dramatically.

Chapter Eighteen

Elvis Farrow, wanting to put as much distance as possible between the Flying Squad and himself, had hired a car from a reputable firm by producing one of his collection of false driving licences. He had realised, too late, that his over-confidence in imagining that the first visit of Fox and Gilroy would come to nothing was a mistake likely to have dire consequences. If only he had taken it as a warning and fled when he had the chance to do so in comfort.

It was Farrow's intention to make for Dover and cross — as a foot-passenger — to France. The hired car would be left in a street some way away in an attempt to allay any suspicion that he may have gone abroad. Unfortunately for Elvis Farrow, the traffic division of the Kent County Constabulary put the kibosh on that little plan.

Police Constables Joe Holt and Peter Slinger had had an unproductive day. In order to discuss future strategy, they had pulled into a lay-by on that stretch of road which links two parts of the M20 and which is still called the A20, simply because it has yet to be brought up to the requisite standard for motorways. Furthermore, because of some adjacent road-works, that part of the carriageway was subject to a temporary speed limit of fifty miles an hour.

Joe Holt estimated that the Ford Sierra passed them at about seventy miles an hour, an estimate with which Peter Slinger saw no reason to disagree.

'Well sod that,' said Holt, starting the engine of their white Ford Granada. Accelerating rapidly, he kept the Ford Sierra in sight while Slinger concentrated on the specially calibrated speedometer with which traffic cars are fitted.

'That'll do,' said Slinger, looking ahead with a yawn. 'That's half a mile at a steady seventy-two.'

Holt flicked the switch that illuminated the blue lights on the roof of the car and closed the distance between him and the car ahead. At just the right moment he switched on the siren, noting with a grin of satisfaction the sudden movement of the driver in front as he stared into his rear-view mirror shortly before pulling on to the hard shoulder.

With that casual and amiable menace with which all traffic policemen are imbued, Holt strolled up to the door of Farrow's car and peered down at him through his now open window.

'Good afternoon, sir,' he said. 'Hurrying for the ferry, are we?' Holt was accustomed to people who booked a ferry six months in advance and then didn't leave themselves enough time to get to the port.

'Yes, I am as a matter of fact, officer,' said Farrow.

'Oh dear,' said Holt. 'Well, we have just followed you for a distance of half a mile during which time your speed averaged seventy-two miles an hour.'

Farrow half-smiled and pursed his lips. 'Well that's only a teeny bit over the limit, isn't it?' he said. His face was wet with perspiration.

'Actually,' said Holt, 'it's twenty-two miles an hour over the limit...'

'But I — '

'That section of the carriageway being restricted to fifty miles an hour.'

Although some temporary speed restrictions are the subject of specific legislation, Holt was aware that the particular section he was talking about was not. And that made for difficulties. It left him with the option of reporting Farrow for reckless or careless driving, which was more difficult to prove, and might well turn out to be a waste of time. It was his intention, therefore, to allow Farrow to proceed with what the police call a verbal warning, despite the fact that, in the experience of the police, there is nothing more sickening than the sycophantic gratitude of the driver who has just been let off.

PC Holt was about to deliver his grave warning, when PC Slinger put in his two-penn'orth. 'Is this your car, sir?' he asked, as he walked up beside Holt.

'Yes.'

'I see.' Slinger opened the driver's door. 'Perhaps you'd just step out of the car, sir,' he said with a smile.

Farrow got out of the car and allowed himself to be steered round to the nearside, policemen not liking their customers to get knocked over while they are being interviewed... mainly because of the writing involved.

'I have just checked this vehicle on the computer, sir, and the registered keeper is a car-hire firm in London.'

'Ah, yes, of course. I'd forgotten,' said Farrow lamely.

'Funny thing to forget,' said Holt, frowning. 'Are you taking this car abroad with you?'

'Abroad?' Farrow sounded surprised, as though the policeman had just made an outrageous suggestion.

'Yes, sir. Abroad. When I asked you if you were making for the ferry, you said you were.'

'Ah, yes. I mean no. I'm going abroad. The car isn't.'

'And what are you going to do with it, then?' Slinger tapped his pocket book with his pen. 'This company doesn't have an office in Dover.'

'Oh!'

'May I see your driving licence, sir?' said Holt.

'Oh, yes.' And that was when Farrow made his first mistake. In common with many travellers, he had put all his necessary papers together. Farrow's were in a neat leather document wallet. He leaned into the car and took it from the front passenger seat, opened it and withdrew his driving licence. Holt made a few notes in his pocket book and handed it back. As Farrow returned it to the document wallet, a passport fell out. Holt, being a courteous sort of fellow, stooped and picked it up. As everyone knows, you don't have to open a passport to see the name of the holder. It is conveniently written in a little white space at the top of the cover. And the name on Farrow's wasn't Farrow. That wouldn't have mattered so much, but it wasn't Gibson either, which was the name that Holt had just recorded from the driving licence Farrow had produced. Holt opened the passport and studied the photograph. 'Not a good likeness, is it?' he said amiably. 'But then, they never are. Still, it's undoubtedly you, isn't it?'

'Er, yes.'

'Perhaps you'd care to explain why the name is even less of a likeness then, seeing that's it's different from the one in your driving licence... sir?'

'Ah!'

*

DI Denzil Evans and company were not best pleased at being hauled off a promising observation that could well have resulted in a few beneficial knock-offs in order to conduct searches of premises. However, as the direction had come from the Detective Chief Superintendent, they had little option but to comply.

The house was a disappointment. It was a tip. Farrow, living the life of a bachelor — even if he wasn't one — was an exceptionally untidy individual, and appeared to have no pride in the appearance of his domain. Every work surface in the kitchen was covered with dirty dishes, and soiled clothing lay in abandoned little heaps in the bedroom. The bed was unmade, and the wardrobe door was open. Week-old newspapers lay scattered about on the sitting room floor, and the only items mildly to excite the searching detectives were several piles of pornographic magazines in the cupboard under the stairs.

Evidentially, the shop proved more productive. There, in a plastic carrier-bag secreted behind a cardboard box of compact discs and tapes in the stock-room, the police found several packets of white powder. None of the detectives was willing to offer odds on it not being cocaine.

*

Concluding that the over-documented Mr Farrow would be of interest to the CID, PCs Holt and Slinger drove him back the few miles to Maidstone Police Station, rather than take him to one of the smaller — and nearer — police offices.

After the customary delays which follow the excitement of an arrest, a detective constable named Riley appeared on the scene. Casually, he dropped the driving licence and passport on the desk on front of Farrow. 'Well, Mr Gibson — or Mr Williams — perhaps you'd care to tell us who you really are?' From his pocket, Riley extracted two packets of white powder which had been found taped to Farrow's body when he had been searched. 'And what you were doing in possession of that?' He held the two packets between finger and thumb.

'I've never seen it before,' said Farrow. 'And I want a solicitor.'

Riley grinned. 'Yeah, I don't blame you,' he said. 'And don't try that old trick of pretending that we've planted evidence on you because the find was witnessed by two other officers. It doesn't work any more. It's too much hassle as far as we're concerned.' He scratched his chest. 'Going abroad, were you?' Farrow remained silent and Riley dropped the two packets on the table. 'Easier to carry than travellers' cheques, I suppose,' he said. He moved the driving licence slightly with his forefinger. 'And this was reported stolen four months ago during a security van robbery.' Riley sat down opposite Farrow and stretched out his legs. 'You want to tell me about it?'

'Nothing to say,' said Farrow sullenly.

'Suit yourself,' said Riley, 'but we've only just begun. First of all, we're going to take your fingerprints.'

Farrow was not, however, a man of any great resilience. 'Name's Elvis Farrow,' he said with a resigned sigh.

Riley glared at Farrow suspiciously. 'If that's a joke,' he said, 'I must warn you that I'm very busy and I do not take kindly to people who waste my time.'

'It's true,' said Farrow, annoyed at being disbelieved.

'How old are you?'

'Forty-five. Why?'

Riley looked up at the ceiling, calculating. 'How come, then, that your parents called you Elvis nine years before Elvis Presley's first single came out? No one had ever heard the name Elvis until then.'

Farrow shook his head wearily. 'Just my luck,' he said. 'A copper who's an Elvis fan.'

Riley grinned. 'Let's start again, shall we? What's your real name?'

Farrow sighed. 'Eric Forbes,' he said. 'But I changed it by deed poll.' He decided to give in completely. 'I've also used the name Edward Frazer.'

DC Riley stood up. 'I think you've changed your name so often, you haven't got a clue who you are,' he said. 'Still, we'll see if we can't help you out.' He put Farrow back in his cell and made his way to the nearest terminal of the Police National Computer.

Five minutes later, Riley opened Farrow's cell door again. 'Congratulations,' he said. 'You're going on a journey to London. Seems the Flying Squad want to talk to you about cocaine, bigamy... and an unsolved murder.'

Riley was quite disappointed that this information appeared to come as no surprise to Farrow.

'DI Mason, British Transport Police, on line two for you, guv,' said the DC as Gilroy walked through the office.

Gilroy picked up a phone and pressed a button. 'DI Gilroy,' he said.

*

Tommy Fox sorted through the several sheets of paper on his desk as though trying to decide which was the most important.

'Now then,' he said. 'We have statements from Silver Barnes, his cohort Mr Lambie, Donald Close and Ivy Barnes, all of which tend to shift the blame on to someone other than the deponent thereof. If we get one from Elvis, we'll have a nap hand. And with any sort of luck, we might just find a common thread that will enable us to make an early arrest in the case of the murder of Muriel Close, née Yates.'

'We've done that already, guv,' said Gilroy, who was getting heartily sick of the whole business.

Fox grinned. 'You're right, Jack,' he said, 'but up until now, we've only been joking.' A thought crossed his mind. 'Jack!'

'Yes, sir?'

'Given that Farrow took it on the toes the moment he spotted us in Croydon, and that he didn't have time to go home, where d'you suppose he laid hands on a stolen driving licence and a duff passport in such a hurry?'

'I've been thinking about that, guv,' said Gilroy.

'Good, good,' said Fox. 'Well think about it a bit more, will you? And for a start, I think that another search of Ivy Barnes' flat at Ruislip, where, you will recall, she was known as Mrs Sonia Farrow, might discover a hidden haul of such documents. Give it your best attention, Jack, there's a good fellow.'

'Yes, sir.'

'Incidentally, Jack, I think taking that obo off Ivy's flat after her arrest was a bit premature. I've got a feeling that that's where Farrow went when we lost him.'

Gilroy sighed. 'That's what I was thinking about, guv'nor.'

Fox smiled owlishly. 'Just have to think a bit quicker next time, Jack,' he said.

*

'I do hate searching boozers,' said DS Fletcher. 'It takes bloody hours, and you never know whether you've finished or not. There are cellars and attics, and all sorts of little cupboards tucked away all over the shop.'

'Shut up,' said DI Denzil Evans.

They weren't keen on executing search warrants in the early morning, but with a pub there was little option unless you wanted to herd all the customers to one side and search them as well.

Frank Goodall answered the door, wearing a dressing-gown and carpet slippers. 'Yes? What is it?'

'Police,' said Evans. He held a sheet of paper up. 'We have a warrant to search these premises.'

'What the hell's this all about?' Goodall was not a happy man. 'Does your guv'nor know about this?'

'Oh yes,' said Evans, 'he certainly does.'

'Well, he was in here last night.'

'Oh? Who are you talking about?'

'The DI from the local nick.'

'Back luck,' said Evans. 'We're from the Flying Squad.'

*

The original search of Ivy Barnes' Ruislip flat had not been thorough. But routine searches following an arrest are generally cursory unless vital evidence is being sought to support what would otherwise be a bit of a dodgy arrest. But now, Jack Gilroy and a handful of other Flying Squad officers took the place apart. They found seven driving licences, all of which had been reported stolen. Four of them were in women's names. They also found three passports. Although apparently authentic, one of them bore a photograph of Elvis Farrow, and two of them photographs of Ivy Barnes. But each of them had been issued in a false name. In addition to that interesting little haul, the police uncovered a quantity of drugs, secreted in a plastic bag in the lavatory cistern.

'Bloody original, that is,' said Gilroy. 'Who searched this place first off?' he enquired suspiciously.

'No idea, guv,' said one of the detective constables. He did know, but had recognised the signs of an impending disciplinary enquiry. In such circumstances, it was always wise to remain shtum. If the DI really wanted to know, he would find out easily enough.

*

'Very interesting, Jack,' said Fox, 'but hardly surprising. Who carried out the first search, incidentally?'

'Don't know, sir,' said Gilroy.

'Well find out, Jack, and have a few words in their shell-like, will you? Bit slack, that was.'

'Right, sir.'

'And now, Jack, we'll go and see Elvis Farrow, alias Eric Forbes, alias Edward Frazer.' For a moment, Fox mused on Farrow's differing names. 'They all begin with the letters E and F,' he said, as if he had just made an astonishing discovery. 'I don't know why he didn't just call himself Errol Flynn and be done with it.'

*

Although Elvis Farrow had been thrown into a panic when he had been stopped on the A20 by PCs Holt and Slinger — a state of alarm made worse by his later interview with DC Riley at Maidstone Police Station — he positively came apart at the arrival of Detective Chief Superintendent Fox of the Flying Squad. The last time they had spoken, it had been obvious that Fox was on a fishing expedition, but now, thanks to Farrow's own stupidity in assuming that that had been an end to the matter, there was a good chance that he was going to go down for a long time. The judiciary did not take kindly to people who supplied the youth of the country with hard drugs, and tended to think in sentences of ten years... and climbing. That prospect did not fill Elvis Farrow with glee. He had been to prison before, and he didn't much care for it. For some reason that he couldn't fathom, the other prisoners tended either to pick on him or make disgusting suggestions.

'I shall call you Elvis,' said Fox, taking some time to seat himself comfortably on one of the hard wooden chairs in the interview room. 'I just can't keep up with all your aliases — ' He broke off and silently studied the pathetic figure opposite him. Farrow was now perspiring freely, and frequently mopped his face with a less-than-clean handkerchief. 'Now then,' continued Fox, 'I want you to tell me what you know about the death of Muriel Close, and when you have done so, my detective inspector here will write it all down and you will sign it.'

'But — '

'Don't argue, Elvis. You're in enough trouble as it is.'

'I've never heard of anyone called Muriel Close.' Farrow's mind, such as it was, went into top gear as he tried to work out what this overbearing policeman was talking about.

'You're not going to be difficult about this, are you?' said Fox in a resigned sort of way.

'Honestly — '

Fox tutted. 'You shouldn't bandy words like that about, Elvis. Not a man in your position.' He stifled a yawn of boredom. 'Very well then, we'll talk about drugs, shall we?'

'Drugs?' Farrow tried to make it sound innocent. 'I don't know — '

'Oh dear,' said Fox. 'Let's not bugger about, Elvis. You probably didn't even know his name, but a creature called Wayne Crick was arrested coming out of your shop a couple of days ago. He was in possession of a quantity of cocaine which he is willing to testify was supplied by you. As a result of that little affair, I and other officers visited your shop to talk to you, but the moment you saw us, you ran away. I suppose you're going to tell me you suddenly remembered an urgent appointment.' Fox looked disinterestedly around the room. 'Furthermore,' he continued, staring back at Farrow, 'when we searched the said shop, we found further quantities of controlled substances. And as if that wasn't enough, when the Kent police nicked you, my son, you had some strapped to your fat little body. So I think a little chat about all this might well be beneficial... certainly to me if not to you. Then we'll get back to talking about the late Mrs Close.'

Farrow sighed deeply, looked sorry for himself, and mopped his face once more.

*

It was a couple of hours after his arrival at Frank Goodall's pub that DI Evans rang Fox.

For some minutes, Fox listened to the DI's report, then he laughed. 'What the hell made you look for that, Denzil?' he asked.

'Copper's nose, guv,' said Evans.

'Right,' said Fox. 'Nick him.'

*

'You say you went to Manchester on the three o'cock train to see the United-Everton replay, Mr Goodall.'

'Yes.'

'It was cancelled. Apparently your fellow football fans started a punch-up at Euston and they smashed the bloody thing up. It was taken out of service... never even left London. The railway police nicked about sixty of the buggers. So you didn't travel on that train, Mr Goodall.'

'But —'

'My officers found a ticket and a seat reservation for that train,' continued Fox, 'but there were no markings on it to show that it had been seen by a ticket inspector. Not that that means anything.' Fox paused to allow Goodall to digest that telling piece of information and then went on. 'Furthermore, it seems that you keep a little collection of ticket stubs for all the matches you've been to, but we were unable to find one for the Manchester match. Now why's that?' Fox inclined his head.

'I lost it.'

'And my officers also found a video of the match that you said you went to Manchester to see. Now why should you have recorded that?'

'I told you, I'm a keen football fan. I wanted to see the highlights again.'

Fox scoffed. 'Highlights be damned,' he said. 'There weren't any highlights in that match.' He glanced across at Gilroy, and waited until he had finished writing. The tape-recorder was running, but Fox was a careful man. 'Now,' said Fox, 'perhaps you will tell me where you were on the evening of the fourth of April?'

For what seemed an eternity, Goodall sat and stared at the top of the wooden table. Finally, he raised his head and gazed at Fox with a baleful expression. 'I think I ought to send for a solicitor,' he said.

'Why?' asked Fox. 'Have you committed a crime?'

Goodall hesitated only briefly before going on. 'Just before I was leaving to catch the train, I got a phone call. It was from Muriel. She said that she had to see me urgently.'

'Where did you meet her?'

'At Waterloo Station.'

'Yes, go on.'

'She told me that she had at last found out where Donald Close lived — it was Cobham — and she wanted me to go down there with her while she tackled him about her money.'

'And so you went.'

'Yes.'

'What happened?'

'Nothing happened. Close wasn't there. So I said I'd go back with her another day.'

'Let me get this right,' said Fox. 'You, a dedicated football fan, passed up a chance to see this match in Manchester to go all the way to Cobham on the off-chance of seeing Donald Close? Why didn't you telephone first, just to make sure he was in?'

'I didn't want to frighten him off. Anyway, I didn't know the telephone number. Muriel said it was ex-directory.'

'And do you know the telephone number now?'

'No. Like I said, it's ex-directory.'

'So you went down to Cobham with Muriel Close, found that the house was empty and came back to London. Is that right?'

'Yes.'

'Back to Waterloo?'

'Yes.'

'Then what happened?'

'Muriel said she was going across to Liverpool Street to catch a train to Edmonton.'

'I see. And what time would that have been?'

'It must have been about half past six, maybe seven o'clock even.'

'And that's the last time you saw Muriel Close, is it?'

'Yes.'

Fox swung in his chair and held a hand out to DI Evans. Evans handed him a small black book. 'Your private telephone book, Mr Goodall,' said Fox. He turned the pages. 'And here is the telephone number of Donald Close.' He opened the book wide, displaying it to the prisoner.

'I'd forgotten I'd got it,' said Goodall lamely.

Fox closed the book and returned it to Evans. 'I see,' he said. He moved a few papers on the table until he found what he wanted. 'I am going to put you up on an identification parade, Mr Goodall.'

'What for?'

'There is a clerk in the Community Charge department of the Esher Urban District Council who will almost certainly identify you as the man who called seeking information about Donald Close, known to him as John Calvin. And known to you by that name too. You're quite a detective, aren't you, Mr Goodall? When Muriel Close first told you that her husband had disappeared with all her money, you set out to find him.

And find him you did. I don't know how, but I could use that sort of expertise in my department. But that's not all, is it?' Again Fox held out his hand to DI Evans. 'This,' said Fox, displaying a small piece of folded cardboard, 'is the membership card for your local karate club. We made a few enquiries and it seems you're quite the expert. Got belts of every imaginable colour, haven't you? And you're certainly capable of delivering the blow that killed Muriel Close.' He threw the card contemptuously on the table. 'I may say,' he added, 'that your club was not terribly impressed with the possibility that one of its members may have mis-used his skills. They take a pretty poor view of that, apparently.'

Goodall looked up, his face drained of colour and his jaw slack. 'All right,' he said. 'I killed her, but — '

'You are not obliged to say anything,' said Fox, 'but anything you do say will be taken down in writing and may be given in evidence.'

'It was her getting pregnant that did it. It was fun until then. But she said she'd left off taking the pill because she wanted me to divorce Sylvia and marry her, but that would have been daft. The pub's Sylvia's — although I hold the licence — and Muriel hadn't got any money. Donald Close had seen to that. She was going to tell Sylvia everything. That's the trouble with taking up with your wife's sister. I knew where Close lived, and I arranged to meet Muriel and take her there. I pretended I'd just found out. I booked the ticket to Manchester and everything, to make it look as though that's where I'd been. I left her body at Close's place so that he'd get the blame for it. It seemed like a good idea, her body in his house, particularly as he'd taken off with all her money. Stands to reason he'd have been a suspect, doesn't it? Anyway, I phoned him, and said I was a solicitor acting for Muriel and wanted to meet him in a pub, urgently, because Muriel had agreed to a settlement. Close sounded relieved, said he wanted to get her off his back. So I took Muriel down there, and...' He paused. 'And the rest you know.'

Fox smiled. 'Ducking and diving to the last, eh?' he said. 'You haven't got it quite right, even now. That phone call you said you received from Muriel. What you'd done was to promise to take Muriel to France to marry her... after you'd got a divorce, of course.' Fox grinned. That's how you persuaded her to meet you. You explained the trip to Cobham by telling her that Close had at last agreed to repay the money. But just in case she'd told anyone else that she was going to France — and she had — you had to fake that call. Not very clever that. That was the one thing that really set me thinking.'

'But — '

'But nothing,' said Fox. 'Poor Muriel Close was a naive woman. First she fell for Donald Close's blandishments, then yours. How she could believe all that guff I don't know. But I'll tell you this much, mister: a jury will believe it. And you're going to have a long time to think over where you went wrong. About thirty years, I should think.'

*

'The Receiver's Department have been on the phone, sir. Seems they want their straw boaters back,' said Gilroy. 'The ones we used at Henley.'

'Sod that!' said Fox. 'Tell 'em we're going again next year.'

If you enjoyed, please share your thoughts on Amazon by leaving *Lead Me to the Slaughter* a review.

For more free and discounted eBooks every week, sign up to the *Endeavour Press* newsletter.

Follow us on Twitter and Instagram.

Printed in Great Britain
by Amazon